Also by B.W. Powe

A Climate Charged

The Solitary Outlaw

Noise of Time (text for the Glenn Gould Profile)

A Tremendous Canada of Light

Outage

Outage

A Journey into Electric City

B.W. Powe

THE ECCO PRESS

THE ECCO PRESS
100 West Broad Street
Hopewell, New Jersey 08525

Published simultaneously in Canada by Random House of
Canada Limited, Toronto

Printed in the United States of America

FIRST EDITION

Library of Congress Cataloging-in-Publication Data

Powe, B. W. (Bruce W.), 1955—
Outage: a journey into electric city / B. W. Powe
p.   cm.
I. Title.
PR9199.3.P64093   1995
813'.54--dc20   94-43664
ISBN 0-88001-418-0

For Robin

Throw away the lights, the definitions
And say of what you see in the dark

That it is this or that it is that,
But do not use the rotted names.

How should you walk in that space and know
Nothing of the madness of space,

Nothing of its jocular procreations?
Throw the lights away. Nothing must stand

Between you and the shapes you take
When the crust of shape has been destroyed.

Wallace Stevens

Study what thou art, whereof thou art a part, what
thou knowest of this art. This is really what thou art.
All that is without thee is also within.

Solomon Trismosin, *Alchemical Wanderings*

Now at the end of print, electronics appears and seems to be
paving the way for the musical polities of the future.

William Irwin Thompson

Outage

I hear the city.

The first Monday in October, and the fall weather has arrived. Arctic light, white light. Pale blue skies, gray clouds tinged with red. I love the cooler wind. It makes the sound of the city sharper and finer, a sound that can enter and carry everywhere, penetrating me. Listen to the air, to what it stirs inside us and outside us, the incoherent fears and hopes, the waves of unspoken longing, the current that pulses toward a blowout in time.

The hill at Riverdale Park, in Toronto's East End, gives me the picture I need. Look at the city, its traffic and towers. On the sloping hill, I stand near maple and birch trees, their veinlike branches spreading outward, the grass slick with brown and yellow leaves. On my left a hospital for permanently damaged patients; on my right a viaduct and a school. The city expands to the west.

I watch the light on the bank towers, a silver and golden glow reflecting on their surfaces. Sheet metal, mirrors. In daylight and nightlight this place is radioactive — a raw nerve, a carrier of chaos. I pick up the discharge of messages, the swarms of data, the shouting, and the rush.

Everything surges here, everything has been changing. Electricity cores through the city's conduits and cells. It has suddenly become a vast electromagnetic field where technological inventions accumulate and outstrip the abilities of the inventors, who cannot imagine consequences. We boost the electronic current through machines and absorb their streams of energy.

Feel the city's speed, its rhythm unfolding in compressed time. The towers form a horizon, a boundary, steel-edged and massive. But inside that zone there's a scattering of personal voices, a dispersal of the private mind and will. Who's responsible for the push for power and space that I see? The answer comes in the collective, "We're here...dissolve into us...it's best to belong..."

Is the corporate embrace, this merger, the same as a community, a harmony, a trust? Can the hightech tribalism become a neighborhood, reforge bonds between people? I wonder if the technologies of the telecity fire a hallucination of noises, a mirage of images, or channel something more spiritually interfused into our lives.

What can we use to handle the oversupply of messages without damaging our responses? What filters through? Is the electromagnetic field an exercise in tyrannical control or the beginning of an authentic human radiance? The cityroar may be a voice of life. I can't say, and I have to know.

End of the nineteen eighties. The decade's climax, apogee. Galvanized premonitions, prophecies in the air. With over sixty-thousand TV transmitters around the globe, our planet now emanates more low-frequency waves than the sun. The world remaking itself into a psychic livewire, new models of reality emerging. People alarmed, adrift, falling out of old stable identities.

Overloaded with sensations and details, I find that I'm questioning it all. No place sounds or looks the same to me from month to month.

Out age. Bring the age out into the open, its obsessions and potential. Out age. It's the time when each person can become the antenna of the race.

Shock

The Scorched Head

Black and blue Monday. It was the day when the world's stock markets crashed. The computers convulsed, panicking people.

Michael Tannikis called me just before midnight.

"Do you know what's happening? Breakneck crisis. The money markets are at war. The machines are avid. It's the permanent crisis, man. The world is burning up. But I've got the whole pattern in my head. Are you listening? Time to talk, time to take a walk."

Michael was a student in my night class at York University. He often stayed late to discuss writing, ideas, and media issues with me. But words shook loose in him when the financial markets went into shock. As if his thoughts were crashing too. He left messages on my answering machine. The phone, in another part of the house, buzzed, clicked, recorded him. When I played the tape back, I heard through the hiss of a bad connection how his voice mixed desperation, hope, and manic insight.

"I'm trying to get hold of you. Where are you? What are you doing? Can't you see? We are being shot up and brought down, and they don't understand. I'm talking white noise, I'm talking exposure."

At around two-thirty a.m., unable to sleep, I phoned the number he'd left and got his answering machine. In the morning there were more messages waiting.

"How much longer can any of us stand to be alone? I'm not on drugs, believe me. That's not the name of the game. The machines are telling us things. We're being transformed. We'll be brand new. We're learning how to dream together again."

The tape hummed, spooled ahead, started again.

"Give or take, give or break," he talked on, his face invisible to me. "It's cycles, man. It's all musical. Like you have to listen first. You have to play. It's all in the flowing. The rhythm's in our skin."

I recognized what he was saying. I understood the references, the concerns. It was as if our minds had started to merge, and we were sharing obsessions. His words twisted through the wires. Michael T. (so I called him) was living in the blast of the new.

Noise City

Radio garbage jams heavens...The electromagnetic roar of the modern world is thwarting scientists' efforts to monitor the faint whispers of the universe...

MAGNETIC STORM ALERT FOR POWER COMPANIES
AND SATELLITE USERS

This was a time when I was monitoring how the electric currents run through our lives. I was struggling with pieces, getting a glimpse of the forces and processes that conduct and entangle us. Pulling in headlines and datelines, facts becoming fax, your head and home like receivers, your mind melding with the electromagnetic waves from satellites, cables, radios, VDTs, and TVs, so that you are caught in the chatter and calls, your ears jangling with the acoustic traces of the past, present, maybe even the future, the instruments of voice and moving image drawing you deeper into their grids.

I'd begun a book that was to describe the electronic conditions and the problems of overload, that would pursue human connections in the data explosion. I set up files, made lists, kept clippings and notes. In my classes at the university, I talked incessantly about multimedia, fluid worlds of information, our inability to interpret — or, more exactly, our inability to unify — networks, responses, ideas. I talked about losing frames of reference for reality. To my wife, Lena, to my friends and colleagues, to people I knew in stores, to my neighbors, I went on as if possessed. I said:

There are lights blinking and becoming faint for no apparent reason in offices and homes. There have been abrupt power cuts at hockey games and the players have been told to play on with no TV coverage and ice turning to slush under their skates. Spectacular historical incidents spark like flares in the night, then fade from almost everyone's memory. VDTs and household appliances are reported to be influencing users, affecting their physical and mental states. There are scientists who discuss recombined DNA strands, restructured selves, silicon transplants that suggest evolutionary time can be shortened, that nature can be accelerated, our bodies propelled into artificial realms, carbonbased flesh eliminated, our minds placed inside mobile computers, becoming half-human, half-machine. There are people whose jobs consist of reading your life for secrets, who scan your credit profile to find anomalies and gaps, wondering about who you are, each of us part of a shadowdata, each of us a code for others to crack.

And I'd explain:

This is the century of communications. We are witnessing wild machine metamorphoses, an ecstatic evolution. Before nineteen hundred, Thomas Edison brought commercial electrical power to New York and Nikola Testa lit the Chicago World's Fair with the first AC power system. Soon after we admitted the telephone and radio into our lives; after World War II, and into the decades beyond, TV and stereo hi-fi; then computers, digitization, microprocessing — the abrupt ability to simulate, replicate, imitate. Balances in nature have been altered forever. The futurists and technologists now speak, with almost mystic reverence, about convergence, every machine in a total linkup. Appliances at home and technology at work surround people with their own personal vibrating spheres. Here's what can bring chronic fluster: CB radios, walkie-talkies, ham radios, air and sea navigation systems, spy satellites, police radios, military talk channels, radar beacons. How can anyone sleep? I'd ask; and there is more to come. A myriad of messages scores through the airwaves, messages that we catch and share, viewers, programmers, and performers alike. These signals feed restive souls. When TV alloys with stereo sound, the telephone combines with the fax, and satellites interphase with cable setups and dishes, their currents and fields bring voices, faces, sounds, and images to the world, the hyperintensity.

And I said;

There are people in the money markets using their computer networks to mask themselves. They create console personae, popping up in the nets under pseudonyms, giving themselves female names (if male) and male names (if female). Yet I'd been finding that single human voices, like those faint whispers of the universe that astronomers tracked, are often jammed by the electromagnetic cry. People losing each other in the spew, people forgetting how to communicate with one another, people blowing up spiritually, emotionally.

And through all this I realized that something unnamed howled, perpetually close to being seen and heard, coming to birth.

So when Michael T. started calling me, I was already feeling dislocated, adrift in random data, living without a structure for the experience. Lena told me that my conversations had become too intense and elliptical. "You're getting paranoid," she said, without smiling. I knew then that our marriage was in trouble. I'd peered into some hole, and I'd recoiled, uncertain about what I saw. I couldn't sit still. The world was unhinged; it had slipped from its moorings. I knew I couldn't go back to a halcyon period when I could pretend that I didn't know people were going mad from the jarring, or numbing themselves, and that the new technologies were bringing something big and ravenous to us, making you feel like more of a stranger than you may have before, and yet at the same time making you feel intimate with the globe — inside its workings, the whirl.

I was hooked by Michael's messages. Even though I knew almost nothing about him — where did he live? what was his family like? who were his friends? what where his motives? — I'd begun to believe that maybe through my classes, in our conversations, and in my writings, I'd encouraged him to be inflamed with chaos.

"Everyone's talking about real problems, real situations, real people, real life," he said on the phone one night. "I want to ask someone, what's unreal? Who'll tell me? Who's going to say what's really happening?"

It was the computers, he claimed, that had run things on Black and blue Monday. The rampaging machines were asserting control.

I understood; I'd had glimpses. The shock of a crash can be an instant of insight. The computers may have been exhibiting an embryonic form of artificial intelligence (AI). It was as if the machines were deliberately generating noise, riffling through codes, permutations, and possibilities, hunting for a voice.

Silicon Deliria

The stock market fall of nineteen eighty-seven was the first global outage. The transmissions of an invisible network went briefly public; the microcomputer converged with TV, and the material market fused with immaterial images and sound bites. This union of computers and economics, of TV and the VDT, with highstakes trading and futures speculation, heightened the rush of events. In a flash, cash-credit flow became an agonizing crashflow.

Moving capital. At the speed with which credit, investments, and bonds hurtled, there were sudden distortions of figures, rapid drops in holdings, lightning action that kindled outrage, a frenzy. Simultaneously, capital cities seemed to be moving: Tokyo, Chicago, Hong Kong, London, New York — not one of them worked like an isolated city in an independent nationstate. The cities appeared to be living entities who were broadcasting to one another, joining up in every direction at once.

I wasn't at the Toronto Stock Exchange on Black and blue Monday. I didn't have to be there to be part of the turmoil. In this public city, with its international meshwork of news and reports, from TV, radio, and print, no one could be left untouched. The computer throe revealed what may have been a structure of connections. The current moved quickly, and slowly, startlingly, and seamlessly, organizing itself into fields. The crash brought total immersion, submergence.

Throughout my neighborhood, in the East End, the TVs and radios fluttered and jabbered. Telephone calls came in from people consumed by the collapse.

I made a record of many of the lines and remarks that I heard during the week.

"We think by headlines."

"There's no ground left to stand on."

"We can't see the end."

"You don't have a situation that's on the one hand or on the other hand. You have an octopus. Many hands, tentacles, reaching everywhere."

This news began in the East, in Tokyo, and ripped around the world into the suggestible city, and into my home.

A wealthy Bay Street investor said: "People are standing around on the stock-exchange floor. They're wondering about how much worse things can get. They can't see any reason for this at all."

I heard how our paranoia was being spurred by words that had lost their conventional contexts. Words were taken from the language of nuclear warfare — words like meltdown, fallout, and radiation. The stock exchange became an animist universe of bulls and bears. I heard neologisms — global debting, disinflation, computer-decision, reconditioning, mainframing.

We were inundated by experts and their opinions, trans-Atlantic calls, static from cablelines, market closures and headline disclosures, and there was no place to hide. I was struck by this paradox: an overload can resemble a nervous breakdown, while our access to replays, on-the-spot interviews, and hookups to other cities can bring a visionary intensity to what we perceive.

An investment specialist said: "Once the great fear started, people were shaken by the computers. In our brokerage I saw people key in orders faster than the computers could take them. When they did register the input, the computers would seem to speed up even more. Those key-in people operated like they had no control at all."

That week in the Toronto *Globe and Mail*, the Report on Business carried on one of its lefthand pages a debate by experts and market analysts on the causes of Black and blue Monday. They spoke of the obvious: overextended credit, excessive speculation, the influence of Chicago's exchange on New York's, phony wealth, bankruptcies, and greed, the phenomenon of twenty-three of the world's largest stock markets falling together as if they'd been knocked over in a surreal game of dominoes. The righthand side of the page carried an advertisement for computers. Black type said:

LET US PUT YOU INTO THE AIR
IN YOUR WORKPLACE OR STATION

The graphics showed a desktop terminal divided from its base. A floating screen, a head leaving its body behind.

No control. That was a key. The computers looked as though they had turned malignant, launching a gadget terrorism. What they were truly doing was restructuring our ground of feeling and response without any of us fully knowing it. Finances and computers drove the TV reports. TV in turn drove the print commentaries and copy. Older brokers, acquainted with jolts in the market, counseled calm, a quiet observance of trends. But while the microchips had grown smaller, our appetite for advice, facts, background, statistics, and editorials, had grown more insatiable. We were each listening, reacting, and even if we were isolated from the causes, we weren't removed from the effects. In that terminal week in October, the dislocation of national boundaries altered our belief that single institutions and individuals determined the mood and tempo of lives. The screech and wail of radio and TV and the computer together, the sheer volume of statistics and percentages, made each person sense that reality had shifted, come unsprung, without our full consent.

* * *

Three months after the crash, the Toronto Stock Exchange recorded a drop that shattered financial records. I thought that the city would again resound with the restless voices, with the market turbulence, that had stirred in Tokyo, London, Paris, and New York. (The TSE, I noticed, wore the initials of T.S. Eliot, author of "The Waste Land.") Economists dubbed this spasm the One-Day Crash or the Twenty-four-hour Drop.

Few people paid attention. The din on the stock-exchange floors and the plunging numbers neither incited the press nor drew the complete media linkage. These dives didn't inspire cries for reform or for introspection, and didn't announce the end of the capitalist system amid spectacle and alarm. The Twenty-four-hour Drops were now part of the routine; breakdowns had become predictable, even inevitable.

These were the operations of a separate universe of economics and computers, a concurrent field, a dual zone. Corporate spokespeople, interpreting the disembodied domain, asserting some institutional authority, reminding us of the presence of banks and investment houses, talked about money becoming fluid, a mere digit in the cosmos of trade. Explaining:

"Telecommunications systems make credit mobile."

"The market forces are interconnecting."

"We have to get used to the leaps and falls."

"This is the reorganizing of the global economy."

I noticed a modulated tone in the comments and descriptions. In press releases and newspapers and on TV the language of nuclear war had been transformed into sensitive terminology — as if the stock exchange was made of flesh. I read about "sympathy pains," "skittishness," "empathetic results." The financial markets could be anxiety-ridden, cautious, buoyant, exultant. There was unexpected talk about penetration, interfusion, interactivity. I identified a shift away from debates about media to awed discussions about living data.

The computers, TVs, faxes, and telephones could reflect and incite the user's emotions and moods. We could feel frightened and depressed, confident and cheerful, and the instant responsiveness of the machines could somehow apprehend this and inject both depression and elation into the system. The financial markets had evolved into a shuddering lattice of warnings and indicators. In the static, you could hear the SOS of those who were suffering; in the tumult, you could hear the cryptic missives of those who were ruthless, callous speculators indifferent to the pain and hope of others. Tapping into sources, tapping out paths.

The headlong ups and downs of the market created a one-day world where people were expendable. But the market also promoted networks of association. I realized that these volatile datafields could shrink time and present the human figure writ large — what William Blake might have called an electronic Albion. Through this multimedia engagement we could hear and see ourselves on a scale that we'd never encountered before. And encoded in the bits and bytes there may be that straining spirit. The machines were fired up, amplifying our every murmur and shout. And all that we are — good and terrible — raged, racing and hustling across continents and oceans.

I recognized that each crisis, or crash, was like a seed, a cell, that contained another larger or similar event and crisis. Complex communication chains of cause and effect provoked greater opportunities for miscommunication. The stock crashes resembled wars, apocalyptic moments where terror and upheaval, recklessness and pride, dreams and revelations mixed. But in the midst of this, you could begin to sense that the seeds, scraps, and guesses, the bedlam and blare, implied variations, extensions, passages, reshaped meanings, a voice that seemed to be calling to us, a new unfolding shade in this blend of imagination, technology, and perpetual emergency.

* * *

After the crashes, nothing looked different to me when I wandered around the city. I'd walk downtown and see how the building and wrecking and rebuilding thrived. Settled low-rises were being razed, and abstract high-rises erected. Our furor was mirrored in this constant refashioning. But the cycles of boom and bust, the crosswirings in messages, the agility of data, also sent many — if not most — people scurrying for cover, searching for insulation, filters, and shields, for ways of escape.

Rage too long repressed consumes people, like an accelerated form of cancer or like a cocaine addiction eating you from the inside. The only treatment for most of us is to pull down the blinders we wear, replay our memories, scan for the pattern, and go on jamming the crucial frequencies into bands that we can hear.

Icarus

Michael T. talked to me through this time. I fed off his mania. He'd disappeared from my class and he only left communiqués on my answering machine. When I checked for messages, I'd see the tiny redlight flickering like a beacon.

"IBM, AT&T, ITT, Pepsi, Coca-Cola, Time-Warner, Rogers Cable, the Turner Network, all the international speculators...all the transnationals...they should be opening embassies around the world. Then we'd really be talking about who's trying to run things. Not just yakety-yak. Show us who's really into control. I mean the fashion isn't for passion, but the season of the spontaneous is coming. It's the power hour now, and no one'll be able to keep out the flow."

Then his calls suddenly stopped.

After that first crash in October, when the frenzy had passed and when the dips and lunges in the markets had subsided, something eased in Michael. The phone didn't ring in the hours before the morning. He seemed to withdraw with the fading of the news.

I waited, phoned his number, and found nothing.

Two weeks later, my answering machine recorded a series of broken remarks from him, statements condensed into obscure bits, like hermetic notes for a work he was composing in his head.

"You could call me Icarus. Too close to the sun. I've been through a spiral. I've been flying and frying. I was going to write I-C-H on my denim jacket. Short for Icarus. My true name, my deep name."

I'd pulled up a chair, and sat listening to his quietened voice. What had happened to settle him? What had he found? What was he trying to tell me?

"I busted up, man. Shifts and riffs. Jamming things into my brain. And you know I didn't want to be another frazzled wire. I just want to live like a human being. I have to find my original self, my first face. Out of this broken behavior. No masks. No posturing. Anyone can fake it. And I need the real business. Direct speech."

His voice sounded less frenzied, almost reconciled, certainly cooled down from whatever wildness had combusted in him.

"I'll cut through the miscommunications. Cut through the lies. Analysis cuts through. I want to go somewhere where the waves won't drown you."

He stopped again. I wrote down what he said, thinking this would be his last call.

The next day he left a gentle monologue:

"I want to record all the tender moments. The fine moments. Like when a tree speaks through the wind. Like when the wind speaks through a tree.

"I want to get older, slower.

"I want to get smaller.

"Like a cat.

"Moving through the grass, next to the ground, close to the earth. Getting older, slower, smaller.

"This is what I'll do. Start the process of living again. Become a person. Become alive again. That's when I'll be real. That's when I'll be human again."

Those lines haunted me. They held a meaning that I needed

to understand. I thought I'd been losing a coherent line in my study of information, of electronic effects — I'd been striving for a clear, unattainable outside position, and I was resisting the deeper and tangled path, the emotional core. While I listened for what may churn in the wavelengths, I avoided personal disclosure and understanding, what was happening inside my home, in my life, in my relations with others, especially my wife — Lena, a lithe woman, so vigorous and impervious, now watching me rout myself toward utter confusion. All of these pieces and vague traces could be like stray shots in a glittering darkness. They left tinges, suspicions, the mystery of the noise in the machines. I felt I had to get closer to the heart of these networks. Naked and squalling, our true selves must appear.

I returned Michael's phone calls, and again got static, the metallic click and tone of his machine. Eventually, the tape ran out on his recorder, leaving nothing.

*　*　*

One night at the university, I met a friend who taught full time in the Humanities Division. We talked in a pub — a dingy place in a college. I asked her if she'd seen Michael. Yes, she said, surprising me. He'd entered her office a few days before, late in the afternoon. He didn't say anything at first, then he began to read from a manuscript he'd brought with him. He looked scrawny and tired, she told me. His speech was jumbled, jagged, elaborate. She'd been concerned for him, and had asked him if she could glance at the manuscript for herself. Michael had handed it over enthusiastically. She skimmed it, finding pencil strokes, inky fingerprints, an occasional precise statement like an aphorism, and sketches of faces and mouths and the heads of animals. One page had a prose poem about the suffering of angels and demons.

"Here's a thing that'll interest you. The manuscript had a title."

"What was it?"

She hesitated, frowned as though remembering some pain or schizoid wrenching that she'd read in the words.

"The manuscript was called 'Scorched.'"

* * *

Finally I saw him.

On a Saturday afternoon I was out walking along Front Street. Near the half-completed SkyDome stadium I saw Michael standing alone, staring up at the ribs of the arena. The girders and cement casings looked raw, wrecked. It was difficult to tell if the stadium was being demolished piece by piece or being hurriedly constructed to meet a deadline. Soon there would be gargoyles — strange and almost unidentifiable sculptures, creatures — hoisted above us, and inside there would be one massive TV screen dominating the north wall, and TVs mounted everywhere in the snaking hallways. Michael circled cautiously in front of the building, seemingly gauging it, appraising it.

He appeared haggard. Without his telephone, his acoustic passion, he seemed diminished, unimposing. He was much smaller, leaner, and darker than I'd remembered. With his amplified voice no longer ringing in my ears, I realized how little I'd seen of him. What was his family background? What did his home look like? What were his connections like with other people?

I understood that this was my entry into cyberspace, virtual reality. Electronics piped you into parallel universes. I saw the rift between the person and the simulated space of tape recordings. I'd imagined that Michael had mutated into a media being whose obsession had been to comprehend how one event could ignite many results, effects, explanations, cords of meaning. I realized that I'd let his humanity elude me.

I spoke to him.

When he turned to me, I saw that at first he wasn't sure who

I was either. Then he eagerly stepped closer. We stood back from the crowds, and talked. I asked him if he was all right.

"Hey, I'm fine," he said. He bounced nervously from foot to foot, incapable, it seemed, of staying in the same spot for more than a moment.

I pushed to know more, mentioning drugs, specifically cocaine.

"No way. More like too much coffee, too many cigarettes, no sleep, and too much TV. And no books, man. I was reading between the lincs, I wasn't reading the lines. If you know what I mean."

I couldn't see this then, but I can almost see it now: Michael had been initiated into the rites of data blackout and illumination, the dark time when you break down from a secure state and become dimly aware of what may breathe beyond you, the energy and pattern behind the visible. Bombarded, irradiated, Michael considered himself a veteran of a sound bite and image hazing.

"Influence. You've got to be influenced now. Got to be moved. Feel it all. Everything coming at you at once. What matters after is your destiny. The future. Too late to stop. I'm talking about letting it all reach you."

He had refused to close himself off to chaos, and to have been so acutely receptive at the same time had been insidiously painful for him.

We parted.

I later learned from the counselor at the university that Michael had been ordered by his family's doctor to rest in bed. He spent weeks sleeping, reading books, I was told. The prescription had no doubt been for a period of silence.

Human Measures

Tonight I want to get away from all the disorder. I'm inside my own room, my quiet room full of books. I've closed the den door, lowered the window so that it's only partly open, drawn the white curtains halfway, sat down, and relaxed in my wooden captain's chair. It's a worn, comfortable chair that my maternal grandfather brought from Dublin to Ferntosh, Alberta, in nineteen seventeen, when he and his Protestant family fled insurrections and injustices, the Irish troubles. I gaze around here slowly, see my manuscript on my desk, my shelves lined with books. The shelves are ordered according to author and subject. I switch on my small desklamp and a subdued glow throws a light as a candle might over the book I've left open from the night before.

My typewriter, writing pads, and pens are reassuring somehow. This small, private room is like an island of refuge. The ringing that has racketed in my ears seems to stop at last. The babble from outside falters and fades; the news doesn't penetrate here; the rumble from the street is distant, muted.

I reach across my desk for the open book, Walter Benjamin's

Illuminations. The feel and texture of paper. I look at the slight shadow the book casts when I hold it under my desklamp. Cardboard, binding, leaves. A static object; there's nothing to plug in. I turn to a page, unhurried, pacing myself. My eyes stalk the letters along the printed lines, forward and then downward.

Silence, solitude, the world of books.

But on the sidetable where I've stocked my files with clippings from newspapers and magazines, an advertisement shouts:

IS PAPER PASSÉ?
No more pencils, no more books...Coming soon!

An article that I've kept from the *New York Times* announces:

JUKEBOX LIBRARIES
The encyclopedia can be recorded on a disk the size of a musical CD. A small library can be contained in an optical jukebox...

And I know, sitting in this room where I write and read, that I have to ask questions about the book itself, about this privacy. Questions about the nature of reading, about the control of information, about decoding and interpreting the dataflow. If you believe that to live truly means you must challenge yourself and your world — and that the process of questioning and recording is central to your search for an enlightened life — then I know I have to ask this:

Could a bookbound awareness become a kind of blindness? Is the concept of the printed word itself undergoing a radical revaluation and change? Is the private world of the book — of ownership and personal copyright, of libraries and collections — a cherished myth of writers unable to follow along with the inventions, innovations, and experiments that occur daily? Writers feel obliged to criticize TV, radio, the computer. Why not the book? The years of introverted reading, the silence, the specialized training. Does meaning stream through the forcefields of the machines? Is it possible that I could carry a passion for books so far that I could cut myself off from life, from an understanding of myself and others?

These are hard questions to ask because maybe they are insoluble, maybe they deflect you from the matter of living acutely, living with perception, and, finally, living with yourself.

Yet this space seems to contract around me, becoming smaller, claustrophobic. My room abruptly feels like a prisonhouse of received knowledge.

* * *

Pitch blackness beyond the window. My house creaks, stirs, and settles.

When I'm honest with myself, I can say that I became a writer in part to maintain this privilege of solitude, the sanctum of books, this looking glass of study, observation, and response through the printed word. But I discovered that many literary people were turning insular and self-righteous when confronted by the hyperintensity of electronic communications. The forcefields are surely overpowering. However, the literary temper — or distemper — was rapidly becoming one that frequently tried, denounced, and punished the entire technological track. The surgical knife of intellectual analysis could function equally as well as an executioner's blade. It could cut up and serve information in murdered gray bits. Deadening ideas, deadened senses; little sense of the whole; a bookbound specialization for its own sake. So many books had been published with titles that proclaimed finales, conclusions, decay and death, an intellectual's Armageddon: "The Last of..."; "The Closing of..."; "The Decline of..."; "The Fall of..."; even "The End of the End of..." Some writers had indulged themselves in self-conscious windups to this self-conscious century.

I'd done my share of writing "The End of the End" pieces, but I was growing restless, suspicious, dissatisfied. There's high drama to anything titled "The Last," "The End." Yet I wonder if our millennial mood, half-troubled, half-elated, could also be a spark, a passage point through which and out of which ideas and emotions rush. A passion for the end may be a passion for breakout and renewal.

It is the reactive temper that I'm afraid of in myself. The snap judgements, the fast condemnations. I'd been finding that if one weren't adept at channeling input and output, at revolving possibilities in the mind, at handling multiple connections from various sources, then it was likely that the literary person, possessed by the medium of the book — black print, white pages — would be imprisoned by the act of judgement. Private reaction and condemnation could become solitary confinement. The more strongly focused the reading eye became, the greater the chance for the intensity of a too-isolated life.

I lean over my desk and move my lamp's switch to its highest setting. The light gleams, the wiring hums. I clutch a pen in my left hand. Begin writing words out on a blank page. I watch my pen, my hand, shape language, proceeding slowly, the etch of a word, sentence following sentence, the structuring of sense.

A human measure...

To locate and redefine an intelligible balance...

I want to find ways of learning about the natural energies, which we call telluric, and the artificial forces, which are electronic, and their meridian, their merger. There are implications of AI, apparitions and vocal presences in the wiring and chips. There are conundrums in a universe where radiation can be both a field and a wave. Computers already transport 1.5 million bits of information per second; but scientists say that within a few years there will be gigabytes and even terabytes — billions and trillions of bits. What instrument could I use to identify the route to a true human expressiveness? How can you walk with any certainty down these paths?

* * *

The instruments of perception and of change.

I look at an article from a magazine that I've left in my files.

Here is how the changeover from the book culture to computer culture — another way of putting this would be to say the changeover from alphabet culture to digital culture — was recognized in that clipping:

DID THE UNIVERSE JUST HAPPEN?

Our model for the cosmos, the author claimed, should be a computer program set for infinite, quixotic, and paradoxical variations, an orderly chaos, an eternal chaotic order.

In the late eighteen hundreds, I recall, the symbolist poet Mallarmé wrote in *Le livre, instrument spirituel* that everything in the world exists to end in a book — *que tout, au monde, existe pour aboutir à un livre.* Yet does the world any longer exist to end in a book? I think of the book metaphors of the universe: Dante's vision in his *Paradiso* of the seemingly scattered stars bound by love "into one single volume"; Shakespeare's equating of immortality with the publishing of a volume of sonnets; the Romantics and their readings of nature's pages and its occult diction; Whitman's "Leaves of Grass" identifying the poems and the pages themselves with the swaying souls of humanity.

To see a world in a microchip. The metaphors, figures of speech, and symbols have flipped in the public's mind. The unstill model of the universe now resembles the dynamic fluctuations of a replicating organism.

And what impels these infinite variations in our cosmic computer? Energy, attraction and repulsion, electricity and magnetism.

Hints inform me: the universe is all of a piece; it does not know fragments.

But what in this is the deep motif, the centering theme, the underlying design and strain?

* * *

Something moves here. I pause, look around my den. I'd switched on my typewriter an hour ago; its flatline hum adds a pleasing low drone to the room.

There are papers on the floor, files piled on top of other files. On the shelves paperbacks lean against hardbacks. These are the books I've loved, the books where I've lived a counter-life, transcendent from ordinary things. Books like monuments; ragged books with a musty smell. I have *The Book of Changes*, works on alchemy, divination, dreams, esoteric philosophy, those underground myths of history, heretical readings of experience, and new scientific writings by chaos theorists on the apparent randomness, the sweeping instability of nature. The words point to rhymes of meaning, arhythmic commotion, conjectures and rumors that could be the advance rim of the essential knowledge I crave.

Time slows in this room. The beige carpet I've thrown over the hardwood floor muffles the legs of my chair when I push it back. The carpet softens other furtive, aloof movements in the house. I imagine a clock ticking here. The second hand clicks with the monotonous regularity of a metronome, its mild sound like the tapping of a pen on a wooden surface.

I watch shadows. The house's groans add to the darkness outside, my sense of seclusion inside. At night everything in my room is vibrant; even the pens, papers, the typewriter and lamp, and my denim jacket hanging from the hook in the door take on a vital human quality.

I'm among familiar things. It may be this that has brought the quiet I've known, the settling in myself. In October, the gold and red leaves rustle over the sidewalks and grass, and I cling to this house's interiors, loving its quirky sounds, the way it slows down at night, the way it curbs my impatience.

(There's more. Lena in bed asleep, down the hall. Lena in another room, a shoulder bared above a white sheet, her long hair across her face. My wife and I, separated in this house...)

But time doesn't slow. It dashes on, faster. Digital clocks don't have to be rewound, and in digital time there's no equivalent to counterclockwise.

* * *

A radio booms out in the street. A scramble of motors and squealing tires. Police sirens whoop by. Across the alley a TV light glints.

And if I were to allow this night noise to permeate my room without a reply, I'd be sealing up the windows, stuffing my ears with wax, slamming and locking the door. We have plugged into the power of the machines. Crowd voices burst in; barriers are breached. Any room anywhere can be whipped up with whispers, mutters, and pleas.

Like others who dealt with the chaos of their times, I needed a human measure to draw straight lines in reality for me. "Euclid is too easy," the painter John Yeats told his son, William Butler Yeats. "It comes naturally to the literary imagination." What the elder Yeats may have meant is that a mind made up of book readings will be drawn to narrative logic and linearity, a single perspective. A mind made by books must translate and control experience through the turn and rule of the printed page. But the secret of being may lie in the unspoken, in the mysterious, in perceptions and processes that are not the result of lineal sequence or argument. If you withdraw too far into a bookish chamber, a room of your own, you could turn in on yourself; if you stand too inflexibly, stubbornly, in the firestorm of information, you could burn yourself out.

* * *

30

Morning.

My night thoughts are softened by a warmer air, a slight wind that ripples the curtains. As I pull them back, I see how in the halflight of the dawn the city doesn't seem so unmanageable, so devouring. The alley outside my window is undisturbed except for the brown-striped tabby that saunters by. The back yards of the redbrick houses, built between World Wars I and II, look peaceful. Clouds drift down; the treetops stand out. The alley is soon covered by a morning mist. The dampness descends, and I find a still interlude before the restless roar starts again.

In those sleepless hours, I can think:

The stock market crashes that heralded the crumbling of national borderlines, boundaries rendered meaningless by the swift wraithlike exchanges of data, the disconnected facts and statistics and opinions, the apotheosis of the microcomputer and its splice-in with TV and the telephone and the fax, the loss of introspective and contemplative time, Michael T.'s heightened feelings, his willingness to be desperate, the stretching and sagging of people's nerves, the hallucinatory tinge to the telecommunications' visions, all the calling ghosts and the hisses on tape...and what happens to people and their ability to feel, their capacity to make contact with each other...decentered selves...nomadic, unstable...

At my desk I note down these junctures and debates on paper. There are factors I could add, and no resolution in sight, no closure I could honestly invoke.

What cohesiveness could I find to organize the intensity of the turbulence? Pattern; incoherence. Wholeness, and breakage. How could I speak truly of the eruptions, the options, the melding of technology and culture, the joining of commerce and machinery and art and political force that I perceived in the crashes, that I heard in Michael's freeform rants, that I'd kept a record of in my lectures at the university, that I'd been trying to write about in a medium that seemed obsolete? And there's another point I must address — why, since I'd begun to confront the data overdose, in the past months, I can't simply shut off the TV and the radio, shut out the telephone, turn down the volume, unplug the cords.

When I sit back in my chair — the wood brittle and cracked, smoothed by use — I see how my notes and questions could be distractions, even a sort of addiction. Transnational stock brokerages and speculators employ those spokespeople who explain crises, and who can misinform us, swamping us with what have been termed misstatements and misfacts. These people could be blinded; it is unlikely that they are any less confounded than I am. Reality can be obscured; our minds deluded. Truths about ourselves then become harder to hear, see, and feel, and harder to bear. All of this for me, and for others, could be a phony shock, a slick drama of jolts, and not the recognition, the individual sounding, that we need...

These concerns claw for attention. Each question, each point, each juncture, could be a sign that many people understand the need to puncture illusions, to snap back the masks of power — to see what may be behind those masks — face our evasions and crackups, clarify what it means to interpret reality during sensory deprivation and sensory tilt, in an information and misinformation glut. It strikes me now that what we can hope to do from any point we start, however we enter this city, is involve and invest ourselves, examine the spread of greed, the need for power in our souls, trace how the electroscape can drug us, and how it can shape and elevate our senses.

* * *

The morning blare begins to build again. Quiet times must always pass here. The city's sound crescendoes to a clamor. There is the shifting pitch of ephemeral remarks and peals of laughter, with the chants of slogans, the incantations of ads, all the rap and grit in the street. This ritual of rising and falling sound tells me how I must admit new angles, words, experiences, ideas. I have to educate

32

myself in revisions and revelation, the often contradictory feelings and occurrences in the city of dizzying and sometimes dazzling motion.

AN AVALANCE OF INFORMATION
IS COMING
    TO YOUR VIDEO SCREEN

Only the fastest will survive

The headlines and blurbs, the traces and particles, the speculative comments, haven't formed a luminous whole for me yet. But if it's true that a personal voice, that individual consciousness itself, can be overwhelmed by rough news, then I'm forced to acknowledge that whatever happens, whatever I do, will have to be measured beside others who are floundering and fighting their way through this turmoil and doubt.

Fastforwarding

Blank Screen

At noon I walk up two floors in my house to my viewing room, the place I've set aside for the TV, my stereo system, a couch, a table, shelves of vinyl discs, CDs, and tapes. I look at the dark-green tube, the black plastic frame, the single cord stringing out to the power bar, the nest of wires and plugs.

The blank screen momentarily startles me. I'd expected to find images jumping, sound crackling, the interweaving of commercials and shows and news, the suave seductions of entertainment and exposure, an opening for vital incident and fantasy in this box that throws life into a constant dissolve.

But the screen admits nothing. The TV isn't on. And yet it suggests the presence of forms ready to emerge, the rhythm of changing stations.

I stand for a while in this room's solitude. With the TV off, the room seems larger than I remember, without much warmth, almost silent, unpeopled. The bright sun, yellow light from the window, catches my eye. Harvest gold remains late in the season. A streak of gray clouds; a few red and brown leaves dangle from the top of the maple tree. But the TV has the greater pull here, and I turn back to the set and touch the remote.

Tube flash, light twitching on the mesh.

I push the volume up high. And because I've cabled the TV into the amplifier-receiver, the speakers amplify the jolt. A cocoon mood wraps around me when I sit close to the tube's heat. Ionized air. The flutter casts its soft blue shine. Gray and white dots wash up and down. Interference images, a flatline of white noise.

A couple of seconds pass before I realize that I'm staring at a blank spot in the cable system.

What is TV? How does it truly affect us? Simple questions, yet they're hard to answer. I sit in front of the screen speculating, drawn to its glow. I could force TV into a precise, literary definition. But the effects of TV aren't precise: they're amorphous, subliminal, nonverbal, unpredictable, sensual, impalpable. Everyone knows about TV. We take it for granted, expressing opinions on its impact, mostly denunciations, despite the fact that nearly everyone watches it and listens to its chatter. TV has much to do with the sense of aimlessness and discontinuity that people perceive, the assault and allure of rampant data, the atmosphere of fear and excitement thriving and storming in our lives. The machine flickers, making its omnipresence felt, like a companion. Or an enemy?

Press the remote. The stations shuttle by. I catch myself thinking about TV as if the screen could answer me. Futurists talk about interactive media, a true fusion of user and machine, where the set responds to your hand and to your private whims and probes, output matching input. The cathode beam seems to travel only one way now, like a monologue.

You switch on TV and your eyes and ears receive images and voices, your body gathers in traces of motion and presence. People move — words spin — everything shakes loose. The questions I've been articulating for myself must center on this: in the flickering, the elements of change, is there a cycle, a movement toward balance, a series of links that will establish a whole pattern, an underlying melody, a rhythm and harmony of feeling and thought?

* * *

Touching the remote again, flipping stations backward and forward.

The swarms of representation, the apparitions of the afternoon.

Entering *in medias res*, I immerse myself in a soap opera. I skip to an interview that's spliced with filmed commercials and review clips of upcoming shows. Mesmerized, I let the programming engulf me. The box frames the floating world, its now.

I keep tapping the button, and keep tapping into the hum of human talk, inside the lawless flux, toward things missed, things felt to be present.

Instantly I become part of the viewing family that TV executives want to lure and hold. The light and sound technologies pervade our homes with their drift, their sense nets designed to entrance us and to web us together. Relays of the mundane and the unknown. I just saw this commercial; she looks like a neighbor of mine; I've heard an extreme opinion that I've never considered before.

Who programs the images and sound bites? The stateless corporations, the transnationals with holdings and network chiefs on several continents, the product of multiple mergers. They have the money to buy space on the tube, filling the air day and night with their content, setting up fleeting coordinates of reference and meaning.

Time slides on. I'm treated to jumpcuts, fadeouts, fast and slow motion. Hurtling images make real time seemingly vanish.

Is TV a medium of visions or of hallucinations? Is it a hypnotic tool that bolts you to your chair before an addictive mesh? I've returned for renewed access, asking if it's possible that TV offers a key to the electric process and myths. It may be an instrument that allows us to see and hear directly into the current and its fields, beyond the corporate attempts at control.

* * *

My room blurs. The house appears to recede into the background. Gone are the clouds scuttling across the sky, the afternoon's yellow light. The vivid leaves seem to dissolve.

Moving through channels, hot colors and pixel density, identifying faces, feeling moods, discovering contrasts, fast-forwarding —

Touch Memory

You, sudden in a TV flash.

I see an image of Lena, unexpectedly coming through with the look of someone visiting a talk show. Ghost, guest. As if out of a dream. I find myself pausing to remember us together, sprawled here, her hand on the remote, pressing the buttons. A memory disconnected from the swing of my search. Her face disappears into the blue backdrop, the fluttering signal, the simulations and resemblances that hover in my viewing room.

I put the remote down and let the talk show linger. TV offers reassurances in its familiar faces and landscapes. It peoples our solitude. But it can play tricks, like a wily prankster adept with special effects. Deceptions, concealments, holes. Images spill through the concentrated beam. In the flicker, with the set's vibration, you sit inside a light that can affect you by stirring memories and dreams, your recollections and inner life merging with this radiant point.

I saw someone who looked like Lena. I'm taking my time getting to the story of an unraveling marriage; I've resisted that side of the trip. But when you plunge into psychic highspeed, you can easily elude what haunts you, your past, your relationships, your motives, their mystery.

Between news items and commercials, a lone figure touched off my memories. Lena was twinned in the look of a woman who was interviewed. I saw a double, then she was gone.

Tapping the remote, and a suggestive fluid image weaves in a memory and a dream.

A TV room is an interior space, a chamber inside a house and inside the mind. You can be lured into absorbing the tube's radiance by the sheer intensity of its delivery. The TV space resembles a circle of magic, conjuring symbols, shadows, masks. If you're suggestible enough, you can slip into a trance, hypnotized by the rays, the constant configurations.

Lena and I were avid TV watchers. Sometimes we'd sit for hours, our minds transfixed, a distance between us. The tube's glitter prevailed, and we sat without saying much to each other. Then I'd start talking about TV, the bombardment of minutae and opinions. We didn't know how to scan this meshing, I said, TV rewires our sense of time and place.

"It's more like a tranquilizer," she'd said, laughing. "It's just a way of tuning things out for a while. That's all it is, really."

There was a path of awareness that I had to discover for myself. To engage the labyrinth of clues that the media emits and issues, to be aware of the hazards of an overload, you have to develop a scale for boundaries. Stay open, stay curious, but don't let genuine human contact be swept away.

I remember touching her, lying down in sensuality, soft skin and tongues meeting, breathing intimacies, burying myself in her wet life, the salty warm taste between her legs, then the damp heat and the hard thrust of our bodies joining...

Pressing in programs, I fastforward the channels.

In my mind I rewind these memories that are like dreams. I saw a woman who resembled Lena, and she vanished. TV exposes a primal, even elemental side of life. You encounter an isolated figure, wild weather in a lush landscape, the shadows in a closed room, people meeting and clashing and making love and separating, people struggling to break through to each other, renewing their connection with the world. This is also what happens: your own stories and projections join the flicker, the banter of stars and guests.

And if I were a different sort of writer, I'd stop to describe what happens between two people when sympathy and warmth decay. Soon I'll restore what I've omitted. Someone there to be addressed. But I tap the button and flip through the panoramas, the faces, the graphics like hieroglyphs, this skittering glow.

Homing

Latent Rhythms

Morning, and a softer light comes through my window. A soprano sings Strauss lieder on the radio, in another room, far off inside the house. I scatter on my desk all the notes I've been carrying in my pockets. The notes contain memories and ideas, and maybe the cues I need to find my way through the effusions of the mediascape, the information spew, images emanating into dark rooms, the sonic messages that beam and bounce off the towers and spires.

Scented air, warmer today. An autumn morning without any wind, the chill. Outside, the deep urban hum, hydroelectric, machine-driven, has already started up. I sort out my notes, reading them over, wondering if the necessary pattern is beginning to gather within them.

Here are some facts. I was born in Ottawa in nineteen fifty-five. I was named after my father, who was working at that time on Parliament Hill for the federal Liberal Party and writing novels on Sundays. He was transferred to Toronto in nineteen fifty-seven. Our family moved to what was then a genteel, introverted city, where you could get a clear view of a lake. My sister was born in nineteen fifty-nine, and my mother named her after her mother. In nineteen sixty-four, after years of living in a three-bedroom apartment on the West Side, we moved to a house in North Toronto, in a nearly rustic area called Glen Echo, not far from Hogg's Hollow.

Glen Echo, the echoing glen.

Now I remember the wind hissing at night through the elm trees on the street and in the ravines, like voices rushing past. The strong, bracing winds rustled the maples, oaks, birches, and willows in late October and early November.

Randomness, drift. These notes don't seem to connect everything for me. But I wonder how memory tracks into the present, about the way thoughts and perceptions intertwine with TV images and pop songs, those hints and fantasies of a mediated existence, how the real and the unreal collide. I need to trace how we lived under invisible pressure, where and when the influences began, the shaping of our selves in the flux.

I try to shut out external input, the chaos, and listen for latent rhythms, for themes and variations. The wind in the trees, the echoes along the ravines. There is the seemingly secure sound of a home in the suburbs, the easy tone in the house itself, the welcoming voices of my mother, father, and sister.

I have to retrieve parts of my past because I know that I've become rootless, harrowed by the blur of events and upset, unsure of what shadows me in the midnight calls and the unsparing reams of data, the interpretations, statistics, pictures, and sounds. My grip on things is suddenly insubstantial.

So I hold on to what glimmers come. They are erratic, unanchored, somehow reassuring and beautiful, the tone and time of a house and family. In the overflow of information it is up to each of us to find the core of meaning, inner form, something to call grounding, home.

Cathode Erotic

Remembering one moment when I truly felt how the current had seeped into my life, molding and shaping, I go back into the experience of watching TV after midnight for the first time with my girlfriend Christine, in the darkened basement of my family's home.

"Keep the TV on," Christine said. She slipped off her jeans and her panties and slid down on the couch.

With that gentle command, we lost our virginity together. Black-and-white rays bathed our squirming bodies. The TV program that was on didn't matter to us. The picture was snowy; the sound wasn't sharply defined. But we felt protected somehow, accompanied by a sound track that seemed specially designed for our adolescent groping.

Our bodies picked up the gray glow from the set. We absorbed the scan and the flicker, and we radiated a gray-blue tint on the couch.

In the next moment, our bodies — I noticed when I opened my eyes again — were covered with what appeared like quivering tattoos. Their shapes shivered. Conductive skin; some instant affiliation, even a foreknowledge, an understanding fired through our fingertips and mouths. She jumped slightly when I kissed her inner thigh, and I was intensified too by her hands running up and down my back.

A commercial flashed across Christine's face the instant I looked into her eyes. She closed her eyes suddenly. Then she pushed around me, drawing me deeply inside her. A news report smothered our groans. When we finished — mostly unaware of what we'd done — we sat up to see what show followed next.

First came the sensation, the touch, the flux of images and sounds, then came the thinking, the explanations. What doesn't follow in my mind is the chronology — the linear passage of time. My mental montage doesn't cut from A to B and C. I'm not sure how old Christine and I were. Moments blend into other moments from later in our time together. Scenes leak into set pieces from movies and TV shows. But I remember feelings, the place: my contact with her skin, making love in the rec room, the TV in the corner, on the couch with its threadbare covering.

Christine stroked my hair and face with her pale, inquisitive hands. The sensation of my flesh meeting hers, the sensual fit, the surprising familiarity. As if entering each other's bodies was the easiest thing to do, almost an unconscious act, maybe inevitable.

"Want to come closer while you're watching?" she asked on another night.

In the renovated basement of her parents' home, we lay in each other's arms, clothed and warm and relaxed, on a brown leather couch. The TV gleamed.

Christine stretched up, tossing her red hair loose. She unbuttoned her shirt and unsnapped her bra. I reached over and cupped her breasts and her erect nipples. She leaned forward and ran her tongue between my lips, then licked my chin and mouth. She smelled of perfume and bathsoap. The blue-gray light irradiated us again and music and dialogue washed over our skin. I touched her legs, sliding my hand up to caress the wet part in her jeans. And she began to massage my thigh, her other hand lifting my shirt and rubbing and clasping my back and neck.

* * *

The dark, quiet house. Her parents were asleep upstairs. All was subdued, softened, except for the tinny sound and the murky tube-light, which was all that the old set could deliver. Beams flickered over the stucco ceiling and the bare tile floor.

Christine and I wriggled apart, a little breathless, then we smiled and removed clothes until we were naked. We took in the rays, the TV voices like overheard conversations, the people on TV like eavesdroppers on our whispering, and our senses were left open.

Our bodies and psyches had become the area of penetration, the screens and receptors and translators on which light and sound played.

"Television," Christine murmured, "does something weird to me."

And she rolled toward me again on the couch.

"Can you feel what I mean?" she asked.

(I could...)

"Can you feel it?" she asked.

(I did...)

"Please don't go home early tonight. Please don't let me go, don't go off in yourself...Not tonight," she said strangely, almost to herself.

(It was already late. I wasn't planning on going anywhere. She didn't want to be alone, and neither did I. I wanted to stay inside her.)

I loved the way the gray-blue light traveled over her white skin, her shapely hips, her silky inner thighs, the soft red hair below her navel. The sensuality of the flicker, the vibrations of sound like an invitation to join together. Our sex-touch had a lightness. It was easy

51

for us to find an aura around our flesh, our bodies glistening in the pathway of the discharging set. After we made love, I rested my head on her, my ear next to her womb. I listened closely — for what, I'm not sure. But I heard her heartbeat and felt her warm skin's pulse.

* * *

The procession of shows on TV created a floating mood. Nothing appeared to be a threat to our lives and leisure. Twelve-thirty a.m....one a.m....one-thirty a.m....

Discovering sex in front of the TV. Sometimes making love like that could become oddly abstracted, almost disembodied. You could feel like you weren't really there. Our bodies were galvanized. Secret memoranda and teachings seemed to leap back and forth between our fingers, palms, and lips. Yet I wonder if our emotions and minds were fully engaged. First came the touching, then came the viewing of the programs.

The black-and-white rays scanned physical outline, the contours of faces and bodies. Movement and musculature stood out, compelled our attention. We were, maybe instinctively, concentrating on pronounced bone structures, eyes that glinted and sparked and glared, rich tumbles of hair, people walking, standing, kneeling, and sitting, postures of action and arrest, postures of power. With the tubelight's glaze and skim over our bodies, we were more eroticized than tranquilized, part participants, part experimenters.

TV watching has been described by media experts as immobilizing, static, passive. The introduction of any electronic field into a home is more like a stimulator. Modulating, modifying; adjustments of feeling, response, and perception. It is the sustained exposure to any one medium that may bring the blunting of emotions, the mesmerism, the passionless removal, the disengagement from reality. But I doubt if most people who spent years watching the screen would say that their TV ingestion was pacifying at first. Black-and-white rays and buzzing sound tracks inspired and provoked moods, a state of sifting and reply.

I retained scraps of commercials, jingles, clichés, lyrics. Disparate experiences remote-controlled my memories, triggering an outpouring of repartee from a sitcom, songlines from a variety show. I'd be constantly surprised by the bits I'd find in my mind, the implants and fragments and tips about existence.

TV grounded us. Only that grounding was fluid. The most successful TV events uncovered the flux of experience. The crisis, the slice-of-life program, the eyewitness report, the sports spectacular, made TV come alive. And the scenes and articulations it disclosed, imparted, and documented appeared seamless, mutable, and chameleonlike.

✢ ✢ ✢

Christine and I glowed when we made love, our liquid kisses reflected back to us on the screen, our pale bodies mingling with its beams, the sexual electroscape seducing and brushing and nestling us, while our ears hummed with the vibrating air, with all the dialogue and jokes and announcements, the bites of music, this technology's palaver, its discourse of light and sound.

* * *

"Come inside me," Christine whispered.

She said my name so quietly that I could barely make it out. I wanted to hear her voice, her breathing. Then she shed her clothes and stood by the couch, holding my head to her.

"I want to feel you inside me."

I licked her tiny brown nipples, and she rubbed her hands on the nape of my neck, under my hair. I worked with my mouth back down to her parted legs, tongueing between her thighs, finding her wetness again.

53

She leaned me back on the couch, unbuttoned my shirt, pulled off my jeans and underwear, and then straddled me. Her hands guided me in. I pushed deeper, and we moved, our bodies becoming slick and damp.

"Jesus, TV makes me want to fuck," she said.

The luminousness from the set wrapped around her body and red hair. She rose and fell on me, looking like a fierce angel in the cathode halo.

Programs teemed. Light was cast over the room. Smooth ambient noise informed our background.

And we would return to that couch in the basement on Friday and Saturday night for years, two people glimpsing and sensing something within and even beyond the other, exploring one another's bodies into the night and into the early morning.

Transforming

Another night, a few years later, another moment. I was watching TV alone in the den, now and then skimming a page of the hardback book on my lap. The TV kept up a relentless backdrop, a mobile pastiche that began with a talk show then coalesced into a movie, interspersed with loud commercials and the station's insignia. My parents had bought a Motorola color set, and its larger screen brought a greater visual intensity. I scanned the reds, greens, and blues, not registering the content of the show.

Then the tubelight blazed these words:

THE TRANSFORMATION IS HERE
THE TRANSFORMATION IS NOW

I sat up on the couch and waited eagerly to see what would materialize. There was something I needed to know here, something essential, crucial, looming.

An image of a new car rolled onto the screen. The car was sleek, shiny, elegant. The rough frontier landscape behind it reflected on the surface. A narrator with a husky baritone solemnly intoned lines about resilience, innovations for the road, retiring your old wheels. "The time has come," the voice preached, "for a profound change in your life."

Mysteries followed. The tires spun off the screen. They looked as though they'd been sheared off the car's body. A black phantom space occupied the driver's seat. The car was piloted by an off-screen controller, an unseen force, inaccessible and yet apparently all-knowing, possibly beneficent, possibly obsessive about authority, domination, restraint. But the engine gunned and the wheels rotated — they seemed to clamor and turn with a life of their own.

A TRANSFORMATION OF TIRES

I thought in pictures and symbols. Circles, cycles, revolutions, spirals; things going round, mutating faster, their substance altered in the whorl. I felt as if I was approaching the rhythm of the world. It was necessary that I listen and see.

A TRANSFORMATION OF LIVING

Words shifted around in my mind: to be informed was to be reshaped. I heard distant echoes of the word "trance," a directive in "live."

Nothing more. Dispatch completed. The tubeglow lit another ad about a hit movie.

Released, I slumped back on the couch, and reread the passage on the page to figure out where I'd been in the book.

*　*　*

One night I was lying between the stereo speakers in the living room. I absorbed sound directly. The Beatles' *White Album* played on the turntable. Side four, cut one, Revolution Number 1. This song reworked the 45 RPM single that the band had put out earlier. The album version was looser, slower, a parody of the original. The title pushed in one direction, but John Lennon's lyrics and sarcastic growl pushed in another altogether. His words rejected terrorism, ideological revolutions based on extremist left and right positions, coercion, and bullying. Yet Lennon confessed that we all want to change ourselves. He hinted that you must let the world grab you before you can find answers to your questions.

The lush stereo sound — guitars and drums channeled through left and right speakers; overdubbed voices in the center — molded more of an acoustic presence in the room than I'd heard before. Between the lines and Lennon's ironic delivery, the song said that change was already vital in our homes, livid in our nerve ends and minds.

Revolution Number 9 tracked three songs later. This music tore away from conventional pop song structures into tape loops and sampling. "Number 9...Number 9...Number 9..." a voice chanted. Lennon howled in the background. Church chimes, garbled speech, distorted orchestrations. The cut was unpredictable, impossible to program on conventional radio. Push this revolution far enough, the music suggested, and you get a recording of chaos that captures life churning close to form, stunning noise on the brink of becoming a sharp signal.

* * *

The diamond needle scraped to the end of the record. Then the needle scratched and bobbed, stuck near the spindle. The hiss in the speakers sounded like a surf at high tide.

These synthetic discs had inspired a language of cuts, grooves, and tracks. The words told of a ploughing, a plotted path that took the listener somewhere. The needle was moving toward the center, toward elusive zones, hidden places.

The hi-fi system worked through a translation of force-fields. Vibrations were promoted through an excitement of speakers. Then that oscillation passed through me. What was struck inside the speakers was converted into music by my ears and mind.

But there was always that hiss at the edge. I'd sometimes leave the needle there, wondering if more would eventually reveal itself.

* * *

I was beginning to learn that the TV light and hi-fi sound belonged to a vast electronic ritual, an initiation into moving images and music, an expanding imaginative process. And I responded to the new vehicles of expression because I thought they were agents. The myths, dramas, songs, and lyrics seemed to bring me closer to messages from an invisible realm.

I remember how certain recordings became important to me. I'd select the *White Album* with its blank cover, the whiteness opening to possibility; The Eroica Symphony conducted by Georg Solti, so that I could reflect on the number of times that Beethoven sent the main theme in the first movement through surprising mutations; Glenn Gould's nineteen fifty-five recording of The Goldberg Variations; Mahler's Ninth Symphony, in Leonard Bernstein's impassioned, eccentric reading; Led Zeppelin's second album, those arrogant rock-and-rollers with their relentless beat and ferocious guitar; and The Who's ambitious opera *Tommy*. They had this in common: embryonic themes metamorphosed into variations. Each disc ended with the hiss that gestured toward the unheard and implied, the enigma around things. These notes and phrases, and the strip of noise, were like seeds that contained multitudes.

* * *

And when I turned on the TV, I'd let the psychic caresses touch me. And when I placed the diamond needle on the disc, I could start a transformation again.

Sensibility

Transformation! I think of Christine, the commercial about tires, the *White Album* songs, and I know I'm turning toward where our sensual preparations began, the on and off conditioning, the buildup and the abrupt release of energy.

Christine and I lived in the technological induction of mind, spirit, and sensibility into an environment that was both electric and magnetic, both flow and field, light and acoustic, a milieu of recordings, concerts, and tapings, of hi-fi speakers, tubes, and screens, of transmission and reception. Only we didn't know it; we were largely oblivious to the effects. Sensibility precedes ideology. This initiation wasn't informed by the dialectical imperative, the logic and forward press of history toward a synthesis, possibly a terminal conclusion. Karl Marx would not have easily recognized the transformations that the current and its fields instated and instigated. Capital may have driven the manufacturing of machines and their mass merchandising. But once these technologies were installed in our homes — the electronic devices giving off radiation, and amplifying, conveying, and often deforming signals — a force was unleashed, unchecked. High voltages can provoke regeneration. Scientists began to say there were more breakthroughs and discoveries per minute in technology than at any other time. Suddenly it appeared that our existence had become a maze of influences and repercussions, charged particles stirring matters everywhere, and that the conditions of our lives were inflamed. And so the protean element we called electromagnetism had stolen indoors, subtly and deeply into the living room and basement, the den and kitchen and bedroom, impressing our senses and sensitivities, affecting what was forming in the slippery center of our private selves. The pull of that power was intangible, evasive, ethereal, circuitous. And when Christine and I made love on the couch in the line of the TV beam, and when I sprawled on the floor with my head between the stereo speakers, we both lived in an influx which composed the deliria and rearrangements of the new, the world's reenchantment. Our lives were screened and irradiated in the cathode glow, in the repeatable cycles of music.

* * *

Songs, ads, slogans, blurbs. These spilled through my mind in those years. I remember the shaping of sensibility, the forging of response, in phrases and remarks that are like captions and notes:

Growing up electrified meant you could listen to the planet, to mutterings on wavelengths that you couldn't completely follow. Growing up with such an acoustic nearness meant having a mind full of melodies, chords, and rhythms, with a fluidity, and sometimes an uncertainty, in your thoughts.

Growing up without borderlines in the mind meant living in the midst of the great twentieth-century transformation: culture and political spectacle and sexuality plus technology. This turbulent alchemy didn't mean an end to politics. On the contrary, we could become aware, through visual and aural replays, the shimmer and accent of patterns, of the techniques of manipulation, of the mania to control.

But growing up with a TV screen and hi-fi speakers meant growing up self-conscious, all too aware of our own flesh, our reflections, our amorphous selves. It meant being exposed. Receptivity can become gullibility — a sort of permanent childlike eagerness to watch life slide and gambol and accelerate by.

* * *

With our TVs, stereos, radios, headphones, and movie screens, we lived in a time when music, motion, echoes, icons, and corporate emotions and symbols were the touchpoints that so many of us understood without explanation. Perceptual changes precede a change of mind. We'd feel experiences before we'd conceptualize them or understand them. Modes of education, contexts of authority, systems of propaganda, were at work, fashioning. But what was most obvious, apparent, was visceral, sensual, ear-filling, eye-filling. And we had access to soundscapes and imagescapes through TV, the telephone, the radio, and later the home terminal, the video recorder and camera. Though our story would be local, and even banal, taking place in high school hallways, in the renovated basements of our parents' homes, in shopping malls and at hamburger joints, that story would also be televisual and oral, soaked in global events and fictitious treatments of history. It would often be difficult to tell the difference between a movie, a TV show, a radio dramatization we'd encountered on an assassination (like that of President John F. Kennedy or his brother Robert), and the real catastrophe. Fact and fantasy fused, becoming a hybrid of mass events and private fictions. You could experience waves of primary effects (political turmoil and stock market crashes) and ripples of secondary effects (depression, exhilaration, other mood alterations). Through an affluence provided by our parents, a wealth that people in other cultures could hardly imagine, we had the metamorphic influence of technology readily available, so that we could make over what we consumed, saw, and heard, and so that we could be remade ourselves.

Living electrified sometimes means breathing in sensations of jolts and strokes.

It means living linked, by extended senses and heightened sensitivities, to what occurs elsewhere.

Living in psychic networks and susceptible interconnections means becoming impressionable, sometimes irritable and irascible, and sometimes numbed, a supersensitivity that comes from being constantly barraged, brushed, rubbed, and influenced. It means having to struggle to regain, or to discover, a personal voice, authentic and without delusion, a responsiveness that could lead you to a closer relationship with others.

Our world was full of visions and dreams, of spells and transports and portents, and it was capable, I would find, of radical disruption, confusion, and breakdown.

A Crack in the Conditioning

Autumn, in the evening, at my parents' dinner table, and suddenly every light in the house flickered off.

"What's happening?" my father asked.

"Nothing important," my mother replied.

My sister and I stared at each other.

"Well, something's wrong. The lights are all going. My God." My father removed his glasses, rubbed his eyes almost violently, and glanced up at the ceiling as if he'd find some answer there.

We sat quietly and waited. The lights in the ceiling shuddered back on. Then they snapped off, and stayed off, and we were alone in the darkness.

My sister shoved her plate away and complained that she couldn't see.

"It's all right. Don't worry. Everything's fine," my mother said soothingly, no trace of alarm or annoyance in her voice. She kept her reading glasses on when she spoke.

But the darkness remained, and we continued to wait, huddling uneasily.

"It'll be all right," my mother repeated.

My parents wanted an orderly, well-tempered world. They tried to find a safe home for my sister and me. In our tree-lined, sheltered neighborhood, there was no street lighting at night. There were no paved sidewalks, and because there was almost no traffic, no stop signs were needed to mark the intersections. Glen Echo was a secluded spot, a haven of light and sound, a fit place for my mental life of music, books, and TV, my floating and drifting in the media streams.

There had never been a mugging or a murder in our back yards. Breakings-and-enterings were rare. I had friends whose parents hardly ever locked their front doors when they went to bed. Hunting rifles were kept under key in basement collections — if anyone even had a gun or admitted to owning one. Rape, incest, and child abuse were secrets that no one dared mention out loud. We engaged the roar and glare of history and crisis mostly through TV and radio. In my neighborhood, the homes were quiet, the people snug and aloof.

I never questioned my situation. I didn't think there was anything odd about it.

The blackout cracked my sense of security. A shortage had intruded on us. The energy feed-in had stopped, and we found ourselves in the gap between connections.

I was aware that there was a split in our world. The TV was down. The radio was dead. The lights were gone. The kitchen had lost its steady hum, and the house had turned cold.

* * *

"It's nothing," my mother said. "A fuse has blown somewhere. A hydro station's broken down. Somebody tripped over a cord. These things happen."

A temporary break; merely an interruption.

My mother was a former schoolteacher who thrived on explanations. Sharp-witted and well-read, she was a model of patience and tolerance. For her a breakage like this could probably be understood. A disruptive effect had to have a specific cause. She said that we each had the gift of reason, and we could study and learn to put things together. Listen, read, and wait, she said. A blown fuse was not only intelligible, it was inevitable. With what I later took to be a stoical streak in her, she shrugged and sighed.

My father incited the fear.

"Can't we do something?"

"Like what?"

My mother's steadiness seemed to provoke him.

"What about the neighbors? Maybe we should call someone. Jesus Christ. Is everything out?"

"It's only a shortage of some sort. We'll fix it. Or someone will. Stop fussing. I'll check the fuse box. And check with the neighbors."

On and off, a reordering of data, the reaction to being abruptly isolated.

By then we realized that the lights wouldn't be back for a while. A cool wind seeped through tiny slits in the back door. The windows rattled. The house conducted an internal conversation. There was the strange diction of brick and wood, the building's structure articulating things to itself.

None of us said anything. Then my mother got up from the table, opened a cupboard, and found candles on the shelf. She lit two with matches and made wax mounds in two small dishes — offerings to the night.

Candlelight made the house look haunted. Ghostly shapes fluttered over the walls, the refrigerator, and stove. We became murky imprints, vague silhouettes, like figures dimly seen in an old gaslit theater. Water dripped from the kitchen faucet. Hollow tapping; water on metal. Outside, branches and leaves crackled in the wind. I heard a dog whine and yip down the street. Through the dining-room windows I saw cars slink by the house, their headlights like searchbeams skimming over the yards and bushes, the driveways and trees.

The cars didn't stop. No one came to the door.

"When do you think this'll end?" my father asked.

An unfamiliar strain of loneliness and panic had crept into his voice. He was talking almost as if we weren't there. He jumped up from the table, angrily paced back and forth, then sat down again. I saw how completely unsettled he was. My father was a gentle man, and it unnerved me to see that he could so easily lose his composure.

My mother stood and said that she'd call the city Hydro number. She went off to the den, but when she phoned out I could hear that she connected with nothing. The lines were jammed, noisy, staticky, she said. The switchboards must have been congested with callers, all of them probably with the same question. When she came back to the kitchen, she confessed that she'd forgotten to replace some dead batteries in the den's portable radio.

Through all this, my sister and I remained silent at the table. I shifted uncomfortably in my chair. She poked nervously at her food. We may have been sharing a single thought: how preset we were in our ways; how much we assumed that there would always be smooth operations in our home. I remember thinking new things about my sister: I don't really know you, I said to myself, I don't know what you think and feel; you're a cipher to me, living a secret life here.

The house grew colder, and its creaks and groans became eerie, mystifying. There were crumblings in the basement. The longer the blackout continued, the more the house became estranged from us. It felt like a laboratory in someone's experiment. As if the light and the heat had been programmed by a diabolical electrician who was running a malicious test on our reflexes.

Suddenly I wondered if this vulnerable universe was perverse and demonic. Nothing was still. The furniture and appliances, the windows and doors, the foundations and walls... everything was alive, inhabited, possibly possessed.

The night had its own rules. My hearing was drawn to the noises that came from the basement and from upstairs. Sounds became emphatic. People once populated this darkness with whispering demons, sprites, spirits, and gargoyles; in a blackout you could turn superstitious and recall ghost stories and nightmares. Our home had protected us from what could be virulently thriving, replicating underneath the placid facade of a genteel neighborhood.

*　*　*

"Anyone... Anyone home there?... Anyone... need..." someone hollered harshly.

We all tensed around the table. I was about to ask who could be calling us, when another voice yelled. This one was pitched higher. It was clearly female.

"Who's that?" my father asked.

Garbled fragments, phrases in the air.

"What are they saying?" my sister asked.

"It's Mary and George." My mother was obviously relieved that she could be so precise. George was our neighbor, an engineer with one of the city's water filtration plants. He worked a night shift, and it was unusual for him to be home at this hour. Mary, his wife, was one of my mother's closer friends.

We'd recognized their voices. Yet we hesitated, unsure about the broken-up words, their tone and intent.

I listened to make sure my mother was right about who they were. Then I heard: they were calling our names, and they were asking if we needed any help.

*　*　*

This moment has lived in my memory because our panic surged when the darkness set in. We'd been unprepared for the termination of service, our plunge into the night. The energyflow had been interrupted. We'd felt the shock. An impalpable network surrounded us. Only when it snapped did I recognize and feel the complete nature of its pervasiveness and its ability to penetrate and vanish. I'd noticed that each of us had responded differently to the isolation, the disorder.

That night with our neighbors, Mary and George, we speculated about the causes of the blackout. In the candlelight we added details to the list of what could happen, how the chaos could come.

Thunderstorms could drench transformers; ice storms could freeze wires.

Peak periods could cause brownouts and drains, when stoves, refrigerators, toasters, and kettles put too much pressure on reserves.

Ground wires could produce disturbances when shook by earthquake tremors or saturated by underground streams.

Atmospheric anomalies could multiply and cause a gathering of air masses that placed stress on the physical structures of working plants and machines.

Faulty wirings could fray in stations not granted enough government money for parts and repairs.

A nuclear reactor, in the developmental stage, could melt down and spark an atomic zero hour.

We theorized and amused ourselves, and let our imaginations run. The conversation was warm, animated. We enjoyed one another's company, and the transforming of the dark.

* * *

The lights fluttered, shooting back on in the kitchen. The even hum of the house came back. Heat poured up through the vents. The light bulbs shone steadily.

My father finally relaxed and asked if anyone wanted a drink. My mother puttered around the kitchen, blowing out candles, while my sister finished her supper without saying a word. Our neighbors thanked my parents for their welcome, then they returned to their own home.

After dinner my father withdrew into the living room to his solitary chair and the novel he was reading. Soon the sweet aroma of his pipe tobacco wafted through the house. My sister curled up on the den couch with a school book. My mother disappeared into the furnace room to inspect the fuse box.

I stood in the kitchen, staring out the window. The sight outside troubled me. Our lights had returned, but the recovery in the neighborhood had been selective. The power was off in other homes. At that moment I thought someone or something shaped these forcefields, or commanded them, arbitrarily sending the current to one spot and not to another, brightening and darkening different places, different lives.

* * *

Radio reports crackled in the house.

Unsettled conditions...downed wires...freak storms...

Announcers and newscasters overlapped, informing us:

Watch out...Don't forget to readjust your clocks...

Reports segued into a commercial, into a song, and back again into commentary, the station's call number, followed by a phone number for emergencies.

Brief terminations...in parts of the north eastern United States...and in eastern Ontario...

Radio voices spoke of causes and convergences behind the blackout, a commentary that carried memories, subtexts, and overtones. Voices referred to the recent past, recalled another breakdown, a crisis when the lights went off in New York City years before, and the darkness descended.

* * *

This is what I understand now. As I try to decipher the code of the electroscape — until I'm whole again and I can translate for myself what the direction of the current may be — I see that even in those days our city had started to hook into adrenaline cycles of surge and crash. My family and their friends could be awash in confusing communiqués. We could ask questions, and we could be genuinely uncomfortable about the answers. Then the moment when our world was split passed, and we settled back into a complacent routine. Switch on, switch off. But the threat of a fuse box chaos could feed our desire to root ourselves somewhere, in a family, a home, a town, or a city, a community that we hoped would never change. I believe that in this blackout each of us around the table grasped that no place is entirely safe, nothing is permanent. The power may temporarily disconnect; the power may circulate and run; the power may reveal its presence in many shapes. We would always be in its path, at junctures. You could flee from the current that can dissolve borders, enter homes, provoke speculations and fears, and you could search for inspiring connections and energy, that which can revive you without making you either docile or destructive, an unconscious vehicle of the charge.

I was part of a time when people felt the possibility of an intense receptivity. Through TV and stereo hi-fi we were given enhanced vision and amplified hearing, through telephones we were offered an extended reach into our time and space, through computers we would eventually have access to information stores. But you could go adrift with the moving electrons, with the blue tattoos from TVs impressed on your retinas, the guitar riffs in your ears and your hands clapping for more. You could be always waiting for more, for the TV light to illuminate you and the right rhythm to carry you along.

These were the probes and tracks that echoed and glimmered and would keep coming back to me. Outages brought jabs of perception, moments of consciousness. Were the blackouts and surges a part of the way that we could comprehend the environ-

71

ment of force? Would we have to learn how to be flexible in our responses and to trust our intuitions? Was there a complex joining of telluric energy and electronic technology beginning to emerge? Was our mediated world providing firsthand sensations and masking reality at the same time? What messages were being telegraphed, compressed, buried, stowed for later use and analysis? Who or what was the sender? What was unfolding here?

I think it was then that I began to be obsessed with X-rays of situations, the struggle of the imagination to keep up with technology, how raw information presents us with massive riddles, these clashes of chaos and order. I was looking for the overriding pattern, concealed, implicit, and numinous.

* * *

Eleven p.m. In the den my father switched on the TV to the news. I'd trailed after him into the room, expecting that we'd be shown what had happened, that sources would be brought up to date. Visual clips confirmed earlier radio accounts. Many people had experienced the same darkness. Reassuring images unfolded from the northern seaboard and the eastern townships. My mother came up from the basement and said she'd found that the wiring and the fuses were intact.

After about ten minutes, my sister packed up her book and sauntered silently to her room. Upstairs she clicked on a small AM radio by her bed. I could hear it distantly in the den while I watched TV, becoming drowsy.

Our top story...police saying to remain on the alert...

Off and on. These were the rhythms of the dance of data, and the rhythms of awareness and reception and of a trance. We consumed the waves. Blithely we waited without fully knowing that we were waiting for anything, or in need of anything.

I fell asleep on the couch, the newscast filtering through my thoughts, and I dreamed of TV, scenes from the blackout, the wind at the windows, all dissolving together into a single spell of suggestion.

We'll keep you up-dated...

Our street was becoming the globe and its heart was the beat of sound and motion that was beginning to pulse through each house.

This just in...

Piano

There was always music in our house, music that was recorded and live, music on radios and stereos, on black discs and tapes, reel-to-reel and eight-track cassettes, in the guitars and other instruments my sister and I had. Music is one key that helps me to recall things. It's music that gives a shape to my memories.

And I remember that...

...my mother played the piano softly in the morning.

My mother had wanted to be a concert pianist. She told us that her childhood during the grueling dust-bowl years of the depression in central Alberta, then World War II and personal sacrifice to that war, prevented her from considering a career that would have put her interests above her family's. She became a grade-school teacher for a time, before she met my father and moved east. So she lived in our house with her common-sense attitude toward fixing the things that had broken, and with her mind full of the Romantic composers. And in the early morning, before breakfast, we'd hear her softly play Chopin and Schumann.

I never saw my mother play. I only heard her in the living

room, where my father had placed the upright Mason Risch piano that he'd bought for her. I don't know why she was uneasy about being watched. We didn't ask her, just respected her eccentric wish. We'd move quietly through the house, washing, dressing, cooking breakfast, preparing for school and work. And in the living room, my mother would take the tempi of the music slowly. She liked to linger over the notes, discovering harmonies, rhythms, shadings in the melodies, subtleties in the structures. She'd play Brahms one morning — the Intermezzo in A Major, if I'm remembering this right — and Chopin the next, until our breakfasts were nearly done, then she'd return to the kitchen, her face flushed and lively.

* * *

My sister and I rarely made comments about our mother's playing. It was understood that if we wanted her to continue, she couldn't be interrupted, and we weren't to watch. This analytical woman, for whom the house was a special domain of both natural and artificial energy, didn't want us to see her in the grip of her longing, her passion for art.

"My hands are so stiff," she muttered one morning when I was in junior high school. She'd altered her routine, and she was sitting alone at the breakfast table when we came downstairs.

"My hands hurt. They're so unresponsive."

Toward the end of that same week, my sister found her alone again at the table.

And suddenly my mother stopped playing the piano.

* * *

Her fingers stiffened. They became gnarled, sometimes clawlike. Arthritis had set in, possessing her hands, it seemed, leaving her wincing in pain whenever she tried to touch the keys.

Slowly the piano turned into a piece of furniture. It was

another place for my father to stack the novels, history books, memoirs, and political studies that he liked to read. A collection of framed family photographs accumulated there — pictures of great-grandparents and grandparents, miniatures of wedding parties and cousins in graduation gowns. The piano keys slipped out of tune. The sheet music for the Appassionata and the Nocturnes were stored in the piano bench. We didn't hear her in the morning, and gradually we began to forget that the piano in the living room was meant to be played.

* * *

Her shoulders lost their elasticity to bursitis. She couldn't hold a pen properly to write the letters and postcards that she'd tirelessly mailed to her family and friends.

In the mornings, without her playing, our breakfast routine became talkative, rushed. Rattling newspapers and sizzling skillets.

Over the next years, she never complained about the loss of her music. She never said anything about it at all. She listened to every record my sister and I bought, and she criticized, complimented, and commented on the playing.

"The Beatles break all the rules. And for no good reason I can see. It's all effects. I'm all for breaking the rules, if you have a good reason for doing so. But they're just piling up the sounds. Neil Young. I think he should sing Kafka. If anyone ever bothers to put Kafka to music. In the lieder form or in a one-act opera. Neil Young was born to play The Hunger Artist. What a song cycle you could make out of that. Could you imagine what some of these musicians could do with a little training? *Moondance*. Now, that's lovely. *Astral Weeks*. What beautiful titles. That Van Morrison fellow can write songs. Moody, yes. But, then, he's Irish. And the Rolling Stones. Well, frankly, I find them tiresome. All that forced energy. Unnaturally angry. I mean, honestly, with all that money. The Who are livelier. That drummer in *Tommy* is the most astonishing I've heard. What holds the band together onstage? He hardly ever plays the beat. They must have a strong intuitive sense of where the other is going...Well, if you want, take Alfred Brendel for Schubert's Sonatas and Horowitz for Scarlatti, and Ivan Moravic for Chopin's Nocturnes. But definitely not Glenn Gould for Beethoven's sonatas. The things that man does to the dynamics are just outrageous..."

* * *

One day I watched from the doorway while my mother sat at the kitchen table, without seeing me, pressing imaginary keys with her hands. As if she were alone at the piano, trying out a new piece.

Painfully, carefully, her reddened hands tapped out a rhythmic pattern on the wooden surface. I couldn't tell what the passage was. It may have been from a Beethoven sonata or a Brahms intermezzo. Her eyes were closed. Her face was set in a mask of deep concentration. She tried an octave leap, winced, then formed a chord. She winced again and then she tried a fast arpeggio. Her arms jerked as though a blast of heat had shot up her fingers and hands. She opened her eyes, frowned, shook her head, stretched her fingers, rubbed them, and closed her eyes again. Her hands resisted her will. They were refusing to go back to their former suppleness and reach. But I could see from the expression on her face that music was running through her mind. The difficult scores that she had memorized a long time ago now animated her thinking, her imagination, her memories, her time alone.

I walked in, surprised her. She was flustered, annoyed.

"I was just lost in thought. Nothing important, really. Did you want something? There's some cheese in the fridge and bread on the counter, if you'd like to make yourself a sandwich."

I had interrupted her, discovered her, and I knew better than to ask about her pain.

* * *

77

My mother spent more time alone at the kitchen table. The arthritis in her knee joints and ankles made long walks and climbing the stairs, or any physical effort, difficult and slow and often tortuous. A systemic breakdown of bone marrow due to diabetes and the thyroid infections she suffered when she grew older slashed into her ability to concentrate for any length of time on scores. Her blond hair thinned and turned white. Her strong features softened under swollen skin. Her sharp wit and skeptical intellect — which could be the terror of milder, duller souls, as I'd witnessed at the dinners my parents had sometimes given — became gentler, easier.

And still my sister would find our mother alone at the kitchen table, tapping out the measures with her hands. And still she'd analyze new recordings, listening for some ideal performance. And still she'd sit transfixed by the confident touch of a pianist's hands on a keyboard.

* * *

Wherever I go and whatever I do, I can still be riveted by someone playing Schubert's B-flat Sonata, Schumann's Kinderszenen, and especially Brahms's Intermezzo in A Major. I can no longer tell if I'm adding this music to my memories, what pieces she actually played. They've become memories that are like echoes of recordings I've heard.

When I hear these pieces, something happens to me. They evoke a serenity and a lightness, some place I've been and may be again. They speak of a sense of belonging, an intimacy that transcends time. They speak of a love that can't be easily taken from you.

It's then that I'm sharply reminded of our mornings before breakfast, when my mother played, when we were together and listening quietly, before her hands grew gnarled and stiffened.

My father eventually bought a combined compact disc and tape-deck unit and had it installed in the kitchen cabinet.

I don't recall that anyone played the piano in the house again.

The Mechanical Typewriter

There was another sound in our house, more pronounced and percussive, the sound of words being pounded onto paper on an old mechanical typewriter. A different music from my memory, ringing, physical, harder.

On Sundays my father's typing echoed throughout the house. When he was a young reporter for the *Edmonton Journal*, he'd taken a secretarial course, acquiring shorthand for making notes and a fast, accurate typing style for writing copy. We could hear how well his work was going by the way he attacked his Smith-Corona with a staccato intensity, the ring coming quickly at the end of each line, the keys hammering out the words that he'd waited for a week to write down.

That day his normally affable manner was deposed by what seemed like a driven spirit. He got up early and had a breakfast of oranges, bran cereal, and fresh coffee. Then he took his mug upstairs and vanished into his den, where he pounced on the typewriter keys.

That's how I heard him for years. The nonelectric typewriter with its metallic clacking tone. I thought that it sounded as though my father was knocking on a door, looking for an entrance somewhere, a passage through his life, a form for his restless mind, punching through the specialized compartments he'd made for himself.

His den on the second floor was austere, painted off-white. His desk faced south toward the street. He had allowed himself only one bookshelf, lined with novels, memoirs, and diaries by authors like Herman Melville, Robertson Davies, Margaret Laurence, Anthony Powell, and Mackenzie King. It was a peculiar collection. They were a group of split people, apocalyptic-mystics, realists, and pragmatic politicians. "They're full-time schizophrenics," he said. As if that comment explained everything, or anything.

I see him at his desk, smoking his pipe when he was typing a first draft. I know that when he paused to think, rest, and stare out the bay window, he tapped his pipe on an ashtray. That would be the one break in his pace. Sometimes he'd tap his pipe repeatedly, loudly, even irritably, and we knew then that his work wasn't going well: he couldn't find that continuous rhythm that he wanted. His time rushed away from him. Soon he'd be back at his desk in his cluttered downtown office, entangled in his week of briefings, meetings, phone calls, and press releases. His business life then dominated his imagination.

* * *

My father rarely talked about his writing. This isn't unusual for a writer, but for him the private search was more complex, elusive, hesitant. Whenever he was writing a novel, my mother would say, "He's having another identity crisis." His five published novels were all different in style. They seemed to me to be written by many people, none of whom knew the others. Each book had taken hundreds of Sundays, and hundreds of revisions. He probed through the language, tapping on the typewriter that he'd hauled around with him for years, making words yield up a story, a theme, a cohesive structure.

I've come to realize that this single day of searching framed his life. He hunted inside sentences and rhythms as if he were trying to catch a voice that would move him, define him, release him from the draining work he did for the transnational corporation that employed him. Shaping a self, pulling a person from the blur.

Monday morning his change began. He put on a tailored dark-blue suit, always dapper, left the house, and marched down to the subway, the business section of the *Globe and Mail* tucked under his arm. And in the discipline of that walk — as people could have seen if they'd observed him — he was mentally preparing himself for the pragmatic mask he was about to don. He entered the sleek tower of mirrors and marble lobbies in the financial district, his other world of office politics and practicalities.

* * *

I don't know if my father really succeeded in compartmentalizing these aspects of himself. There was a gap between his idealism and his backroom life at work. I heard it in the way he sometimes assaulted his typewriter: he was trying to make sense of his split life through writing. Acutely sensitive and uncertain, he'd toughened himself to live with his two identities.

* * *

I met that efficient political self outside his office one day.

I was going to a meeting with a publisher, when I saw my father striding down the street. He didn't see me, so I stopped him, saying simply, "Dad." He backed away, like a man who'd been cornered. Then he looked curiously through his thick glasses, no recognition at all in his eyes. "Dad," I said again, carefully. I was about to laugh. (I remembered the joke about the absentminded professor who didn't recognize his own child on the street, so intense were his preoccupations.)

My father's eyes were cloudy, startled, sore. He stared hard at me, nervously straining to clear his gaze.

For a moment I was embarrassed. He truly didn't know me. I stepped back.

Then he said my name, slowly, with shock in his voice.

"Bruce."

Since my first name is his too, the word hung between us, suspended, like a word that could cause as much disunity as unity. We'd had difficulty recognizing each other on the frantic street. I was aware then of how connections can come and go in the shuffle and push of that space. Too much information swirling around, demanding attention, will make anyone restless, withdrawn, and anxious. We'd had to forge back in our memories the family link, the community we'd known. And more: I recognized that both of us had the ambition to write, and this created a bond that was often no bond at all. Both of us had created a book-bound structure of words, interior realms, solitudes that could wall out others.

Later my mother told me that my father's dim sight was due to cataracts, that he was almost blind. He was already nearsighted, and his refusal to acknowledge his growing blindness to his family had become a form of self-protection. With a stoicism that was unusual for him, he complained only when he bumped into things.

I can visualize him typing on Sundays, peering closely at a black and white page. His sentences must have looked smeared, obscure to him. He may have been trying to see his voice. He hadn't recognized me on the street. Behind his glasses, my father was withdrawing into a world of gray shapes and haze.

* * *

One Sunday I went to my family's home for dinner. When I walked in, I heard the familiar tapping drift from the second floor. My father came out of his den and called out hello, a shy warmth in his tone. Then he returned to his room and resumed his writing, with few pauses, the pounding leaving a trace of his pursuit, the track of his uncertainty, unease, and desire.

My father submitted at last to cataract surgery. It had become necessary. Afterward he told us that he saw with new eyes. But he couldn't read for many weeks following his operation, and it was many months before he began to write another book.

Hidden Harmonies

It's strange for me to realize how much I heard them. I listened to my parents through walls, doors, and floors, when they touched or tapped the keys of an instrument. My mother and father were good to my sister and me. Despite the attention that they devoted to their playing and typing, they were generous people, and they made time for us. Our family had a closeness, in an understated and undemonstrative way. But they were obsessed, and they handed obsession on to their children. Hidden harmonies are sometimes stronger than those that you immediately perceive or understand. Throughout our house, my sister and I heard our parents while they were absorbed with entering other worlds, listening for tones and overtones, testing the notes on the staves and the words on the page.

I never asked my parents the obvious question: what were they looking for? We were so careful about respecting one another's privacy, that merely asking a question could be difficult. I'm not even sure that by looking at my roots I'll be able to explain my sense of rootlessness. What is important must be the knowledge that in my family there was an attempt to reach beyond ourselves, to what was enigmatic, elusive. Trying to understand your parents may not help you to understand your own peculiar destiny. But it can point to paths traveled, the messages that were unconsciously handed on. I know that the idealism I inherited from them both — the dream of a world of music, of imaginative books with a vital readership, of a true call and response between individuals, of writing myself into a clearer, more receptive self — has led me to discontent. Dissatisfied, often disappointed, too easily disillusioned by people and experiences, I've moved my address constantly, lost friendships and loves, found myself wandering. I've sometimes felt like a data addict, greedy for stimulations, action, and news of crisis. It's been said that a person may be measured by their motion from a still-point. If there's no still-point of affection or faith in the heart and mind, then that person will swing unhinged in any wind. I became all too comfortably critical of the status quo as I've observed it in my city and my culture. I say "comfortably," because it is frequently easier to react and condemn than it is to engage and comprehend.

And yet I can't answer the most obvious question I have about growing up in Glen Echo: what was it that my parents struggled to find? I didn't feel the importance of asking them when I was young. I haven't felt the importance of answers until recently.

It seems to me that I've always listened for what's on the other side of a wall, a closed door, or a screen. My parents began their search during a depression and a war — obstacles that were outside them; my restlessness began in affluence, TV watching, the music I heard on tapes and discs, an ethereal confusion. Now I see that no matter what your background may be, your life could become blocked and fragmented, how you couldn't always achieve a whole vision, how we embroil ourselves in memories and frustrated hopes, locked into journeys within, pursuing strange glimpses, moved by a mysterious rhythm, heading for overload, blackout, bafflement.

Drumology

Sonic Rite

The roar in the night. Music pours from car radios and boom boxes, bringing guitar licks and drumbeats and shouted lyrics. Up and down the street the cars and people rove. It's Saturday night and it's a time for listening, watching, and moving. The night rolls in, and I follow the steady beats of heavy metal, hip hop, rap, thrash, trance, and blues, leaving my house, stepping outside.

The roar doesn't disappear during the week. But on Saturday night it reaches its climax. The sounds and rhythms peak, rattling people, making them jittery, edgy, curious. I've seen my neighbors stare out their living room windows, waiting expectantly, keenly. We're drawn to what in the sound recalls marrow knowledge, a visceral code, an ancient beat that promises a release of energy, a root rhythm in the technological blare.

Where will this sound lead us tonight? What could these signals become?

I hurry to the thronging corner. The snarled traffic looks like it had all been heading into the citycore. I stand at the curb and observe people inside their stalled cars. Drivers incline their heads, passengers lean toward dashboards, people nod and mouth words to songs. Expensive stereo systems turn a car into a traveling concert hall, an auditorium on wheels. I glance over my shoulder and see some people tote boom boxes that have CD players and miniature TVs tuned to Super 8 tapes of MuchMusic. We've released recorded music from living rooms, dens, and basements, the confines of cramped spaces and wall sockets. The car stereos and boom boxes now battle one another, each seeking to be heard over the other, veejays and deejays vying for possession of the air.

The traffic inexplicably kickstarts itself. Cars revive, dash ahead. The drivers hurtle themselves somewhere. They look as though they're out to track down a vital route, or location, or call.

I absorb bits of lyrics, riffs, and drum patterns, the shape of a rhythmic phrase. I'm familiar with most of the songs. They infuse my mind. I listen to the wail, these whirling pieces — this rush sound — for some possibility of a transcendent acoustics, a music not yet heard, a harmonious overtone, an expression of heart and mind joined at last, a melody and a rhythm that will finally articulate meaning, intentions, structure, aims.

I start walking to where I can get a cab. Then I find myself walking faster, speeding up, as if I've been injected with the street's pitch. There is a message in the roar: get going, come along. Obey, chase the songs, the tones, the fixated, and fixating, drums.

* * *

"You want ecstasy?" the woman asks the man ahead of me at the danceclub door.

"The band or the drug?"

"X-T-C, X-T-C."

"I do, babe, I do."

Initiations, indoctrinations. There are secret worlds inside the clubs. You better know the house moves, how to talk, what to wear. Once I'm inside, I feel an intense self-consciousness come over me when I notice the mirrors on the walls. We're surrounded by glimpses of ourselves, flashes of flesh, sudden doublings. Voyeur spotlights single out huddled figures. At the stand-up bar people keep their sex watch, hungrily eyeing how others dance, strut, prowl.

On the floor people dance disguised. They wear stage makeup, charms, chains, amulets, black leather, black shirts, head-bands, fringes, a tribal garb meant to shimmer with warnings and enticements, to project latent power. Men and women don death-head brooches, voodoo rings, spiked gloves, and motorcycle boots, like a pack of tamed Hell's Angels under the roving strobes. These styles say: mask yourself with an aloof mood, an aggressive stance, a seductive pose, when you enter this cosmopolitan night.

The din envelops me. I'm pushed around the floor by the hardbeat, the thumping, compulsive repetition in the music. The walls themselves seem to shake. I've submerged myself in the vibrations, and again I'm amazed at how taken up I can be. I find communication through words difficult at first. My ears buzz and I'm not sure about my thoughts — are they mine? — they're infil-trated by the song's words. You feel the music inside you, becoming it, intoning the chants and refrains. It's impossible to be detached. I have to struggle to hold on to my internal voice. I've been in rau-cous danceclubs before, but this noise level must be over 110 deci-bels, well over the pain threshold.

The highdecibel level reminds me that the dancebar is a planned space — tooled to the psychology of sound. Even if the club's designers have worked haphazardly, they can guess and intuit that certain keys, rhythms, and tones will have specific effects. The power to make listeners submit or surrender to com-mands and pronouncements was an attribute of the gods in pagan cultures. Only the gods could make thunder; only the gods repro-duced their voices at will. Here a deejay, closeted in a concealed booth, steers the music from behind a mixing board.

I see bodies sway to the beat like mediums in a trance. I've entered an acoustic maze that's both sensual and ethereal. My only guides are echoes and tones, the cues that are written on waves. I trace the effects of the cadenced sound, and I'm mesmerized by the constant thudding, the music's utter lack of variation. I sense that everyone here, these highdecibel initiates, understand the consistent elations and depressions of the rhythm.

Down the corridor that leads to the toilets, I read these words scrawled on the wall:

MAY THE FORCE BE WITH YOU

MAY THE FARCE BE WITH YOU

Someone has scribbled on the opposite side:

MAY YOUR FACE ALWAYS BE WITH YOU

Game playing, masks. This irony is one of the postures of those who've been inducted into the rock-and-roll cyber ceremonies. The songs simulate life and stimulate people into becoming performers eager to demonstrate their dance skills, how they can skim over these floors. But I want to know about the emotion that channels underneath the games, the authentic strain, what urges there are toward perceiving and knowing, what rawness drives the dance.

In the washroom I see a glass vial, an inhaler, and a spoon lying in a sink. Someone seems to have left this equipment to show off. Ripped toilet paper. Tissues wadded in balls. An overflowing toilet. A syringe in the water. People have covered the mirrors with Magic Marker ink.

DEATH CRAWLS
ROMAN CITY PARANOIA
JACKING OFF L'AMERICAN
DREAM

These lines read like a lyrical hangover from an old garage band's song. I have to be careful about seeing too much in the scrawls. A literary cast of mind will interpret and reinvent these experiences through language and argument, assembling logical lines that will move from one paragraph to another, linking ideas. And this isn't a literary place, neither nonbook nor antibook. It's an intensified magnetic field, a house of amplified noise.

* * *

People spin, galvanized on the dance floor. We're treated like objects and screens, blank slates under the strobing and the flares. The lasers like ray guns, the TV cameras, remold us into living reflectors. Constantly on stage, replayed on monitors, we can see ourselves as things to be recast, restyled. Machines and fashion. We wear the scenery, the colors and parts of the TVs and speakers — black, silver, gray, and red; clips, buttons, and straps — while waiting to be spotted (by whom? by what?) and sequencing our heartbeats to the speakers' overdrive.

Her skin glows as though massaged and burnished with exotic oil. Her slender figure tenses. She sits down at a tiny round table, slips off her black pumps, her bare toes going en pointe, every muscle taut, her posture giving the impression of a coiled spring. She watches herself in the mirrors, aware of her pose. Her body twitches, uncoils, like an instrument being played by an invisible hand.

I linger next to the speakers' dark meshing. Two Sonys show rock videos. Contorting images streak across a singer's face. Her mouth gapes but the song that comes out isn't the same as the one that, like a miked heartbeat, relentlessly builds through the towering banks.

"I like it rough," a woman says.

"I like it punk," her friend replies.

Both women have stripped down to black lacy bras, black spandex shorts, and cowboy boots.

"Head banging."

"Fucking heaviocity."

"No shade of a shade for me."

In the pressure and vehemence of the volume and the pulse, I hear how two women compress their talk into mocking bits, sarcastic fragments, the language of graffiti.

I watch men, backlit and briefly spotlit, hover around video games, the machines of artificial warfare, electronic storms. In this small video arcade, these players get the chance to score fast victories, direct hits on starships, in games called Megadeath, Thor Rock, and Alien Tracker. The men bash the machines, press buttons, laugh. The blasts and bells signify the end of their cartoon enemies.

I feel the power loosed in this space. All these technologies. "After the new wave comes the microwave." I know that there's some truth in this graffiti. Microwaves heat food much more rapidly than ovens. The microwave bombards what we eat with electrons. It gives off low doses of radiation; and it can resemble an up-to-date TV, with touch sources, presettings, digital timers. We are primed and aroused in this forcefield, and we go along with its waves, becoming its partners and acolytes. *We are asking for install-ation, man...Into those raster line vibrations, man...*

The drumsound overwhelms me. I have to withdraw into myself, protect myself. The synthesized drumming, like a voice, has intonation, emphasis, meter. But it can't answer my questions about what's behind the masking, the shimmering, the beat, the clipped sentences. I remember something from a book I'd read on the Eleusinian Rituals, remembering only bits of the statement: "The Mysteries were the channels through which...philosophic light was disseminated...and their initiates were resplendent with intellectual and spiritual understanding." What is understood here? What is being disseminated?

I listen to exchanges between people who, in some nameless agitation, hop from one foot to another.

"Let's declare all rock-and-roll bands a pollution-free zone," a man hollers to his friend.

"A mobile-free zone," he says.

"Antideath in concert."

"Free zones for life."

"Bring a rock-and-roll-free zone to your city."

"Antideath," the man had said. I wouldn't have expected anyone to talk strangely like that. He'd called out the word over the music and the clamor. In all the moving and the lights.

Sex with Angels

Deep night.

Inside this club — another one downtown, closer to the towers and the lake — I find a cavernous, shiny place, packed with jostling crowds. This place echoes with a mosaic of music styles. I hear tribal house, rare groove, bleep techno, new jack swing, technologized songs and hybrid beats, pure aggression with manic, primitive drumming, psychedelia and black punk. The deejay guides the music with opinions, insinuations, his voice vivid and sharp. People disappear into the rhythms. They dance like blurs. Some massive sexual merging goes on. Men and women roam around the dance floors — built on several levels — hunting, talking briefly to strangers, appraising one another, probing what the other may be, may carry, may hide, may subtly expose. These are zones of incognito, stealthy identities.

I stop at one of the stand-up bars that's made of mirrors and chrome.

"You see those chicks over there?"

I turn and look at the man who's spoken to me. He's tall,

presentable, well-dressed, casual. His brown hair is prematurely thin, receding.

"The ladies here are outstanding." He shakes his head. "Like a fashion show. Dressed up but ready to sweat."

"It's all look and no touch." I remember a cartoon from the *New Yorker*. A man lounges in an easy chair, his hands folded primly in his lap. Naked, he stares at the bright hole in his room — the TV set. The caption reads: "Safe Sex."

"That's not true."

"No?"

"I say it ain't so."

He talks like a tough guy, citysmart. But if I were to evaluate him by his clothes and his appearance, I'd say he was a business-man of some sort.

"People come for the buzz. You hear about it. The rumors."

I don't follow his drift.

"It's all word of mouth. And it changes. One place in this week. Who the fuck knows?"

He's pumped, prattling, with a tinge of need in his voice. He must be eager to tell me what he's found or lost here because I've paused, loitered beside him in this bar, become his audience.

"Let me tell you something. You should have seen her. No one could dance like she could. A redhead. With wild hair, all curls. And the brightest green eyes you ever saw. They were extraterres-trial. She'd watch you and watch you without blinking. And there was this sexy glow to her skin."

He says his name is Jack Latour and that he's a partner in a public-relations firm, a small marketing company of hustling entrepreneurs. They've survived ferocious economic times — and, he insists, they're thriving, making money, buying condos and European cars with cellulars.

"You should have seen her. Man, she could dance. This is the weird part. She had a real fuck-you walk. But her dancing was so easy. Natural. All from the hips and thighs. Most people dance from their shoulders. Like they're doing karate in hyperspeed. About as sexy as going on a long-distance march with backpacks."

I glance into the mirrors behind the bar. Reflections, doubles, mirages. I've reacted to the cynicism in his tone. But is he so cynical? He may be concealing himself, actually terrified of being pulled out, exposed, and restrained by the fact that we're strangers. I stare at our multiple images in the mirrors. Duplicated, wrenched, misshapen, our reflections become numerous and unfathomable.

"A lot later I found she was wearing the skimpiest nothings under her clothes. I mean strings. She was flexing her power on the dance floor. Driving guys nuts. Doing it consciously, unconsciously. I don't know. Making us see her anyway."

Jack Latour's eyes turn steely, predatory, watchful. Then he turns away from me and glares furiously at the dance floor. A change of music: improvised scratching, a smooth bass kick. Hip hop segues unexpectedly into Madchester, a blues-pop combination.

"So unaware of it and so aware of it. The effect she had. I mean she fucking knew. I wanted to eat her with a spoon. She was so tasty."

"Now," the deejay shouts.

A silver-flecked globe wheels in the ceiling, casting lattices of spinning light. Flashbulbs pop in a display of fireworks. Confetti showers down from racks hidden behind the light fixtures. Dry ice smoke oozes up, billowing like a fog. I see one couple through the smoke in the center of the floor embracing, reaching inside each other's clothes, wetkissing, fondling each other's legs, boldly making love. Confetti streams around them.

"Some wedding," Jack Latour says.

* * *

"Yeah I was looking for the magic fuck. I started hanging out, watching her, chatting her up when I could. But she'd just move around and around. It was eerie. I didn't know what the hell she was doing."

I'd like to walk on, but I think that Jack Latour is beginning to get to what these maskings and circlings mean, why we search through the night. I'm struck by how people test one another, how we dazzle ourselves, cartoon each other, become infatuated with gestures, looks, steps, the daze of styles. How do you reveal the other, strip off the false layers, keenly appear?

"But we clicked on the dance floor. I followed her, she followed me."

I lean my elbows on the bar, rest my chin in my hands, and study him. He's jabbering so fast that I realize he must have snorted coke earlier.

"So we're back at my condo. I have this great view of the city, you see. And she's letting me do everything. No conversation. I felt like I was raping her. Taking off her clothes, jabbing into her. We finished real fast, and she starts talking. Her voice shocked the shit out of me. She babbled and babbled in a highpitched way. I thought she was talking Greek or Russian. Definitely not English."

He stops, peers at me, frowns, squints at the bar, orders another drink.

The pop music slides into industrial rock, warehouse grit. Then it jumps into fastdance minimalism. "Move," the deejay exhorts.

"I kept asking her, 'what did you say?' I couldn't understand a word at first. And she looked different too. Who the hell was she? I tell you I was a little scared."

His expression becomes forlorn, almost broken, even ashamed. Has he been talking about himself when he suggests multiple personalities, a splintering? Maybe he is so cracked a personality, in so many pieces, incoherent in his core, that he sees only fragments of identity in people, their rude emanations. We each radiate a power, a charm and seductiveness, or a repulsiveness, to others. In this danceclub the electric forcefields are concentrated so that the sound waves rebound off us and our impulses. Our unconscious desires, and uncertainties, may find amplification and distortion and echoes in the acoustic surroundings.

"And here's the strangest thing. We went at it all night. On the floor. In the bathroom. On the kitchen table. Sometimes it was painful. But she stayed with me the next day — a Saturday. We couldn't let go. Even though she babbled in a way that I couldn't understand."

I interrupt and ask him about emotion, the charge of response.

"Are you talking about love? Finding love here?" His voice drops. His manner softens. "Well, we're supposed to be cool. The tragically hip. It's better to be zip. So keep moving, keep it light. But I'll tell you I woke up one morning and I was hooked. I couldn't stop breathing her in. I'd lean over in the morning and inhale. I didn't want to ever forget her scent."

(And abruptly I think of you, Lena. His voice taps in my memories of how you and I met at a dance, a party after a wedding. There was nothing brutal or incomprehensible about how we connected. You spoke to me first about someone we knew in common, and when I saw you, I was startled: my first thought was that I would marry you. We danced close and around us there were crazy people. Filmmakers, TV directors, agents, fledgling starlets, scriptwriters, and lawyers, doped up and drunk. Amphetamine eyes blazed. Couples laughed, stumbling on the floor. We were celebrating a friend's marriage. And I remember thinking about you, Lena, a stranger, that you'd better hold on because life will only get crazier, become more of a blur. Hold on, I said. And you did, thinking — you said later — that I was making a brazen pitch for you. But what I'd meant was hold on to our lives, grasp the future. We had to protect our souls or they'd end up attuned to breakage and the whirling, to the cadences of confusion. I thought that marriage was a leap into belief, stability, and attachment. It was grounding

— an individual would stop passing through and anchor here. And Lena, though I'm reluctant to deal with you, I know you're near, on my mind, behind these events and meetings.)

* * *

"And one morning she's gone. Just like that. My condo's bare again. That white space. We're not talking gypsy flako. She had a good job. She made money. But she was asserting control. Bye bye. No reason necessary. No hard feelings. That's what she said on the phone. She'd leave messages on my machine. And you know sometimes I still couldn't figure out what the fuck she was saying."

Each person is a center, a compass, both a threat to others with their strangeness, their need to be possessed and to possess, and a promise to others, with the worlds in their eyes. Love. That's what the lyrics in the savage songs endlessly repeat.

"I wanted her to really see me."

Did you see her, I wonder to myself.

"Here's the irony. She was beginning to make me gentle with her touch. Slowing down, feeling her. She was telling me things. With her body. With her hands. But it was over. Who was she? I don't know. Now I keep coming back, thinking I'm missing something."

The music promotes and badgers the word "love." We're incomplete beings hoping for completion, and we let the songs move us to forge bonds with someone, to become part of another. Yet I hear that word growled out, turned into a snarl and an obscenity, then reclaimed in all its purity and hope, chanted over and over, until its original urgency slurs and it loses its value and intentness and ardor.

* * *

Jack Latour says nothing more. I could see that he was close to vaulting over into guilt, even despair. But I figure, harshly, that he's only been nudged. He's just had a glimpse of a path. Maybe it's one of our jobs in life to get a clear view of a route for ourselves. It could be that he can't stop trying to explain to himself what happened. It's almost there — the passion to understand, to love, to know. But when our space is this fierce and demanding, it's easier to chase fashions and assume the cover of the dark.

He stalks away into the crowd. And it strikes me that I'm watching him walk back into the megamachine of light and sound. He could ramble through these danceclubs in the same way, and the spark of emotion, the glint of fear and worry could be stamped out in his voice and eyes. He could trail from club to club, baffled, always wanting things. Suddenly I realize that I've been observing more about the music and the environment than I have been about the people. I've watched the performances, the styles, and the TVs. People. What are we becoming in these laboratories of hybrid songs and spotlights and video? The dance of data can roll forward, melting us down into its loops, the spin and flash of the instant.

I feel for Jack Latour, hoping that he'll discover that he has to refuse to be recycled, allow himself to crash, to despair for his life, so that he won't be snared into wandering from place to place. I wonder if he'll have the courage to crack. But who am I to know if this is what he should do? I'm only beginning to know how to crash...

* * *

The dancing brings partners together, and the dancing jams them apart. Step closer; breathe again; step apart. Upbeat, upswing.

"Jacuzzi time."

"Hot tubbing night."

"Shimmying it. You got it?"

"I got it, yeah."

I stand back, and the voices in the din briefly become remote. Again I have the sense that the conversations circle around a subject, only that subject remains a mystery, potentially disruptive, so cloaked and dangerous that no one dares to truly let it rip open.

Still people come here to find the pulse in the sound. The pulsing travels through the conduits, the speakers and screens, advancing through the words spoken and what's left unsaid. The search endures in those who watch and wait. From the speaker banks, the low-frequency bass runs can diminish your ability to think, but they can increase your compulsion to physical action and reaction. Our chance to recharge our minds and emotions can be supplanted by a seamless rumble. (Corporations use Muzak in buildings to cushion the hard-edged cityscape; softer, acoustic music helps to modify, and even amend the city's merciless pace.) I consider how desperate so many of us must be for a release, for an expression of self and spirit. Inside the Saturday night beat I recognize the need to escape loneliness, an urge toward renewal.

Got hotwired livewired flesh
Come to me tonight nowhere anywhere
And shake your body, any body,
No body, any body

The deejay uses key changes in the music to inject mood changes into this place. A sampling of a Puccini aria, Nessun Dorma from *Turandot*, and its moving, melodramatic high notes — an aria that never fails to haunt me with an inexplicable nostalgia for beauty and peace — fuses with the bass line of a hip hop piece. The music yokes together ages, emotions, effects, Romanticism and late twentieth-century bodybeats, yearning and lust, the ethereal and the sensual.

This deejay jumbles modes dangerously. He tangles minor keys for mourning with major keys for heroic action, unaware of

103

the repercussions of each key, the psychic purpose of the musical medicine.

I see a clock near the control booth showing us that it's after midnight. I've lost all track of the hour. We occupy a hermetic, experimental zone, and only the dancing and the music remains.

* * *

A woman with a spectrally white face stands apart from her group of friends. Spellbound, she watches the crowds. I like her young unlined features, her straight black hair cut close to her face. She looks as if she's never seen the sun. A night follower, fan of the artificial. But her face is almost serene, her eyes bright, amused. She wears scarves around her black sweater and black miniskirt, layers of scarves that are like rings.

I ask her about this place, a halting, awkward question.

"I can't explain it. I don't like to sleep. I don't do drugs. I like to stay awake. You arrive here or you don't."

I'm drawn to her voice, its sensuousness, the way she shifts her tone, lets her voice rise and fall. I want to stand close to her murmur.

"Some come for the sex, some for the music, some for the hit. Sure people talk talk. They chitchat. They come and stick their fingers in a socket and feel a shock. But that's not what it's about. The music is the traffic."

I tell her that her scarves fascinate me — the elaborate knotting around her.

"Scarves instead of tattoos or chains. Chains mean you go for the mind fuck. But just because the music's hard doesn't mean that I am. I wear them because I'm tied to music. They mean I'm a slave to mind love."

I start to ask her to say more about this mind love — the invisible cords that may bind us to the dance and the flow — when the deejay jarringly interrupts the music. His voice booms over the loudspeakers. He intones, incants, and samples gunfire, police sirens, political speeches, and half-a-dozen hit songs:

"Vision ignition, ignite your eyes, ignite the skies."

His word scat proclaims, "The vision fire — tell me no lies — the wind is the real — now is the god — the real is now — sex the skies — sing your eyes — come on feel the crowd — feel the noise — now you're real — how does it feel — to sex the skies — sex the lines — fire your eyes — feel the fire — feel the god — sing the skies — amen, omen — omen, amen —"

Mantic words.

They seem involuntary, charismatic, issuing out of a pool of unconscious associations, and of memories that may only be vaguely known to the speaker himself. These mutterings are a calling forth, a summoning of a magic language, of prayers and auguries. The words invoke deities, elements. The chant appears to establish a correspondence that we have suppressed or forgotten, an underworld network. The speaker trusts his words. It's as if the sampling and the runic formulae will drum up meaning, a frame of dreams, intuitions, and reveries.

I look for the girl wrapped in scarves. But she's gone. The deejay's word delirium has passed, and from ecstasy we scuttle back to isolation.

* * *

Women dance with women. Couples swirl by, bodies sidle close.

> *I'm the image machine baby*
> *Insert your picture here*
> *But don't forget, don't forget*
> *To keep your reality switch on*

In every club I've perceived the erotic voltage. Amorous cycles, without the traditional vows, the sacrifices. This is what these places are about for so many, if not everyone. Even with the threat of infections that come from touch and penetration, each body a transmitter and a receiver, even with plagues that can decimate whole groups of people, rogue cells running wild in our blood system, there is here the pressure for immediate intimacy. Healthy, perverse, voyeuristic, grinding, some people meeting for the first time, making love in the hallways, in the washrooms, women with men, women with women, men with men. There is sex sometimes without touching naked skin, achieved through words and the dancing, and there is a sexual search for the other, entrance again.

I step away from the post where I've been leaning and I look back at the mirrors. They twin us with our ethereal doubles. Reflections and games, eros and angels. The diabolical twin of this sexual music is pornography, the brutalization of the senses, where longings and fantasies can reverse into a destructive trance.

I see her come out of the shadows. She sashays slowly, walking in a beautifully balanced way, apart from the myriad mirror-images of others. She is maybe in her mid-twenties, with shortcropped blond hair, and she is aloof, poised in the manner that she parades herself. She has wide bright eyes and the high cheekbones of one with a northern European background. I keep watching how she moves. As if she's going to meet her lover. She wears black high heels, black stockings, a short black leather skirt, a white silk blouse. I think she looks strong physically, and that she's showing off, her sensual strut. Then I'm set off, asking, am I romanticizing her? projecting an image on someone? turning her into a stereotype from a video? This may be how people begin to appear in the sound-and-light show like beings from a dream.

She disappears. And I'm left with the imprint of her poise and presence, a woman at home in the shadows and the rhythms, freely moving, beyond anyone's projections, reveling in herself.

Drumming Time

Drum machines snap us into a fierce highlife. The synthesizers on this track sound like the talking drums in Africa that pounded cryptograms of greeting and sympathy, wisdom echoing across valleys, rivers, and mountains. The drummers conversed, even argued, with other drummers, and delivered praise, stories, spells, the accents of history and magic. I feel the technologized drums in the pit of my stomach, up my spinal column.

I watch people, half-rapt and half-blank, shake, vibrate, stamp around the stand-up bar. They drum their fingers on tables and chairs. Other people tap their feet, keeping time. Percussionists call this independent coordination — the frenetic individual movement of various parts of the body. I observe how some people appear to drum to a private pulse, following an interior rhythmic dialogue, an internal music that differs from the thrash-track that's now playing.

"What are ya thinkin' about, Frank?"

"Everything and not a fuck of a lot."

The speakers generate sound bites for the dancers — short-lived samplings, spasmodic, teasing. The deejay demonstrates that he possesses the power of generation, unlimited musical reproduction. Old styles segue into new styles: music from the nineteen sixties and seventies is reshaped for tonight.

I'm abruptly aware of a generation gap. A ten-year age difference in people can become like half a century. I'm struggling to get my bearings in my thirties, while people in their middle twenties, and younger, devour the whir. Most of those I see in this dancebar appear at one with a pinball machine temperament. They take the monitors and the musical mosaic for granted. I'm all too self-conscious about how books and movies and TV shows, black discs and CDs, rattle against one another, influence one another, create friction.

People here slip inside the crossover of styles. The dancers are truly wavelike. For them there's only tide, only the stream. They aren't concerned with Aristotelian distinctions, Cartesian categories. This dancebar represents a whole for them. They accept that popcult is culture. High and low castes are dissolved. Everything is a matter for the recyclotrons of invention and consumption.

I glance at the chrome post beside me. A red lipstick smear reads:

GET READY TO LOSE YOURSELF
WELCOME
TO THE HOLLOW DECK

A cigarette girl, strapped to a tray full of thin cigars and European cigarettes, swings her items in front of me. "Cigars, cigarillos?" she whispers in a husky voice that is obviously not her normal speaking tone. She wears a flimsy red dress that billows around her legs. Her black hair bobbed, her lips outlined in bright red, she looks like a film-noir femme fatale. She's aware that she's

108

acting out a part for me, for anyone. When I say no thank you, she saunters on to another table, and repeats her performance.

I stare up at the monitors.

The TVs are showing pictures of popcult figures. Heads blend with more heads. The crowd screeches with recognition. The heads dart by: John Lennon, Prince, James Dean, Marilyn Monroe, Kim Basinger, Batman, and stars I don't know. The heads soon incorporate other faces — imitations, lookalikes, clones of Elvis, the Beatles, the Rolling Stones, Bob Dylan, Madonna. Faces reel by. This vortex of heads from movies, TV shows, and pop music posters startles me. Eyes stare out from the pictures. Preternatural eyes, watching back at us. The eyes have been highlighted by computer animation. These famous faces flow in a procession on the screens, like heads from a mobile museum of popcult, the shades from movies and music now in a monitor visitation.

The flux of faces makes every figure appear nebulous, indeterminate. All the stars become amorphous. I see an image of a demonic Michael Jackson from his old video "Thriller," but it has been altered again to more resemble the devil — Satanail, the fallen angel, elder brother to Christ, according to Gnostic and Manichean legends. This liquid array of faces suggests dualities, changeability. Popcult thrives on the ability of its stars to be many sided, chameleons, morphological entities who can be screens for our projections and translations of intent. Of course, I recognize that in true popcult fashion these faces have been doctored with a satiric halfsmirk, ironically, skeptically, with a wink and a nudge, to let you know that the sliding images shouldn't be taken too seriously. The stars represent mercurial corporate interests, but they are symbols of vitality and transmutability too, and we have through our machines the immediate power to enhance and demolish their images, and then to revive their presence. There is no death in the cult world, only regeneration.

And I think of how in this maze of faces, you are apt to ask: who am I? what is authentic? what sort of control do I have? how much meaning can I load onto these stills, the wheeling images? what powers — technological or chemical, astral or telluric, political and cultural — influence us? The forcefield in this danceclub informs us that, if you can afford the price, we may be able to do anything to ourselves. Maybe we can reforge all that we are: mold a new face, a new body, and emanate a new soul. Those who live inside the pop sphere — those who own a TV, a radio, a stereo system, and who go to the movies — sense what the cult figures intuitively and sometimes consciously understand: make yourself over. The roar in the night carries the call to ally yourself with the artificial and the natural together, renew your pact with the machines.

The cult landscape is one of masks and metaphors. Absorb yourself in the racket and motion, and you could easily be distracted. But the cults summon deeper designs, obscured truths, esoteric messages layered over by the sexual icons, the rippling scenes in the TV images. I sense this: the music, the dances, the mirrors and pictures, the flaunting of affluence, are the external representations, the shells, the outer skin, of what beats and moves within, inside us, through the world.

* * *

I stand up from the table and squeeze through a clump of watchers near the dance floor. At another stand-up bar, I order a drink and survey the scene.

Dancers look arrested, suspended, breathless. There's a pause, a lull, for some reason.

"Sixty seconds to airtime!" the deejay shouts.

What airtime, I want to ask someone. Bewildered, I gaze around to see if anyone knows what the deejay means. People appear expectant, eager.

"Boys and girls, you've got to hustle."

The deejay tightens the anxious mood.

"Thirty seconds!"

People juggle for positions in front of the monitors.

"Twenty-five!"

We are being jolted toward the instant, made aware of the push of time. The clock hands turn, digital numbers flip by. The chatter in the crowd has become a murmur in the wake of the countdown. The cigarette girl freezes, as if she's in an acting class, obeying an order to play statue. Behind the bars, the bartenders rivet themselves to where they stand.

"Ten-nine-eight-seven-six." The crowd bellows in unison.

"Two-one-"

A shiver of screams.

"Airtime!"

Bursting onto the monitors, projected onto the walls from hidden projectors, comes a video surrealism of heads ripped open and blasted into pieces. Plastic and latex bits scatter in jets of blood. Limbs and skin erupt in sores. Blood drips, splashes, filling buckets and flooding into white rooms. Bones crack. Faces melt. Wounds fester. Babies eject out of wombs, trailing gangrenous umbilical cords. A green mutant crawls from a woman's vagina.

Movie footage shows creatures and androids and replicants from *Metropolis*, *The Bride of Frankenstein*, *Blade Runner*, *Star Trek*, *Robocop*, and *The Terminator*. Ordinary people grow superhuman through skin grafts and drug injections. Robots march beside swirls of devils and angels. The natural, the supernatural, the pagan, and the artificial clash until it's difficult to tell where humans end and machines begin. Patched, scarred, and steel-studded bodies. Ghastly human hands with greasy machine parts. Roads lead to squirming skin and silicon veins. Wiring spilling like black hair from car windows.

I can't do anything other than watch. On the monitors the computer animation conjures heads again. The famous faces are welded into the humanoid discharge.

The masks tear away, corroded with what looks like battery acid. Politicians and business leaders convert into hydras, sea demons, Minotaurs. The heads, tinted green and blue and red, explode again to shape vultures and eels. Faces mutate. Animals and humans and machines multiply into single entities. Pop faces balloon upward, then condense into tears and stars. The stars heat up, approach supernova. White light flames into silver eyes. The eyes roll in metallic sockets and pop out. Then individual faces emerge again. The faces have been captured, culled from the crowd in the dancebar. Video cameras in the ceiling turn the audience into players, exhibits in the demolition and the scorching.

I've waited long enough to witness this animist eruption through graphics.

And what are we supposed to do now? Ask for a replay, make requests, sit down, relax, order more drinks, light a cigarette, start a conversation with someone we've never met before?

I pull away and find a vacant table and chair.

The detonation on the screens, I realize, has been a secular expression, not religious. It seemed more like a game, a display of technique. Mystery rituals were an initiation into the divine purpose on earth. They confirmed the bond with the sacredness of life. Through these rituals, the neophyte gradually learned that each of us is a vehicle for knowledge, that we are invested with the purpose of raising our minds. The show on the screens has been a reflection of what TV and computer graphics and canned music can do — the interaction of the human face with electronic circuitry.

Some dancers pack the floors, but others trail back to tables and chairs or off to washrooms. People look like vague human flickers after the spectacle, ephemeral beings who follow the ceremony.

The monitors fade to black, and the music eases off.

A softer, soothing hush sweeps through the speakers, a sound like water.

"Chill out," the disembodied voice of the deejay says. "Tone down, slow down, come down."

* * *

I get up hesitantly and slowly step away from the table.

"Would you like a drink or something?" a waitress asks me.

I shake off the video hallucinations, the mirages of destruction and metamorphosis.

"Yes, I would," I say, but I want to ask her about the violence in the video. I want to know if she cares about what the message may be.

"What can I get you? What do you need?"

Suddenly her every question sounds ambiguous, overlaid with meaning.

I see that she's freshfaced, small, with long dark curly hair. She wears glasses and looks studious. Her spandex bodysuit, black and sleek, is torn in strategic places, exposing a hint of bare thigh, the pale top of her breasts, her freckled shoulders. She has an overwhelmed and lonely expression. I'm grateful to find that she's a person and not some monster descended from the monitors. However, could I cross a bridge, draw her out, discover how she feels? Does she know who or what she's working for?

"A double vodka and tonic," I answer after a few moments.

She smiles, and again she gives me a lost, puzzled look. Then she backs away. I understand that she won't make contact, can't break her pace or diverge from her automatic reactions, because then she would have to ask questions, make comments, interrupt her routine. She goes over to a floorside table, bends over, talks to two women who sit there. She nods, smiles, nods, takes down their orders.

* * *

It's late now. Yet the crowds haven't diminished; they've grown. Muttering people cluster at the entrance. They are late-night travelers cruising the bars that stay open after one-thirty a.m.

I continue my thoughts:

Popcult appears to have the dazzle of pagan ecstasy. These

releases of the self, the unleashed emotions. But it's difficult to tell what is real and unreal, authentic and contrived. *Ex-stasis.* The word means to come out of yourself, to break free from the body's restrictions and the mire of social convention, the spirit's entrapment in the slavery of drudgery and routine. The ecstatic frenzy was a way to bring on sensorial derangement and then the power of insight and prophecy. I'd like to believe that this dancebar channels some of the vital current; I'd like to believe that this artificial paradise will inspire the need in its patrons to passionately pursue meaning. But I'm not sure it's possible. I'm gripped by doubt. People dance on and on. It seems absurd to me to be asking these questions, while I stand listening to the push of the drums, their insistent intensity.

Tempo change. An adrenaline shot.

The deejay modulates the music into a rap track, an enraged poetry that the rappers bluntly express. These voices sing from a knowledge of blockage and frustration. The musicians chant, *rap against the power, take the power, rap for your power,* and they must be banging lead pipes, rattling garbage cans, thumping boxes, smashing glass, knocking against whatever imprisons them, their hammering like fists on a wall.

Last Call

"Last call for the night."

I watch cigarettes glimmer briefly like signals in the dark. At secluded tables in corners I see the shadows of strangers gather. People slow down, get ready to vanish.

"Last call."

The deejay replaces the polemical rap with a technologized remake of an old pop song. We're left to feel, at this early hour of the morning, the approach of the end. The theme of this song is mourning, a quiet awe at the passing of things. The song seems to touch a chord in people here: we know that all ecstasy depends on the moment, on the ache of what must remain unfinished, fragmentary, indefinite.

"Last call for the night," the deejay repeats with surprising irony — no alcohol has been served for a few hours. "We have to clear out, clear up. So lend a hand. It's time to save the last dance, the last chance, for you."

The song ends, and I realize that the point of the corrosion of faces I saw earlier is time. We are time haunted, time ruled, time consumed. The faces that bolted by reminded us of fame and stardom, of burnout and suicide, and of the obsession with remaining forever young. So many faces in the flux left the impression of the human hunger for recognition, for some control over our fates, to have a portion of our strange selves imprinted on our memories. The media craves the sheen of youth. TVs and movie screens elevate any look that shines. But the heads rushed by, warning us that time will erode us, exhausting our bodies and spirits. And so the message behind the array must be that we will be smashed apart, and we may only be remembered and reinterpreted in archives, to be reborn and resurrected in movies, videos, and digitized recordings.

One night, one stream of data, one set of places and events. I've been propelled through styles, songs, and fantasies, the semblance of a ritual. I'm surprised that everyone has kept up with the promiscuous mood changes, but it's time for people to arrange themselves into groups, to find comfort and company, move on.

Through the night I've shifted from one mood to another. I've felt my anger become enthusiasm, my passivity become playfulness, my memories turn to sexual longing. My concentration was shattered by the blare and then I'd focus again on the drumming.

Finally it's the loneliness of this place that edges into me. I feel the drift in the people who shuffle furtively around the dance floors. The styles, the masking, the computer graphics, may hide that drift, but it's a wandering that is at the heart here. And though the deejay wants to transform the end of the night into a terminal game — as if he wishes to impose what sounds like a personal infatuation with absolutes and finales — his voiceover only lends poignance to the quietened talk, to the people who linger behind, in no hurry to go.

I see people cling to each other. There's no music left. Yet they slowdance and close their eyes, their hope for love or magic dwindling.

It's over. We may be absorbing games of attachment and fusion through music and dance, but we breathe in the scene and then breathe it out, and we're borne along, late into the dark.

CDs stop silently. There is no hissing static, no direct indication that the music is finished. Only the digital numbers on the black box — a device that cloaks its internal processes — tell the deejay that the play is done. A stylus doesn't run down grooves toward a spindle at the center of the circle. If the deejay decides to start a CD up again, he has to push the button that says Play-Repeat-Play. He has an arrangement of sleek, dark turntables to back up his ensemble, the batteries of influence.

Dancers stray off the floor. Their conversations lapse into dangling fragments. These people appear to have discovered that they are strangers who don't speak the same language. The shared emotions, the collective impetus, have been defused. Waitresses collect the ashtrays and glasses left on the tables and stands and counters. The glasses rattle; the sound resembling wind chimes.

"Illusions, delusions, thrills, chills. Until we meet again."

I watch the deejay slip CDs into clear cases and seventeen- and twelve-inch discs into bare sleeves.

And I sense how we've been left incomplete. The mystery of the music has been stripped from us, and all that stays is our emptiness, our sadness in a stark, enormous room that could be a high school gym. Black cords droop from silent speakers, like the uncoiled innards of a once tightly constructed mechanism. Everyone adjusts to the gritty industrial glare of the regular lighting.

We want the world to be kind. Then we encounter its blindness and implacability, and often its destructiveness — yet it always beckons, holding out the promise that we will find it comprehensible, welcoming, habitable. We come to places like this so that the music will remind us of our first excitement about life, and so that the dancing will reunite us with the unexplainable sensuousness and ethereality of sound and rhythm. In the crucible of music we believe our loneliness and confusion will be transformed into ecstasy, and we're cradled for a time in the flow of the dance and in the shadows that hide our scars.

"Did you lose something?" It's the waitress who spoke to me not so long ago. "Come on, we all have to leave." She's polite, but oddly stiff. She looks glazed, and I'm sure she's anxious to escape.

I gaze around, doubting if I'll ever be back. People hesitate, maybe hoping that the houselights will dim, the music and the dry ice and colors will return, and the dancing will extend to sunrise, so that the afterglow won't fade from us so soon.

* * *

I walk out into the street. The highdecibel levels have dropped, but there's a ringing in my ears; a constant reminder.

Crowds huddle on the sidewalks and steps and on the patches of grass. I catch some of the come-ons, the teasing and innuendos, the cooings and rejections, the last-minute exchanges.

Two drunks lurch near a derelict who panhandles the dancers. One drunk veers over to a bush to vomit. The parking lots across the street look as if they're in the clutch of a morning traffic tie-up. Blue and white cruisers prowl by. From inside the cars, the police eye what must appear like the aftermath of an indoor fiesta.

To get to the root of the rhythm...

But the roar has tapered off to a whisper, and we're like puppets whose unseen cords have been slashed away, and instead of tumbling to the floor in a heap, we walk under lamplights and the sky.

Starframe

Cool air, and the stars.

I look up at the star field in the cloudless sky. They're spectacular, these clusters. I look, and I'm taken by their stillness. Here on a corner, outside the club, I feel an unexpected calm take hold of me. That calm seems to ease from a moment of detachment when I'm free of the rock-and-roll heat, and I see the silent stars.

But there isn't any stillness in the universe. I realize when I scan the Milky Way, the clusters low in the east, with Mars clearly visible tonight, that the quiet is an illusion, a trick of the eye.

The crowds and traffic disperse, leaving the street to the police, the drunks, the prostitutes, and taxi drivers. The pumped din of the club gradually fades from my ears. I gaze up again, and I recognize that the stars only appear placid when you try and read them without the help of a radioscope. Radioactive with subsonic tones, the stars make a kind of music. Like a hum, the astronomers say, or a hiss that can flood a tracking device.

No one can hear that hum without the right instruments, of course. You'd have to imagine it or listen to it on a taped playback.

But to imagine that hum now, after the highdecibels of the dance-bar, gives me some peace.

A breeze rises. The bracing air helps me to wake up, and I walk on.

Then I find myself remembering the legend of the philosopher and mystic Pythagoras. He and his followers studied music and astronomy, seeking the latent order in nature, the complete listening. They were said to have discovered the harmony between the planets, the ratio of tones that was the key to the balance in the solar system. That key, the intricate ratio between ourselves and nature, would open the musical order of the cosmos.

And I remember that radio astronomers say a cosmic music does exist. The electroacoustic blare may sputter and dim, sliding into a backdrop of blips and hisses, but the stars, the planets and their moons continue to leave their sonic trail.

I step off the curb, crossing to the north.

Glancing up again, I become oblivious to the neon signs, the light from the apartment blocks, the closed storefronts.

If I could listen to the stars for myself, I'd find that their steady hum wouldn't end. The radio astronomers claim that once by accident they recorded the afterecho of the Big Bang, the cosmos striking into being. That primal roar found its way into every one of their recordings.

I remember that the astronomers said that they had trouble measuring the strange hum. Layers of interference jammed the airspace, obscuring the echoes, and the scientists were left with static.

* * *

I pause at the corner. An intersection, lights changing. Signs says Don't Walk, Don't Walk. Traffic rumbles by. A lone cyclist passes wearing headphones that look like a crash helmet.

And it comes to me why I recall this:

The Pythagoreans spoke of attuning themselves to the

movements of the stars and planets. They were searching for the correspondence between the mystery of the soul and the mathematical precisions they'd found in nature, the link between the dancer and the dance. In our hearing we'd find the center of learning, and through our lives a rhythm runs like a deep, elusive stream.

I wonder if the danceclubs reflect the ancient concerns, the old knowledge. A dance of attunement, a dance to achieve harmony, a circling with others that imitates the turn of the planets around the sun, everything in our lives an echo of the movements in nature.

Anyone who seeks such a tuning would have to be capable of returning to a point of repose. Dancing was how you could attune yourself to the natural cycles of destruction and creation. But what happens if you whirl to the electromagnetic pulse? What if the rhythms come from the snarl and kick of the city? Will this bring a balance or an imbalance, the overload of the channels?

More questions. And my request for truths.

I suddenly notice that it's cold enough to see my breath. I'm not dressed warmly enough for this weather, and I'm tired. When the lights change, I cross the street to where it'll be easier to flag a cab. Running through my mind, these notions of harmony, the correspondence between dancing and the stars.

A few blocks up, a late-night bar closes. A neighborhood place, more subdued, without lasers or video. In the parking lot, a half-dozen people chatter to one another. Laughter, good-nights, blurred speech, names. People file out to their cars and pass on to boozecans and all-night cafés, to their apartments and houses.

Ignitions catch; motors sputter. Radios start up inside cars, the vibrations audible through closed windows. Tires on cement, exhaust pipes, engines revving, echoes off the buildings.

Above us another music, the planets and stars and their radiophonic hum.

Radiant Point

Occult Scanning

Channels 2-7

The low-quality X-ray flares up. I've aimed the remote at my TV, the infrared matching the signal receiver. Pressing the button for channelsearch, I trigger the scan, then turn down the volume. Everything is pantomimed. I'm aware of gesture, the geometry in cityscapes, jagged and fluid shapes in landscapes, the shuddering structure of endless movement. What you hear affects what you see. These images without a sound track become a series of outlines melding, mutating into a single edgeless show. The subject matter in this soundless stream is impermanence, anarchy.

Channels 8-13

Yet the TV brightens and tints this place with its lattices of light. The electromagnetism that vibrates off the screen is a little touch of eternity in my room, part of the energy that makes and remakes the stars. The signals that form on the screen surface establish a symbolism — logos and encounters and figures irradiated — and it strikes me that the light coming through the tube is similar to what you would see when you observe light's effects on the stained glass of a medieval cathedral. But in a Gothic cathedral it is sunlight and moonlight that illuminate the passion play depicted in the glass. The windows reveal the allegory of the soul's struggle toward courage and wisdom. Light pours into the dark interior that is meant to represent our loneliness and ignorance; that glow robes a person's pain in the covenant of hope and deliverance. While I watch the colored flutter, I wonder if the tubelight scans a passion that the audience unconsciously recognizes, another initiation mystery, a secret story implicit in what appears desultory, rudderless, evanescent.

Channel 14

A quick memory. I was four years old, sitting quietly on the couch of my family's living room, waiting for the world to commence. My mother switched on the set at noon. Spontaneous combustion. The images burst from a single point in the center, a point like a core of compressed matter. In the afternoon, my mother switched off the set. Quick implosion. The picture folded in on itself. All the faces and animals and machines were sucked inward, vanishing down the hole. One point stayed, quivering at the center, its high hum sustained.

Channel 15

What does the word *television* mean? A distant seeing; seeing at a distance. In the nineteen twenties, the first TVs were called Iconoscopes. Their hazy pictures were called shadow plays and silhouettes. The earliest viewers were sometimes named teleseers and ingazers. These definitions, and their overtones of meditation and mysticism, help me to recall what the pioneers in TV research — Vladimir Zworykin, David Sarnoff, Philo T. Farnsworth — wanted to achieve with their invention. A condition of involvement, an audience sharing in light and motion. TV commentators brand the average viewer a couch potato, a vidiot, a boob tuber, a mediacrity. But the original motto for the act of viewing was "seeing things as they happen." The phrase invokes a witnessing, the mediumistic experience, a transporting directly to the moment. The teleseer would find a box that could spring surprises and gifts. The box, like Pandora's, could hide nightmares and demons. And it could become a trap, boxing you in to its caricatures, its repetitions.

Channels 16-17

Bodies fill the screen. People battle against a barrier. Images of an anonymous gathering at an outdoor concert. The crowd pushes. Masses act enraged, hurt, helpless, incapable of stopping their heave. Then an edit. I'm checked over datelines, passed over borderlines without a passport, all restrictions relaxed between nations. Crowds mull on a beach at a resort hotel. The camera darts and zooms around plush environs, inside the homes of the wealthy, the influential. Privacy dissolves; all lives go public, become a public possession. Rapid cuts. I see spectacles of vicious beatings, images of the homeless and the destitute. People photographed in hordes, bodies multiplying. Impressions flung together; panic, sympathy, and awe intermingled. The medium is both a bridge to events and an equalizer of events. It gives me a passageway, the opportunity to roam and investigate, and it makes everything appear possible, permissible. Masses squeeze forward. This seems to be randomness accelerated, uncertainty and transience exalted.

Channels 18-24

As I sit in the stuttering light of my TV room, I recognize how many times I could use the words "both this and that" to describe what the TV images divulge. Paradoxes, contradictions, twins. TV shows life to be diverse, possibly schizoid, both shattered and fluent, always flowing. I can't say with any certainty that one image will follow another, because TV is "both...and..."

Channels 25-27

While I press the button, channelsearching, I think of the TV critiques that I've read in books. Most of them concentrate on the question of content. The books discussed variety shows in the nineteen forties, sitcoms and dramas in the nineteen fifties, documentaries in the sixties, the rise of the news hour in the seventies, the comedy-dramas about people working in TV in the eighties. The articles studied biases, tendencies, the buried agendas. Screen time makes all existence appear like a fictional script that constantly breaks into erratic incidents of affection and anger, failure and triumph. But when I stop at a station to view the news, I begin to see that the frameworks, the structures of presentation, seldom alter. So what holds us? What theme and emotions do we sense within the formulae and the haphazardness?

Channels 28-29

Images of war, of killing and rape, reinforce our sense of entrapment in insoluble horror, in self-contempt, weakness, and irrelevance to the cosmos. Those who are not friends to humankind will find confirmation of bestiality, egotism, mendacity. But images of celebration among companions, of welcome in families, of crusaders and honest citizens, also suggest charity, compassion, decency, conviviality, our profound relevance to the destiny of what plays out here. Those who wish the world were kinder, more humane, will find promises, the tracings of a generous, enlarging spirit. As if our evolution was unfolding toward goodness. In one harmonious flash TV leads us to see both sides—some evocation of what may be a larger cohesiveness.

Channels 30-34

Through the TV mesh, I've absorbed visual inventions that follow more visual inventions. Crowds churn, and individuals disappear. Masses and stars. Soon the tempo of the freeflow dominates my attention. You risk distraction when you watch. I have to concentrate my mind again, focus on the channels' pull, the spin of light.

Channels 37-48

Blurs, pictures writhe, colors squirm. Programs jammed, movies blacked out. Indications of stories continuing, even when you can't see them. In this near silence and glow, I reflect that there may be no absolute answer to the questions that TV stimulates, nothing reducible to a literary synopsis or paraphrase, no theoretical system that will entirely encompass the liquid imagery, the flux of associations and facsimiles.

Channels 60-

The enigma of TV must be for us what the mystique of the moon was for primitive people. The beam travels everywhere, like a shaft into shadowy rooms. One machine has become the third parent, an overseer of the globe, a device that feeds on scandal and joy. It is an amplifier of our nature, magnifying and hustling our desire to record, to abuse, to enchant ourselves. You watch with crowds, the millions you never see, never touch, never can know, sharing their time of terror and fret, of peace and community. The TV light comes to help us dream; it appears similar to the alchemist's *lumen naturae*. And we ask ourselves if TV covertly uses us, incites us to conniption and calm. And we watch the data web renew itself every day, while the indefinable continues to stir us through the screen.

But I've been amazed to find through the crowding, the shuffle, and the emanations, how subtlety endures, how there is a volatile transparent quality to the images. We seem to be seeing through. This subliminal factor makes TV crafty, enticing. What it elevates is the human gesture.

I see a quick smile, expressions of wonder and hunger, softer eyes and brooding moods, a furrow of pain on a forehead, expressions of petulance and disgust, laughter erupting, moist kisses and pecks on a cheek, skin that looks sallow, expressions that are furious, and passing, always in instants of response, interpretation, and questioning, the singular miracle of one person's face.

Test Face

"What's that face doing up there?"

"What face?" she asks.

"The one repeated on all the monitors."

"Oh, *that* face. It's just a pattern. We use it in the control room to test the focus, colors, the camera angles, depth of field, that sort of thing. Why?"

"It seems to be moving."

"It *does*?"

Twelve monitors lightgun their images of a face. A young man's, cleanshaven, bland, his eyes staring without blinking. A panel of screens filled with a tinted face, a black-and-white face, a face hovering in white.

"It can't be moving. It's just a still, you know. Something we can adjust."

I stare at the bank of Panasonics in the editing suite. The CBC logo is stamped in the center of the open door over a sign that says Entry Code — No Code, Do Not Enter. An acquaintance, Ava Bernstein, the executive producer of an afternoon rock-video show, has invited me downtown to see a show edited. I'm struck by the multiple takes, the face reproduced on monitor after monitor; each looks slightly different. The face floats, uncoupled, disembodied.

Ava touches the dials and knobs on the mixing board. Her hands flutter expertly.

"No, no, no. It just *looks* like he's moving."

"So many screens at once."

"You got it."

"The lights flickering."

"Too many TVs." She smiles, her hands resting on the panel, one finger on a switch. Red digital letters glare. Dozens of timers and clocks. Cigarette butts and coffee cups and fast-food wrappers. The hightech studio looks like somebody's basement.

"Do you know who he is?"

"Who?"

"That guy."

"What guy?"

"The head."

"You're kidding."

Her eyes haven't moved from the monitors. She seems as enthralled as I am.

"Well, I was wondering who he is."

"I've never thought about it before. Some actor. A guy they pulled off the street. Andy Warhol's cousin. A relative of the chairman. He's just up there. Mr. Bland in person."

"And you never asked who he is?"

"Why should I? Weird question. I mean, after all, he's been here as long as I have. He's just *a test*. We could have used someone else. Or Garfield the cat. We needed a face, any old face."

"A young one. With no character."

"Yeah, yeah, yeah. No character. That's the point. I mean, what is the point?"

"That he's a blank."

"Oh, I see. Nothing up there. Mr. Zero. About as interesting as white bread. But, then, this is the CBC, right?" She laughs, and looks from me back to the Panasonics, the Beta boxes stacked on the console, then at me again.

The duplicated face, backed by the power of the monitors, has an uncanny presence in the room. The face, in fact, doesn't move, though expressions appear to ripple across it. A frown, a smile, a sneer, a wink. In one monitor he looks angelic, innocent, otherworldly; in another he looks like a greasy cyberpunk, his features splashed across a computerized Wanted poster. I glance from screen to screen, and see how the changes in hues and tones, the shadows and spots, could make up a storyline. A tale of corruption, a young man gone wrong. "Naked City." What evil lurks.

"Do you get tired of seeing him?"

"I never thought about it before. I don't argue with something that's just *there* like that. Do you want me to shut it off? If it's annoying you..."

"It's the repetition that's so...compelling. You can't get away from him."

"Like Big Brother. Or the Mona Lisa. I hear you can't get away from her stare either. But he's not really interesting, is he? He's...nobody."

"Or everybody."

"Oh, please! But, sure, I see your meaning. Maybe that *is* the point."

* * *

"The thing about TV is that we've made this *thing*. And we don't know how powerful it is."

Then Ava Bernstein begins to tell me how we can create a mystery out of a blank face simply through the focus of the radiant technology.

"Let me tell you what I've seen. For this rock show we do, we get five to ten thousand letters a week. *Five* to *ten* thousand letters. And most of the letters are totally obsessive. We can't tell if these kids are projecting their feelings. What they're making up. Just responding to this incredible image. But they write. You should see the piles. They write and write. You'd be amazed at the effect the most perfect dummies have just because they're on TV. Total nadas. Zoned-out heads. I'm talking specialists in stupidity. Kindergarten dropouts. But somehow they come across."

Ava's voice, tough and blunt, is edged with irony. She's a small person, her black hair long and permed; she wears a loose-fitting black jumpsuit, a black jacket and scarf. Animated, enthusiastic, she swings back and forth in her cushioned swivel chair, talking, giggling, gesturing. She tells me that she's been with the CBC for five years. "I'm a good soldier of the corporation," she says of herself. She'd been trained in film-script writing at university, but her career path, she explains, took her from movies to TV. I like her voice, her passionate talk about the medium of her choice.

"It worries me sometimes. I've seen whole groups become politicized because of rock-and-roll shows we did on apartheid in South Africa. Peace movements springing up because of a video. Nelson Mandela and Madonna mentioned in the same breath. I mean, honestly. And I scoffed at them. TV ignoramuses. Those *fashionable* causes. South Africa this week. Eastern Europe the next. Starvation in Ethiopia. The Middle East in the morning. No nukes. Save the whales. Justice for the aboriginals. What have you got? It goes on and on. Suggestible kids. Low-identity profiles. No memories. No rational basis for their reactions. No continuity. They're not really thinking. None of this is *logical.*

"Then I started to think about it all. The effects. And you know, I realized this may be the first time these viewers got anything. They'd never grasped what apartheid means. What a war does. So who knows if we're a service or a disservice? What we give them is fashion."

"Fashion?" I ask, curious about what she means.

"This year it's equality and justice. Next year it's peace. The

133

year after that it'll be sexism in the workplace. Ideas and values becoming fashions. But is this so bad? Is this so wrong? We influence people on an *unbelievable* scale. We tell them things. Even if it's through the flinch of an eyebrow by the bimbo on the set who makes three times the money that I do."

"She's one of the presences on the screen."

"Yeah, well, whatever you want to call it. Talk about presence! The amazing thing about her is that when I write copy for our anchor bimbo — okay, that *person* — I have to put it in her style. Seriously. I write in the slang. She can't talk spontaneously. I've got a studio monitor that plays the ahs and ums. If she can't see the script on the monitor, mistakes and all, she's totally paralyzed. Out to lunch. I swear she'd have a nervous breakdown right there on the set if she had to make it up."

"Yet these people have a presence on TV."

"So you keep saying. Yeah. Kids write like she's some sort of guru. Big sister. Monitor mom. Let me tell you, when all the letters roll in, I take them seriously. Our anchor bimbo would have a *fit* trying to answer those letters. Now, some people can wing it. Some do improvise. But it's always a surprise to see who works on TV and who doesn't. Generally it's the prettier the better...the blander the better. You don't want Robert De Niro reading the news, right? The whole country would have a heart attack."

* * *

Reading faces.

The impact of light shooting through the tube.

Presences holding sway on a screen; viewers projecting a meaning on that mesh.

Sounding out intent.

We are image-struck in a control room. I try to accommodate this sense of being image-bound, shadowed by faces. The Panasonics appear suspended against the black backdrop, the painted flatboard. Signs say Vid In, Vid Out. Digital letters say Destination, Auto-Edit, Review. A reporter I recognize from the national news hesitates in the hall and stares at the head, her figure in the doorway. It's as if she expects to see a new series of images unreeling. She sighs, then leaves, and we're left alone again.

Only because we're image-bound, we aren't alone. I look at the Panasonics, once again detecting a shift in the young man's expression. It's impossible: the face can't move. Yet the image quivers, the control panel hums. A monitor life.

The philosopher critic Walter Benjamin, in his essay "The Work of Art in the Age of Mechanical Reproduction," said that the aura of authenticity around an art object would erode due to mass repetition. Culture would become billboards, commercials, and postcards. True art and beauty would be churned into the uniform, the disposable. Significant statement and the unique point of view would be flattened into the inoffensive and the acceptable. Variety would give way to monotony and homogeneity, like a Cuisinart culture.

I reflect on Benjamin's critique and its profound suggestion. But as I stare into the monitors, their intense gleam, I observe the aura surrounding the blank face. The cathode light lends a fascinating authority to it. The emanation elevates his features. It gives them their singular shine, the semblance of motion, the vibration that provokes thoughts, memories, opinions. The face says nothing, yet it speaks, borne in white space, the shimmer around it telling us that the image is changeable, tentative, impermanent, multiform, both unique and repeatable.

* * *

"Have you thought about what's happened to him?"

"I never thought about him at all until today," Ava says.

"I wonder what his life's been like."

"It's a bit eerie, isn't it? Who the hell is he? Maybe he doesn't

135

exist. He could be something the computer-animation boys dreamed up one night."

Encountering appearance, the evidence of a presence. This is the true strangeness of TV: the primal intensity of the human face. Time rushes by while we look and listen. And we scour for traces of kindness and cruelty, engagement and longing, gentleness and genius, the ability to love and hate in those who trip across the screens. TV packs our lives with a myriad of strangers. We become the hosts of familiar and unfamiliar guests, our minds jammed by their sullen, resistant, or eloquent silences, by their talking, singing, gossiping, and whispering.

"Put him on the air and you give him substance," Ava says. "That's why we sometimes say, 'Get me some talking heads to fill this space.' We use witnesses, experts, interviews on the street. You can only take about thirty-five seconds of anyone on camera. A minute is a lot of airtime. Most viewers turn off. They don't want to see someone's face up there for so long. I really believe you can have too much of someone on TV. It's like a prime minister or a president who's been in office too long. You start seeing *their* face everywhere. After a while you're sick of them. So the trick is to show these faces, but not to overdo it."

Here Benjamin would be right: the repetition of a face in the media could invite skepticism, mistrust, a lack of faith in that individual's authenticity. After a time, a person's image invades your private room. Overloaded, you reach for the remote control. Then click off that look, reject the overexposed image; scrub the screen, and start over again with someone new.

"You can put almost *anybody* up there and make them seem important," she says. "Again it comes back to the point I made about it —" she gestures at the Beta videocassettes "— this thing that totally changes how we communicate. Put a camera and a microphone on someone, give them airtime, and bang!...the ten-second star is born."

She swivels nervously in her chair and glances at me as if

to confirm that I'm listening.

"That's why politicians and terrorists can be so successful if they understand TV. Interview someone with a real steaming problem. Then add music. Jump cut to a mother crying. And look out. You've got controversy, phone calls to the station. TV is powerful because nearly *everyone* has a grievance!" She throws up her hands in mock exasperation.

"And the more telegenic you are," she continues, "the more mediawise you become — I love TV's buzzwords. They're so vivid — the more likely it is you'll communicate without saying anything. Just stand there and look right."

"So you can make anyone a star?"

"Hey, no, that's the mystery. Real stardom is decided by the viewers. Like my anchor bimbo. Personally, I wouldn't talk to her about anything other than the best method for birth control. But put lights and a camera on her. And that smile. Those eyes. That voice. And people fall in love with her."

"Maybe the TV screen reveals qualities that more analytical people can't read."

"Analytical?" she asks.

"People using argument to understand, rather than music or images."

"Yeah, well. TV *is* stranger than we know. That's why I stay in it. Despite all the terrible hours and pressure, I love reaching into everyone's lives."

"These techniques can be used for propaganda purposes. Politicians, corporate spokesmen — they can use TV to hide facts and distort reality."

"Like negative advertising in political campaigns?"

"A ruthless leader can affect us through TV without us knowing why or how. He could look soft and gentle, and he could be a dictator."

"Charisma is what TV's about. Appearance is what it's all about," she says. "You have to get that before you can get what's happening to politics, news, the whole process. No point in imagining a time when everything is changed by TV. It's already made the great difference."

"So by interpreting charisma, we might begin to get at what's inside a person. Vengeance. Murder. Manipulation. Or sincerity. Compassion. The desire to see justice done." The soul's intentions, I think to myself.

"Something like that."

"But good actors can disguise and protect themselves."

"I don't think you can completely get away with that on TV. I'll tell you why. These faces get so near you. I mean, look at the movies. The *monumental* images on the screen."

"Screens over forty feet high."

"Sure. And what have you got with TV? Twenty-eight inches. Maybe thirty-four. Yeah, there are big screens. Wide screens. But movies are different. They're larger than life. TV people are *intimate*. They're with us every day."

"Like a family."

"Yeah," she agrees softly, "or like the family you've never had."

I watch her turn a dial. She may be about to tell me the so-far-unmentioned story of her life, possibly about walls, locked doors, and estrangements.

But when she doesn't add anything, I say, "TV can be used for unscrupulous ends. It creates the illusion of action and involvement..."

"Sure, sure. Four arguments for the elimination of TV. You can do dreadful stuff. Lie and cheat...But it comes back to how a face like this guy's plays on the monitors. TV goes *right* into your head. Once the signal is in there, you sort out the crap. I believe in common sense. That you can reach the good and the bad in people. It's like I said about the letters we get. They're out there. Figuring it out. And you know, my anchor bimbo is okay in that department. She cares, in her dim way. This is her first serious job.

When she looks into the camera, she looks like she's searching for you. It's amazing. But she isn't false. She's just this pill who makes money by looking straight into the camera, coming through the tube, all smiling and knowing."

* * *

She stares at the control panel, the digital numbers, red letters clocking time. She seems depleted by her outburst. She sits, thinking to herself, swinging back and forth in her mobile chair.

In the pause, I remember the exploding heads, the videotape at the dancebar. The crowd was captivated by the metamorphosis of celebrities into mythical creatures and then excited by the apocalyptic ruin, the faces' meltdown. We'd been transfixed by how the stars could be corroded, the fragility of their charisma.

I make a mental leap to the symbolism of the mystery rites and the Cabbalists, the theologians of the human junction with the cosmos. They were students of the human face, and believed that they could foretell a person's destiny from the wrinkles in a forehead, the cut of a hairline, the curve of a mouth, the shape and color of the eyes. Age lines could display tendencies, possibilities. A human being was a textbook through which you could understand the celestial design. These doctors thought that the secret of your identity, the rise and fall of your fortune, the center of your character, could be imprinted, even gouged, into your moles, wrinkles, and scars.

Scientists discredit the occult obsessions. Yet in modern medicine, a doctor will sometimes use a technique called thermography to detect an illness by heatlines. The shadows and pouches under the eyes, the discolored patches of skin like a bruise, might show a body and soul about to be gripped. Thermography probes the facial surface, anatomizing pores and spots, looking for the marks of inner turmoil.

TV producers and directors put the human face at the

center of the picture. Place a person in a lush landscape or an austere room, into a threatening circumstance, danger lurking. Then disclose how that person will reveal the range of his or her emotions. The occult explorers believed that the stars and the elements of earth, air, fire, and water — what they called the Invisibles — touched our features and hearts. On TV, we constantly watch people touched up by makeup, reshaped by lighting, close-ups, and editing.

This freeze-framed face. Hypnotic, phantasmic, reborn, refashioned, resistant to a normal life-span. The face is seductive because we've made it so through our technology of attention and magnification. But I grasp a humanness in its expression. We are evolving — or rediscovering — a webbed world; it is impossible to escape the feeling that people can be here and everywhere, our imprint extended into all things.

I gaze at the young man's face. No one could preserve such a pristine aspect. Yet what's in a face can lead to knowledge of the heart. He may now have a look of wildness, or of wonder, his stare enriched by worldly indulgence and hard learning, or he may have a look that's been grooved by sorrow and remorse, some lasting hurt, his features showing the deep lines of loss and mourning. Whatever has happened to him, he will probably never know that Ava Bernstein and I once spent time musing on who he was, on what he'd become, and on how the cathode light and the monitor hum had transformed the effect of his unblinking appearance.

"Sticky buttons."

"What?" I'm shaken out of my thoughts.

"Some dude spilled coffee on the board. Buttons like glue. I mean jeez. Go figure."

* * *

"It all makes me think of *The Wizard of Oz*," Ava comments.

"How?"

"The scene in the Wizard's palace. Dorothy, the Scarecrow, the Tin Man, the Cowardly Lion. In front of this huge head. And all these fireworks."

"The mask floating in smoke and fire."

"That's it. *Wonderful* bit. And Toto runs over to the curtain and pulls it back. And there's this little old guy pulling levers. The voice shouts, 'Pay no attention to that man behind the curtains...I am the great and powerful Wizard of Oz.' Then the old coot confesses it's him. Nothing's up there. Well, maybe that's what we're doing. Projecting that someone's up there, or that something's going on behind the mask."

Inside the control room we've watched a test pattern for more than an hour. We could continue proposing scenarios and conspiracies, inserting grids of interpretation, like theorists scrambling to impose logic, order, and sequence on the unknown. But this face may give us nothing more.

"He seems half-alive," I say. "That's what all the monitors do. They almost bring him to life. But he seems...incomplete."

"Well, if you *think* you'll find something up there, you will. Believe me, you'd get used to the setup after a while. The hours by yourself."

I glance at Ava and suddenly recognize the look of solitude about her.

"Do you spend a lot of time alone here?"

Surprised, she turns to me and slumps a little in her chair. She smiles faintly. I see the kindness in her face, her desire to be generous, the humor. Despite her hectic work, she has a living center in her, vivid in her eager eyes, her smile, her words.

"Late nights with coffee and doughnuts. Cigarettes, pizza, and take-out Chinese. Hey. It's my life. I breathe TV, I eat TV. And don't mention the coke, the bennies and tranqs. And the divorces galore. I spend a lot of time getting the show out. It matters to me. It's how I do my bit."

She swivels away in her chair, maybe uneasy that she's

shown me her feelings. Then she straightens her back and says nothing for a moment.

Finally she asks in a gentler tone, "Are you heading somewhere with these questions? It's like you're really after things. Like it's personal. So essential to you."

I nod, and I don't answer her. I'm not sure that I can yet. She swivels back and turns to watch me, waiting for me to reply; then she looks at the Panasonics, sits up in her chair, and starts talking, becoming animated again.

"These images *are* half-alive. That's what you must mean by their presence. Maybe that's how we'll get to know about ourselves. Through the images. Is that where you're going? I'll tell you what I've found. Maybe it'll help. TV is *pure* emotion. That's why I stay. That's why TV drives everyone nuts. This deep stuff just keeps welling up."

Virtue Room

"Virtual reality. When you wear a VR helmet you won't be outside the screen anymore. You'll be swimming in the image."

His eyes widen, the glint of obsession behind his thick wire-frame glasses. His words dart, their quickness in the air.

"With VR, spectatorship will end. By wearing headware, wetware, the body and the mind and electronic engineering become one."

He calls himself by the code name Virtu-Man. A self-proclaimed software architect. In this converted warehouse by the lakeshore, I'd expected to find my contact, Virtu-Man, wearing underground clothes, Italian sunglasses in a shaded room, a black leather jacket studded with computer insignia, the arcana of communication systems. Instead he dresses like a bank executive.

"VR is about designing our perceptual space directly. VR means you won't be separate from TV. This is the beginning of total integration. Perpetual feedback, permanent immersion."

I've come to probe him about the future of the tube. The intimations and signs.

"VR frees the body. Hit a button. A new image concept appears around you. I'm streamlining the physical. You'll be able to meditate anywhere. On a mountain, by a river, in the desert."

A white table, two wooden chairs painted black, a plain room, except for the reams of printout paper, the diskettes, the computer manuals. A terminal glares green light. Digital lettering announces You May Begin Anywhere.

"You could explore your own preferences or perversities. Become a Marquis de Sade, doing VR sado-masochism, having sex with anyone you can imagine. Or a Glenn Gould, a celibate dreamer spinning in cyber-heaven."

Virtu-Man's studio — his name is actually Ted — is like a monastery. Exposed walls and floors, wood and brick; bareness everywhere. He sits rigidly, his hands folded on his desk. His voice jumps with enthusiasm, but his body appears immobilized, tacked to the chair.

"VR means liquid architecture. Making your space absolutely fluid. Psychic architecture. Pieces moving around you on the shifting interests of your personal taste. Neural networks becoming liquid because you just keep flowing through options."

I hear the evangelical tone, the note of the puritan convert, the searcher who thinks that he has found a lasting truth. Again I notice how he rarely flexes or alters the position of his body, how he remains fastened to one spot, stuck while his words wheel and soar.

"Freedom. That's my universal value. My definition of freedom is a high correspondence between what you want to do and what you have to do. It's maximum overlap. Of course, people spend their lives playing video games. Total addiction. Rainbow chasing becoming a way of life. We have to watch what happens when you gratify your sensory needs. People wander off. Like crack addicts. Blowing the social system apart."

Traffic jangling outside. The computer's consistent drone.

The light off the fluorescent lamps in the ceiling. Radiance from the terminal. It's light that can mesmerize us, sound that can haunt us.

"I'm inventing the idea of the complete technoperson. Who reinvents for himself the nomadic lifestyle. Who recreates his preferred world anywhere. Who leaves physicality behind. Nomadic cultures have a strong sense of values. They roam, but they're close-knit."

I've listened, said nothing. I'm trying to pull in the sway of people's voices now, the layers of innuendo, the stories that make claims, the words that embrace the present and breathe in the future, the tones that are no longer self-protective but stripped away almost to their core, the beat of belief, the bass-line of the self. The Virtu-Man has wrapped himself in technology. He is, to my amazement, happy in his effusive futurism. He uses words that have accumulated meaning for him — cult charms and jargon, the language of the initiate. Some of what he says perplexes me, leaves me skeptical. But I follow where his tone goes, what it reveals, the rhythm of his sentences rising.

"Technomads, technognomes. Those who love mental traveling. Those who need physical consistency."

His hands clutch and unclutch. Nothing else about him budges. Just his hands, fine boned and small, pale like a baby's. He steeples his fingers, then he interlaces them, squeezing them tightly.

"Technognomes stay in front of their computers and TVs, repeating the same sequence. It's the missionary position for computer addicts and TV nuts. But the prototype of the technomad is the person walking around with a Walkman on. Creating a partial new world in his head. With tapes, you make variations. With a turn of a dial, you choose another psychic environment. A happy-sad dial, an urban-rural dial. The technomad assumes that he can live in any other space sufficiently."

* * *

Virtual: from the Latin word, *virtūtem*, meaning virtue or quality. There is also *virtù*, an old Italian word that refers to the love of art. The virtue room; it could be a space to find excellence and self-mastery, where consciousness can be attuned to the highest pursuits, a peak of intellectual evolution. Technological virtuosity finally supplants animal being. Are these the implications? The mind thriving in abstract idealist regions, freed from flesh. And room: the word links with rumor —

I'd like to see the technology demonstrated, but he explains how he doesn't own the instruments himself.

"Only corporations can afford to do this. AT&T, Disney, the military. They're building a nomad society of the mind. Go through a door in a mall in Denver and end up in West Edmonton Mall. The difference between malls is infinitesimal. The total standardization of everything. It's the great revolution. A standardized society is a peaceful one. We become passive outside, active inside. Always watching for potential dividers. High resolution stuff that creates divisions."

He squirms, pushing his chair back. The plastic legs make a loud squeak on the wooden floor. I'm startled by the scratching noise. It reminds me that he still hasn't moved. Somehow he talks without shifting his weight, without expansive gestures of any kind.

"A universal city starts in the suburbs and stretches downtown. Television is the vehicle of this standardization. Sitting on standardization committees in corporations gives you the real power in the world. I want to make my mark. It's cheaper to design everything on a grand scale. Mental variety, technological uniformity."

Suddenly he's silent. As if even he's astonished by what he's just said. I don't offer a commentary to him. He lives in a remote mental space, a mediascape made up of responsive rooms and Utopian zeal. His lecture, chant, needed acceptance only. It's enough for me to record his discourse of the new and to watch him in this stark studio.

"I see the future. TV is only the prototype of the great machine that will one day appear."

His fervent voice becomes louder, his gaze directed beyond me. His delicate hands twitch.

"Turn the dials. Go anywhere, everywhere. Shifting our psychic architecture to mountains and rivers. Then to beautiful homes in Victorian England and to beaches in Hawaii. The mind released. Terror curtailed. Each person a wanderer in pictures and dreams. Remaking well-being. Creating fluid architecture. Traveling, traveling."

Late-night Conversion

"Touch the screen."

Alone in my viewing room, I've been flipping stations with my remote when that command stops me at the Christian Cable Network. I watch a televangelist plead with his cathode congregation, a deep American southernness in his voice, a soothing slur that only a member of your family might use. He murmurs, moans, and begins to forge his viewers into a flock.

"Our 1-800-line is the direct line to Jesus Christ Our Lord, toll free to the Savior. You have the power, God's power, the power to come back into His arms. Six-six-six is the line to Satan. In Jesus Christ there is no darkness. I call to you, call on you, pick up your phone, call Him, call us."

The video pulpiteer spreads his arms, like a great bird of prey. He sways. Close-up of his charismatic appearance, silver hair and blue eyes. He grips the microphone.

"Come touch the screen."

He invites the viewer to feel the tube's static. Instantly I lean forward on the couch, impressed by this messianic figure who beckons me to press my hands on the vibration, become a partner in the church of the airwaves, God's channel, where content, image, and sound bite join in a holy roll.

"Welcome, you lost sheep straying in the fields of despair, to the true fold of our Savior, our Lord Jesus, His strength, His mercy."

I witness an uncanny event in the TV glow at midnight. The video preacher understands that across the continent, scattered masses of people sit dazed, frustrated, and anxious. He raises his hands and makes his appeal. He wants to intone us into action. Come close to the tube's heat, find ethereal company here.

"Keep touching until we're one."

I aim the remote and skip ahead to a late-night movie. I see a silvery Greta Garbo, her still-seductive figure, the enticing emotion in her eyes, the shiver in her livid sexuality. The Pentecostal fervor of the fundamentalists doesn't speak to me: they form a closed group, anti-intellectual, intolerant, reductive in their thinking, reactionary in their pronouncements. Yet I flip back to the station, moved by the preacher's entreaty. He seems to know something. He thinks he has found the key.

"We're one family under God, but some of his fold have become homeless in their hearts."

He paces the stage. This TV preacher is a believer who wants to heal you, entrance you, mend your soul's wound. I listen carefully and recognize that the televangelist is informing his flock that this is a crucial time of social breakdown and moral disorder. God harrows us with the call to purpose.

* * *

The televangelists are building a series of transnational corporations — sectarian monoliths. These preachers have combined spiritual, commercial, and political concerns to buy a satellite, broadcast stations, prime-time and late-night slots. They know how the alchemy of TV will convey elemental effects. The flicker and hum suggest a telecasting of sensation, an experience at once urgent and mollifying. Televangelists use the tube like a haloed billboard, a kinetic advertisement for the God of born-again Christianity. They solicit support from viewers, asking them to send money so that the sect's architects and engineers can erect universities, hospitals, and churches, institutions christened with names like the City of Faith, the Prayer Tower, and the Crystal Cathedral. They construct theme parks that resemble a fantasyland for the faithful, hotels that are like a paradise for credit-card Christians. News services interpret world catastrophes according to their revivalist theology. They field candidates in elections, hawking their credo of oneness.

The preacher hints in a whisper that the essence of TV is conversion.

* * *

"I know where you live! The Lord commands us. Look into your hearts. Give up the corruption and come back to the family of Jesus."

I imagine the soulsick viewer isolated in an apartment, worried about money and a job that goes nowhere, wanting to return to wonder, sweet promise, and warmth. All he knows is his critical awareness, the burden of entanglement with the merciless world. He turns to the TV light and the evangelical gust. Estranged and aroused, the viewer yields to the voice of redemption. "Your time is now," the preacher declares. The spirit has been freed in the tube.

The watcher sees a group relieved, a crowd believing. They sing Holy Holy Holy. He feels exalted. He finds vivacity, belonging, solutions.

"Pick up your telephone and we will respond with letters, invitations, membership."

It's so obvious. The world has gone mad. But the words from the set announce, "I know you. God believes you are alive. He is reaching out. He will confirm you." At that moment the viewing room converts into a temple.

* * *

Televangelism thrives on strong leadership, the potency of a single face. The exaggerated gestures and subtle expressions. The video pulpiteers, Jerry Falwell, Robert Schuller, and Pat Robertson, have become notorious, loved, and feared, wealthy celebrities and ambitious politicians. When one TV preacher is discredited, another one takes up the ministry. Critics sneer, and yet the congregations welcome back the sullied, the criminal, the broken. This protestant revivalism evolved out of the Bible Belters and tent orators of the American Midwest and South. Religious radio always had a large audience, but the televangelists understand how TV can captivate legions. On screen the preacher's face will radiate answered needs, the end of anarchic data.

I aim my remote, aware that any point I can turn the show off. Instead I ponder the preacher's appeal to soulsickness and love.

His preaching fits the tube's flash. He homilizes with flare and gusto, and the TV field shocks and strokes our responses. The preacher stares into the camera and spreads the gospel of attraction and belonging.

I surprise myself by feeling sympathy for what he says. His passionate language admits weakness, confusion, yearning. How do we know that spiritual energy will not unnerve us? Divine intent may be rattling, and daunting, striking us unexpectedly.

The preacher exudes zeal. Shots cut back and forth from his enraptured face to the studio audience. The church of the airwaves claims that only love will satisfy your craving, the need for meaning. Only with us, he says, will your life have fixity, borders, consistency.

"The godless are leading our children astray."

Another tone beats back the appeal to unity.

"Our cities are cesspools of disease, unholy circles of lust and addiction, populated by gays and lesbians and reprobates and sinners. O my brothers and sisters."

"Amen," the crowd replies, like a choir well-versed in the call and response, primed for the routine.

Their preacher urges obedience. "You know Armageddon is near!" Now this TV host becomes a wolf, preying on lost sheep. "The gospel is your anchor in the fiery flood of the future. We must sign up, resist the brandishings of unbelievers." Yeas, hand-clapping, cries. "The beast is among us. The Book of Revelations tells us. Watch your TVs. The fire of Armageddon is coming."

In the video preacher's words I find that the longing for redemption becomes an unconscious longing for destruction. He draws a dividing line between the fallen who know about the impending fury and the fallen who do not. I watch this dreamer of annihilation relish the approach of a millennial whirlwind. His call to love changes into a sermon of doom: darkness must descend over those outside his electronic flock.

I pull back on the couch, angered by the abrupt emergence of a vengeful faith, the spiritual bullying. The preacher's voice swerved from an honest urge to relieve suffering to tyrannical censure. It's a pop theology that switches moods as fast as a thirty-second commercial spot. The fundamentalists know that dread and death will make exciting TV.

* * *

I wave the remote. Press the volume button. A green indicator stripe spreads across the screen. Sound falls. The preacher's mouth jacks open. His hands flail. Sweat beads on his forehead. His face is stretched like a rubber mask. Close-ups show choir members shaking, finding pleasure in his promise of punishment. Here is a

TV image of agreement, a congregation of the credulous and the uncritical.

I understand the dangerous force of such an image. The televangelists pray for rebirth, for the recovery from soulsickness — then for the burning of the world. The camera captures the appearance of piety, the flock with their heads bowed, their minds apparently accepting violent prophecy, lips moving in unison.

* * *

Clicking off.

The set darkens.

I sink back slowly in the couch, removing myself from the maze of prayer and euphoric choirs and commercial gospeling.

I consider this need for ecstasy and ritual that I've found again. In televangelism the pattern of isolation and the yearning for transcendence recurs. Fundamentalists offer a firm answer, singularity instead of multiplicity, an absolute in the chaos. They absorb the desperate into a homogeneous whole. The irony is the televangelists use the radiant technology, the medium of flux and multiple meanings, to resurrect walls, hard definition, a restrictive moral order. It wouldn't surprise me if they had a plan to televise Armageddon, should it happen to occur. What begins for them in true spiritual anxiety ends in a crude collective that revels in the condemnation of others and waits for rapture and oblivion.

* * *

Pressing the on button.

Flesh tones, moving limbs, a soft, erotic moaning. A movie dubbed on the multicultural network. I take a moment before I identify the early-hours show: *Last Tango in Paris*. Its images appear cramped and hurried on TV. Maria Schneider and Marlon Brando grapple, naked on a bare mattress. Orange-gold heat seeps

153

off the walls. The lovers throw back their heads, shuddering together, a simulated ecstasy. Skin tones shimmer, an illumination of thighs and breasts and hands. Eyes closed, the two stars look as if they could be praying or murmuring words out of an orgasmic trance.

The expression on faces, the entwining bodies. A cry for order, the turmoil of desire. They're here, side by side. More than a mirror to life, TV tantalizes your feelings, sparking extreme reactions, spellbinding you with its moods and spectacles. The TV light spills electricity, and life clings.

The televangelists recognize that the TV aura may stimulate spirituality. They want to institutionalize that light — to direct it and make it the vehicle for their melodrama of salvation. They present a version of the initiation mysteries — with a literalist twist that takes symbolism to be a fact. The manipulation of the viewer is so blatant that it shouldn't be successful. But it is, because they have perceived the pain that people feel: the bafflement, the lack of tenderness. The televangelists know that there is strangeness in the world, but they want to package this enigma and turn it into a commercial for their fundamentalist God and the terror of his pitiless retribution.

Tapping the button.

Channel 107

At the high end of the cable system, the screen slips into snow. Gray dots flit by. The tinge of a threatening shadow awakens in the background. I stare and listen and detect some spectral image slinking out in the fierce storm of static.

The Sixth Window

Evening and I sit switching the TV off and on again. Remote, monitor, speakers. It's become a routine: the screen glittering, music rising and falling. The house dims again, fading away from my focus on the tube.

Suddenly I find the sound too loud, the picture dulling. Impatient, I leap up from the couch, crossing the floor to shut off the set at its source. I'm tempted to reach around behind it and tear out the plugs.

The quiet of the room takes over. An eerie silence, a startling hush from the TV and the stereo speakers. The silence comes off the furniture, the walls, the carpet, the shelves. Everything has an extra texture, an edge. I'm aware of the coffee table, the couch, the ceiling, as if the whole room has been abruptly demagnetized.

The house slowly makes its presence known to me. Air ducts and vents, the tapping and creaks in the stairwells and walls.

I look at the screen. Maybe I've misunderstood the effects of TV. Magical acts supposedly change the substance of the objects they touch. The mystical experience is meant to reunite you with the numinous in all things. What does TV do? It forms the sixth window to our senses. When it's shut off, its electromagnetic field is muted, and I'm returned to this brief quiet and the objects in the room standing out starkly.

The dark-green tube waits, arrested and contained. I've learned this: TV is one of the primary instruments of the current, letting the pulsations and flickers of life freely enter my home. It's also an agent of noise, interference, and distraction.

Both...and: the condition of paradox.

I'm following these streams, citystreets and paths on the screen, through dancebars and hotcores of symbols and artifacts, TV images and highfrequency tones, chasing down the secret measures, the music that may be behind it all.

"In brief, conceive light invisible, and that is a spirit," Thomas Browne wrote in his *Religio Medici*. A quote I've copied down in my notebook.

TV ushers the things of the air into a room, making one small place an everywhere. The airwaves can be loaded with tricks and fakes, floating heads, idols of light and darkness, limitless diversions and utter disarray. The riddle of TV endures because the screen conveys anything, everything. TV reveals illusions, like an investigative eye, and it is an illusion, a spectacle of effects. All electronic inventions extend our capacities, but are their effects always humane? What does TV truly enhance and to whom does it belong?

* * *

Probing, tapping. I remember the head hovering in the monitors and Ava Bernstein's zeal for her work. She thought that she could touch people through the screen. I think of the TV futurist, whose body seemed locked into his chair, while his breakaway mind flew on into the next century. He believed that TV would one day liberate our dreams. Then the televangelist imploring us to touch the tube, using the cathode ray as if it were a halo. And I think of the woman who resembled Lena, crossing like a ghost through the images (my evasions, how I've avoided her). TV helps you to free-associate. You need a mind that can improvise in the way that jazz musicians play to respond to the whirl.

I stand close to the screen. The sounds in the room are vivid. I must be getting used to the absence of TV. My house feels warmer than it did, but abandoned.

I step away from the set and walk toward the staircase. I've spent too long trying to discern the intent and the gist here, to understand both the simulacrum that TV creates and the nature it exposes, the aural and televisual essence.

* * *

Horns, wheels, and crowds. Throbbing traffic. The rhythm of the street again.

I stride past the Jehovah Witnesses temple, the Maple Leaf Tavern, the McDonald's. It's good to feel the brisk wintery air. Traces of stars over the rooftops. To the northwest the sky blackens. The white tinge around the clouds usually means a storm. Snow may blanket the city tonight.

From where I walk along the sidewalk, I can see the top of the 102-story CN Tower, the city's beacon. Aircraft warning lights flash red, white. This telecommunications spire is a symbol of the powers and the mystery that call to us, scattering over the airwaves.

We are inflamed receptors, moving in pools of electromagnetism, and we need conduits and networks to forge alliances, bonds, and communities. The telecommunications systems feed on our receptivity and on our vulnerability. TV isn't an oppressive monster: it's a conveyer, heightening the current that drives and flares through our lives. Nothing can completely control or determine its effects on the individual mind. Once the means of communication unleash the signs and sound bites in the air, they become variable, eruptive, elusive, sometimes ephemeral. This is

157

because the electric current just "is"...alive. TV augments, repeats, and distorts that "is." The constant amplification and ingestion of the current can make the viewer feel livid and crazed.

Traffic crawls. The narrow road is lit up by neon and Eastern pictograms. Elaborate signs of dragons and snakes. Vietnamese cafés, Korean food stores. Cooking from the restaurants, bitter scents and spice, the tang of an exotic aroma.

I walk on, aware of how vulnerable I've been to the surges of electronic light and sound. I'd thought that I could record and analyze these elements and that I'd be only slightly affected. But I sense the power of the forcefields, their seductiveness and danger, how you can be mesmerized, even dominated. We don't know what we do to ourselves by allowing these untrammeled charges into our homes.

It's the latent beat and harmony in the current that I don't comprehend. This sound within the noise has to be both ancient and new, rooted and rootless, somehow structured and yet shapeless, maybe belonging to no one, leaving trails. We have to learn how to bring our imaginations, our need for meaning and cohesion, together with the electrical breathing...

I stop and wait for a traffic light to turn green. Walkers and shoppers spill over the sidewalks, stepping out into the street, so that cars, vans, and streetcars have to bump forward cautiously. People bustle into the vegetable and fruit markets. On this cold night the corner stores teem like an Old World market.

I listen to the sellers and the customers barter and joke in Chinese, Italian, Japanese, Greek. Words crackle, the voices steeped in day-to-day pleasures and needs.

North toward Riverdale Park the throngs and languages fall away. Beyond the market the city spreads south to the lake, north to the hills. A streetcar's wheels spark when it curves around the corner.

This is life outside tonight. And when I cross the street to the west side, where the park slopes down to the expressway, I think of the TV flux, and I realize how much time I've spent inside over the years. In a room watching. Night after night I've withdrawn into the rays, spending hours alone, or with friends, or with family, immersed in the cathode radiance.

And if I listed the programs in my memory, what a chronicle I'd make. Dramas, comedies, adventures. It would be a collage of the prime-time dream.

The list would encompass two decades of TV programming. Private eyes, secret agents, and supercops in The Man from UNCLE, I Spy, The Saint, Danger Man, Mission Impossible, Ironside, Hawaii Five-O. These shows had the common note of good against evil, of solved crimes. Then there were the family shows, the sitcom view of home life and work: The Dick Van Dyke Show, The Andy Griffith Show, My Three Sons. Each week occult doctrines were leaked, extraterrestrials landed, and the future was imagined in Star Trek, The Twilight Zone, and The Outer Limits. Loners and lawmen rode their horses through frontiers of showdowns and homesteading during Maverick, Have Gun Will Travel, Bonanza, Gunsmoke. In Combat, Twelve O'Clock High, and The Rat Patrol, soldiers on heroic missions fought against a dangerous other, through landscapes of smoldering ruins. Get Smart, Hogan's Heroes, and M*A*S*H parodied movies. The stories had resolution, a closing of their narrative circle. They were morality tales that left an impression of disorder resolved into order. This was the idealist content of TV shows — an empire of righteous people, correctable wrongs, satisfied wants, families supported by unseen depositories of wealth. The past, present, and future were summoned, captured, conceived. History became a blitz of myths, with science fiction and the borderlands and the streets of San Francisco at once synchronous, glittery, and temporary.

The paradox of TV is that the light-sound flux, the images and bites flowing through the technology, went beyond story lines, the content. We were unschooled naturals in unrecognized transformations of sensibility. The stories on TV may have imposed order, but the effects of the cathode ray were turbulent and open and obscure.

At the top of the hill in the park, I see the city boldly silhouetted against the backdrop of clouds. The wind races up, the air stroking my cheeks.

Across the valley, the city glows.

* * *

Walking along a residential street. On both sides the Victorian row houses loom in the darkness. TVs flicker inside the renovated homes, so many people watching. Trees shake in the wind. The leaves on the ground rustle, making a metallic sound, like rain tapping on a tin roof.

I slow down and look up through the tangle of branches. The maples, oaks, and birches are close enough to each other that their branches intertwine, reaching over fences and bushes, ignoring the property lines. The old trees form patterns of entanglement. Suddenly when the clouds pass, the intricate patterns are distinctly illuminated by the silver moon. The full moon is luminous tonight, a beautiful disk surrounded by stars.

I think of how TV beams come through the tube. The moon glimpsed through the clouds. The incandescent arcs of the streetlamps giving off white light.

Complexity, paradox; codes, meshes, and chords. A rhythm keeps building in these recognitions, the pattern moving toward articulation.

What is TV? It's the sixth window through which the flux rushes. Sometimes the window opens wide enough for you to engage a crisis, to encounter the alive eyes of a young woman's face and the pale skin of a dying old man, and sometimes TV arrests you in its sedative glare. The window opens and the flux sweeps in landscape and cityscape, an isolated individual and a crowd, the private and the public, the dreamer and the dream in fusion.

What about the inner life of the TV audience? The ingazers seated in front of the tube, the teleseers clicking their remotes.

I sense what must be the desire in people to find new routes. The flux and the glow lead us forward and backward, jump-cutting to every aspect of life. This movement speaks in murmurs and overtones of discovery and intuition. Each day and night of TV absorption may bring the possibility of tragic intensity, momentary ecstasy. TV is a place for the tired and the depressed, for the curious and the critical. The surplus of images and voices may weigh us down. But the tube takes into the hum of human speech, reassuring and shocking appearances and features, ignitions of fantasy and action, the domain of the invisible.

What about the viewer's passivity, the tranquilized mind? What about the narcotic of TV, and its replacement of life?

I turn the corner, heading southwest, and I reflect that the viewer may be involved in more of a meditative state than I'd considered before. TV creates a mood that may be a preparation for awareness. This may be the beginning of the recognition of complexity, of flux, immersion, sign, and bite, the communication pathways that model our reality.

Passing houses and storefronts and parked cars.

The streets look almost as if they've been evacuated. Dark clouds scramble. The moon appears, disappears, reappears again. A blue corona gleams around it, steady and brilliant and clear. I feel more of the cold wind, the dampness thoroughly penetrating my coat, sweater, and jeans. An argument blurts from the shadows in an alley, a man and a woman rage at each other in what seems like an old nagging fit. Through a living-room window a TV flutters. Its blue shimmer strobes on the walls and glass.

Sound and light, echoes and apparitions, glimpses and tracks.

I walk home, while the clouds seem to be driven across the moon's surface toward a still-distant and mysterious destination.

Hypertext

Ghosting In

See the inflamed megacity from above.

Suddenly you've shed your skin and you've become a silicon entity of the sky, orbiting in tandem with NASA ships and optical-reconnaissance satellites, like one of the Keyhole series that carries microphones and infrared cameras, joining the night seers who read the signatures and symbols on the ground and listen to the city's wail.

Satellites transmit to satellites, signal relays skim the dark. Radar imaging creates a vivid facsimile, precise targeting. Each computerized ship dispatches waves to ground computers for inspection and feedback. The machines deliver insights independent of their earthbound programmers. You skeet among the ships, cross their orbits, infiltrate their maneuvers and systems.

Below, the city looks like an agile creature of space. Fantastic contortions, steel curlicues. Citylights sparkle and buzz, but the lights don't offer any warmth. Your robotic eyes level out over a twelve-lane highway. Darting cars, headlights blurring. Neon letters identify global traders, the corporate logos charged like totems of tribes staking out boundaries.

And when you look down, it seems that all the stars have fallen from the night, and their glitter has been pulled down to the ground, so that the city becomes an alternative galaxy, a surrogate Milky Way.

But it's you who is falling. You race into the cityfield beside the lake's blackness. Use your augmented eyes and ears to hear whispers behind closed doors and zoom in on objects the size of a button. The closer you come, the more you sense how the grid could supernova. Satellites and towers commune. Computers drone inside offices, store binary codes on memory chips, plot hookups to other modems, feed on human history. The city is pro-gramming itself to make more megaliths and metallic brilliance.

A blip starts a countdown.

You swing into the dark that burns, veer by the tower and the stadium, wind whining, the smell of metal overheating. Your machine arms tear off, the air blistering your entry into the night that means terminal time, only the black contains the pull of an even larger consciousness, a huge unutterable thing, closing in faster...

Dionysian Architecture

My house, my bedroom. I check the clock on the bed table beside me. 11:37 p.m., the silent lettering tells me. I came to bed only twenty minutes ago, falling asleep immediately. Then I dreamed of the city and the satellites. I was flying, feeling my body become a machine, flesh jettisoned, watching myself ghost in, smashing down from the night sky.

Noise ripples in through the slightly open windows. It sounds like cars, telephones, people, wires whirring, all at once. The jabber outside contrasts with the reassuring quiet in the house.

Moist, heavy air. As I lie still, slivered by fear, breathing deeply, absorbing the blanket's warmth, I sense how the air jangles. It's weirdly galvanized, like the time before a storm in a forest when the animals crouch or pace, peering out, waiting.

I inhale, shut my eyes, exhale. Then I open my eyes. Disoriented, I glance at the things in the bedroom, looking for stable objects, needing their stillness. The bed, the white sheets, the open cupboard door. Sitting up gradually, I rub my eyes, feeling my skin, muscles, bones.

I turn over, stretching, clearing my mind. When I push up and think, mentally clawing back my fear — the terror of seeing my body dissolve, of becoming metallic, shiny, inhuman — I find some continuities beginning to emerge.

I'd dreamed of machine beings over the city. From the aerial view, I'd thought that the cool lights had teemed with communiqués, the computers and satellites transmitting to one another in digital ciphers.

Affinities, relations. I remember that the architects of the ancient citystates wanted to reflect in their plans what they took to be the cosmic order. Their layout of a city symbolized a faith in the universe; their plans mirrored what they saw as either the universe's cruel implacability or its harmony and beauty.

I think of the Pythagoreans again, the mystic musicians tuning themselves to the planetary music. They believed that city's settlements should be arranged according to the ear and not the eye, arranged for balance and rhythm and echo, a human scale. But the builders of Toronto, I consider, reflect in their shapes the powerkick through the inscape of structures: the lights on the towers, around the malls and their entranceways, glow and quiver like the emanations of a computer and TV screen, constantly altering perspectives. This city's designers have erected a Dionysian architecture, where objects appear to meld, blend, and shift.

* * *

I stir, restless, knowing that I won't be able to get back to sleep tonight.

Do satellites and computer banks talk to one another? Can they play an aerial symphony that develops from AI? Are there spirits haunting the circuitry, generations from technology's cells? It doesn't seem likely. And yet the city replicates, spreads, its exuberant productions, hybrids, and giantism seemingly indifferent to our anxieties and projections. The computer futurists call their zigzagging paths through data a hypertext — links traveling in many directions at once. Lines of meaning and possibility criss-cross like the intricate supports of skyscrapers. Like a hypertext, the city says, You May Begin Anywhere.

Swinging my feet over the edge of the bed, I feel for the solid surface. Hardwood floors, smooth and cold to my touch.

And I think now that there is a deeper message filtering through in the waves from TV, music, and the city. I realize these waves may be moving toward this: electricity is a form of con-sciousness. Electricity may be a life or even life itself, racking us, seeping and bursting out of any outlet it can find, lighting up our minds and constructions.

Ancient philosophers called electricity fire. It was their mysterious life principle. This spark or agent could become a del-uge, an inundation, an ocean, or a river. The universal circuitry could tear down and build up rapidly, abruptly. That energy's dis-charge in the atmosphere, the ancients said, was the coiling and uncoiling of a Great Snake.

Is this recognition of electricity, then, a variation on what philosophers called the *élan vital* — the creative essence? No; we have built structures that amplify energy. In its elementary state fire slyly leaps, teases, devours. It is directionless, variable without a smith or forge to shape its motion. But the city is a sort of giant forger, and technology acts like a duct. We have concentrated and facilitated a fury, and our own greed and voracity can coincide with its blast.

I press my hands on the side of the bed. Safety, consistency. Yet a modern physicist would say that the floor and the bed are made of vibrating particles: these patterns are unstill.

And there it is again: my uncertainty, the confusion, my doubt. A perception emerges — electricity is a form of conscious-ness — and I'm not sure what to do with it. The pattern I've identi-fied of flux, immersion, sign, sound bite, and computer byte, the workings and shapings of transmission, reception, and a myriad of interpretations, seem to collapse. TV, recorded music, computers, my past — nothing fits. Everything breaks back into fragments.

I breathe slowly, regaining my calm, steadying myself. Out there the city cycles on, the streets like channels that direct our moods of exhilaration and collapse, the buildings spiraling upward, demanding that you adapt to the complexes of steel and glass and neon, the environment of force and sensation, the fire's lick and touch.

I'll have to pick up these thoughts again. I'm still staring into an enigma. A voice from nowhere mutters, "Not now, not yet."

Derelict

Two nights after my dream, sleepless, I wander downtown. These networks of streets, twitching lights, layers of sinuous space. Old cities in North America looked cold, uniform, vertical; the new cities sprawl, flash, and amaze you. Cross at a corner. I make mental notes about what could happen if humans and machines merge, thinking about whether electronic technology accelerates the partly conscious current and forms forcefields that give the impression that AI already exists. Crowds, people shouting, jostling one another. Walk ahead, focus. The small cafés, bars, and missions. I notice a drunk slumped on a bench, a man mumbling alone. There are many derelicts in this city now, but I sense something familiar about him, his face, his voice.

He sags, rouses himself to shout, then crumples back, murmuring to no one.

"Michael?" I bend over him. "Michael?"

He groans, looks up, blinks, and shuts his eyes again.

Michael Senica. I'd worked with him when I was a student and I had a summer job tending the grounds at Sunnybrook

Hospital. Idyllic slow days in the sun years ago.

Moved by our old connection, and by the coincidence of meeting him, I help him to sit up. His coat is dirty, creased, sweat-stained, his pants splotched with grease. When I check his wallet, I find it has money, credit cards, a home address. I look into his fleshy face, sunburned raw. His features appear to have somehow become part of the earth.

The cab that I've hailed drops us at a high-rise, the address in Michael's wallet. I support him at the lobby door, in the elevator, and on the ninth floor where I let us into his apartment with one of the keys that I've taken from his coat pocket. Immaculate rooms. I remember his Filipino wife, a young bride he'd brought illegally into the country after he'd answered a lonely-companions ad in a local Croatian newspaper. Pale, slight, she'd uttered nothing more than a soft moan when I'd first met her at the hospital.

Is this why he's drunk? A shattered marriage?

While he bunches up on the plastic-covered couch, I rummage through the books that have been strewn across the coffee table. Goethe's *Elective Affinities*, Rilke's *Sonnets to Orpheus*, among others, in English translations. I smile at his choices, remembering how he'd quote from them. I slide a chair near him, make myself comfortable, and glance through the poems.

Michael was a schoolteacher who'd been a political prisoner under Tito. Though he must have been only in his early forties when we worked together, his health had been ravaged, and he'd looked like a beaten old man, whitehaired, potbellied from beer drinking. He'd been kind to us, the students. He'd tell stories about dissent and oppression, seething discontent in Yugoslavia, and I'd loved how he'd lecture us in the workroom. His unexpectedly relevant words come back to me. "You don't know history...You live without ideology...the know-nothings...But it's better that way...To be able to forget..."

Eventually he grunts, stretches, opens his eyes, and says my name like a question. I tell him where I found him. He grins, embarrassed, twisting upright, shaking his thinning hair. I watch his face. After all the imaged faces I've studied on monitors, I identify in his the imprint of one who's trying to beat back desperate memories. The gouge of suffering, and of some unusual strength.

"How many years since I've seen you?" he mutters.

"I don't know. A long time."

"Thank you for helping me. But what were you doing around here?"

Surprised at how sober he sounds, I tell him of my late-night walks, my questions about the power that snakes through the machines, my hunt for pattern, cohesion, the structure, the key.

"A crisis." He sighs, and looks me over as if he's never truly seen me before. He gets up unsteadily and heads to the kitchen. He forages in a cupboard. Tap water, cups, a spoon clattering on a counter, and I smell the aroma of strong coffee.

"Somebody's paying you to do this?" he asks from the other room. "Some sort of grant. The government maybe."

"Freelancing, teaching. Money for a book, and my savings."

"A book. And you think this is a revolution? Just finding life?"

I describe how I think there's a wisdom that has been submerged in the information spill, our haywire world.

"I heard you are married...What does she think of your...walking around?"

I don't answer him. I know I can't, or won't. Lena: I'm blocking her out, refusing to examine what's behind my questions, my drift.

He's silent when I say nothing. The kettle lets off steam, and there is a click, the shutting off. I wait for him. He returns with two mugs, hands me one, then drops down heavily on the couch, shaking his head.

"You TV kids."

He lights a cigarette, hawks up spit, and starts talking in a burst, like a man recently released from solitary confinement.

Intervocal

"In Yugoslavia I was in jail. On an island, offshore. I am there three years, eight months, six days. I talked too much. I criticized the government, the army, President Tito. They came for me. This was long before the wall came down. All the chaos you talk about."

"I don't think you ever told me everything about this."

"I tell you now. Jail the first day. I had to lie on my bed until nine in the evening. I had to wake up at four in the morning. They opened the door for only five minutes. I couldn't turn around. Then they shoved me back in the cell. Gave me dog food to eat. Inside the cell there were toilets without seats. The smell all day, all night."

"Was that the worst day for you?"

"There was no worst day. Every day was the worst. Well, maybe the worst was when I was transferred to the island. The other cell was an army cell. Because I had been in the army, that's where they took me. No one beat you there. In the police jail they beat you. They didn't need a reason. They were the police.

"The police put seven of us in a bigger cell. With fifty people. All politicals. Then we were on the ship. That ship was full of passengers on holiday. They never knew we were there. Then we were off the ship. Every policeman had to know your face. You got a paper saying I am a political prisoner because of Article 175. Which means I insulted the president. And article 118. Which means I am a friend of imperialist countries. Every time I met a policeman I had to stand with my cap in hand and say I am a political prisoner because...Soon the police got tired of my talk. They'd shout in my face, 'Shut up pig!'

"Do you know this? I had to work twelve hours voluntarily. The police would ask you if you wanted to work. If you said, 'No,' they hit you. Then I had to work another five hours, voluntarily. If I didn't go they made me wash windows. This was very bad. The police had clubs there. They beat me. On my legs. My arms. My back.

"One day I worked with a wheelbarrow. A policeman was sitting under a big umbrella. He was drinking beer and eating sausages. He knew every political prisoner had the right to have a visit from a parent for an hour each month. My mother and father came. They brought cigarettes and sausages. The policeman asked which do you want? Cigarettes or sausages? I need the cigarettes. So I took them to my cell and they were gone in five minutes. The other prisoners took them. That is why the policeman drank beer and ate sausage. That is why he sat there in front of me, under an umbrella."

* * *

Michael smokes cigarette after cigarette, squeezing each one in his yellow-stained fingers. Black tobacco, a European scent. He leans back, speaking to the ceiling as if he's reading a cue card, then leans forward, talking as if he's addressing the rug. His voice, gravelly and deep and worn, mixes bitterness with resignation.

"Seagulls, there were seagulls near the prison. They lived on a cliff near my cell. One day after I'd been good I was allowed out for a walk. Plus, minus — plus, minus. If you had plus marks for being good, the guards let you out. If you had minus marks for being bad, they locked you in. Always being judged, watched."

"You were never really alone."

"Almost never. Except when I went out to the cliff. I climbed it. I found hundreds of eggs. Hundreds and hundreds everywhere. I broke them and ate them raw. I'd never been so hungry. I had lost weight. I ate a hundred, I think."

His voice drops to a whisper, so I have to strain forward to hear him.

"You say you teach. I was a teacher in prison, you remember. I taught the gypsies. Mathematics. Simple addition. Numbers."

Michael is teaching me, cunningly arranging things into his perspective, putting my experiences in place. I should be put off, taking his recollections in a way that would end his talk. But I'm impressed by his voice, with how his wounds are close to the surface, how his tone slides up and down from anger to matter-of-fact storytelling. I push aside my judgement, my need for clearer questions — even my desire to break in — and take him in uninterrupted. He needs me to pay attention tonight. He's not giving me some glib testimonial about endurance, like someone getting ready to write a sentimental greeting card. Unfulfilled, he is speaking with irritation and intelligence.

He blows out a thick haze of blue smoke. The pungent smell.

"I have a story. About giving a gypsy an imaginary apple. I said, 'Here is one apple for you.' And he said, 'Where? There is nothing there.' So I said to him, 'You must pretend it's there.' I picked up some air and I said, 'Here is the second apple.' And he said, 'I see nothing there.' So I began to shout at him, 'You must pretend you see something. If you can't imagine more than what's there, you'll never understand anything.' So I said, 'How many apples do you see now?' And the gypsy answered, 'I see nothing.' The fool. What can you say to a man like that?"

(And I'm reminded of another person's voice, Michael T., and his cracked lucidity. The echoes in their names. But Michael T. had shortcircuited his mind. For him a pattern that became visible in the electronic media meant a conspiracy, a network unified by a single malicious intent of producers and transnational corporations. He'd imagined too much between the lines and he couldn't reconcile all the resemblances and connections he'd found in the signs and sound bites.)

Michael Senica lights a fresh cigarette, pausing, looking down at his books on the coffee table. His stubby fingers brush slowly across the ripped cover of Rilke's *Sonnets*. A caress. He touches the hardback cover almost lovingly.

"Do you know what I'm saying? As soon as I got out I thought of Canada. I thought of space. My friends here said I'd find a job. I said goodbye to my mother and father. I met Croatians who didn't speak English. My new world I found different. I begin to think it was better not to have memories like mine. And when my wife is away I drink too much."

This is the first time that he's mentioned her. I check my impulse to ask him more, aware that he's being guarded about his marriage.

"Sabrina."

"Who?"

"*Sabrina.* That movie on TV. With Audrey Hepburn, Humphrey Bogart, William Holden. I love that show. So much nothing. It was the only movie we had in prison. I see it every time it comes on. *Sabrina* in black-and-white."

He revolves his half-smoked cigarette, watching it burn down in his fingers. Ashes float like dust motes to the carpet.

"I know what you say about TV. Music. Power. I've been lucky. I work at the hospital. My friends show me marijuana plants in the garden. They tell me about the whores the housecleaners run for patients at night."

He stares at me.

"I hate the politics of the old country. They say the wall is down. But walls are hard to bring down. They exist in everyone. Some people want them. Walls to jail ourselves. Toronto is like Utopia to me. Beer and TV. I come home and feel safe."

Finally I know how removed I am from his experiences. He was right when he said that I had little understanding of the brutal politics he'd seen, the prison camps and their vicious guards. My engagements have been traced by a culture of simulation — and sometimes unreality is easier to grasp than history.

* * *

I ask him if he wants more coffee, another cigarette.

"No, nothing...I'll just speak my perfect broken English..."

He's exhausted, misunderstanding what I say, picking his words awkwardly. His gestures have become sluggish, like someone moving in slow motion.

In his apartment I sit for a time and watch him slide into sleep. He burrows into the couch, scratches himself, shudders, and begins to snore. He looks almost the same as he did when I saw him earlier on the bench. Disheveled, drunk, alone. I stand up. On a chair in the dining room I find a blanket, toss it over him, and then I ease out the door. There's nothing more I can do tonight.

Near morning when the streets are nearly bare and the whir of crowds and traffic has almost been stilled, you can hear one person's voice clearly and see into the city shapes that surround us. In the hallway I rattle the door latch, ensuring that it's locked. I hesitate, wondering if he's all right, then I make out his mumbling inside. His words come sporadically. Suddenly I hear a feckless shout, a calling out. As if he's starting a conversation with someone. Or as if he's remembering what it is that he truly wanted to tell me.

Minaret

The tower lights flash, red and white in offbeats. Once for a welcome to visitors, once for a warning to aircraft.

From the window of my reading room I see the stiletto shape of the CN Tower. The late afternoon sky blackens behind it, snow clouds gathering in the west. This city's Statue of Liberty is a telecommunications pillar, a tourist attraction, a listening post, that competes with the high tower in Moscow and the cenotaph in Washington D.C. Structures, symbols. Like monuments assembled to embody and calibrate human ambition and the pulses of data. The minaret has resurfaced here, the old Middle Eastern form that signified God's nexus with humanity. *Manaret.* An Arabian word for lamp or lighthouse.

I've come back to this room because I want to find my familiar solitude with books. The peace in this aloneness, a point of separation, the privacy and silence that came for me from reading and writing. I switch on my desklamp and relax, watching the city through the window — the one-hundred-story gadgets, the cylinders, boxes, and spires, the massive irregular figures.

"You TV kids," Michael said in an ambiguous tone. I'd wanted to tell him that I believe we live in a culture of immersion, computer byte, sign, and sound bite, of discharge and admission, electrified anarchy. This world can offer what seems like second-hand experience, with a firsthand effect of psychic clairvoyance and disturbance, a stroking of your senses.

I'd wanted to tell him more. But he'd needed me only to listen. My attention had been enough. And what could I have said to explain what is happening?

Windows.

I could have told him about stepping outside of your perspective. Going beyond your frame of reference wrenches you out of synch. This room once gave me a window on life. And when I come back to retrieve the solitude that I'd found with books, I recognize once more how they supplied me with alphabetic links, linear time, the hierarchies of mental structure. But I should have told him how I thought that the book culture had been displaced, that there is no ideology on TV. Writing and print will always have roles, but a wildfire evolution is under way. I'd been reluctant to make this leap: to say the pattern of transmission, reception, and multiple interpretations simultaneously represents a break from the past, a beginning, and a recalling of ancient myths of a primordial universal mind. I'd tried to find words for what may lie outside the reach of books —

*　*　*

I turn off my desklamp, brush my papers to one side, and stare out the window.

The roofs of the houses form terraces leading like steps toward the citycore. The bank towers climb, and over them all the CN Tower soars, a landmark where no one lives or stays. Its observation platform revolves. Lights wink in their computerized sequence.

I remember how the Middle Eastern minarets symbolize a fixed tradition and faith, what appears to us to be a warrior religion. Muezzins call the devoted to prayer, chanting the name of Allah. Their cosmology is ruled by ritual, repetition, and scripture. Priests recite suras from the *Koran*, and the faithful respond massively. These recitations are ceremonies of certainty, carrying codes of confirmation and permanence. The minarets establish a pathway like a funnel between the earth and the sky, between humankind and the invisible.

This tower is a source of ghostly voices, turbulent speech, stray notes, and static, an infinite variety that may bear no single message, only the enticements and variations of energy, complex and nomadic, a stir and sound more enigmatic than any structure that we could make.

I glance down to the alloy and then up to the tower, the compass point signaling constantly. Thinking of the new myths that are hard to articulate, thinking about Michael, his suffering, his criticism, his implicit demand that I look for more than what's obvious, visible, there.

* * *

Redlight, chromeflash.

City of Mirrors,
City of Swarming

Clouds swarm across the windowfaces. The sun blazes and the wind blows in from the north. In the towers the windows reflect the splashes of light and the moving clouds. Unsettled, the clouds shoot by and then slow down, their images in the windows contorted like people's reflections in a funhouse mirror.

Today I'm seeing the citycore as if it's uncharted territory. I've walked these routes often enough, but the new buildings have been erected so quickly that it's almost impossible for me to recall past imprints here. Glass windows mirror the crowds and the clouds together. The mirrors exaggerate the width, length, and depth of the street, making it appear grandiose — a supercity's boulevard.

I scurry along Front Street and gaze up at the buildings' façades. The lunch-hour traffic is a blast of metal and color. The glass and steel of the north corners distort the press of people and machines. Liquid walkers float on the surfaces; taxis drip in what looks like an atomic meltdown.

What do the architects want to reflect? Clouds forming and

reforming, people in masses, turbulent skies, dynamic streets, unsteadiness and flux. The effect is hypnotic. See yourself race. See yourself become part of a steel structure. See your appearance bend, alter. The smooth, bright exteriors radiate wealth, extol mobility. The building styles, various and improvised, form a city of images.

I pause for a moment in front of a golden bank tower. So many mirrors and glass doors incite a feeling of hustle; everything is shown rushing. Toronto is a massive copy of any aggressive metropolis — New York, Tokyo, London, Paris. You would find the same structures and moods in the corporate zones and edges of those cities too. Nations linking, minds linking, cities becoming facsimiles of one another.

In these mirrors, I observe reflections of individuals milling, looking as though they've become members of groups, tribes, packs, corporations, transnationals.

I turn north, up Yonge Street. Impressions of Mercedes and Gucci shoes and high heels buckle into an impression of junkfood shops, strip joints, record stores, and theaters. Glass, mirrors, and chrome continue to replicate all appearances, expanding the look of this main artery.

A neon sign crackles:

GET YOUR LICE
OF LIFE
HERE

The S in "Slice" darkened, blown out.

I see mirrors, frames, and advertising signs creating counter-images, echoes, another labyrinth of effects and illusions.

Sunlight dazzles the corner. I veer left on Dundas Street and walk toward the mall's arches, the crystal entrance. A musician wearing sunglasses flays a drum kit, pounding his snare and cymbals, cracking his sticks — a nervous, arhythmic Morse code.

Preachers and sidewalk florists and hot dog vendors shout at shoppers and walkers.

I stop to watch the restless scene. Five punks bracket themselves in a semi-circle. Two boys have Mohawk haircuts, dyed purple with green tips. A skinhead girl has a swastika tattooed on her forehead. Another girl's hair is razor stubble; her white makeup makes her look like a corpse. A boy wears ripped clothes, shreds, a black leather jacket draped insolently over his shoulder. Their shirts and jackets are studded with names: Tilt, Reject, Drug Slug, Malled.

Their postures tense and they start toward me, sniffing like cats, scuffling forward, cuffing one another, grabbing hands. I stay where I am, letting them pass. They shuffle and sneer, widening their circle, swinging around to close in on a man behind me, sucking him into their net. I wait for an explosion of violence, but nothing happens. The gang giggles and scoffs at the man, an executive who grips an expensive leather briefcase.

"Jesus is a lie!" a thin man, dressed in black, hollers. He wears a long gown, tied in with a red sash. "The Christmas miracle is a lie! Jesus is a cheat. Christmas is a fraud!"

People sidestep the ghastly figure.

But the five figures assemble around the strange thin man in black. They spit at him. The sound hisses through their teeth like oil frying in a skillet.

"You a straw boss?" the skinhead asks.

The preacher appears paralyzed.

"You unfucking for real?" The girl with the jacket that says Tilt reaches over and fondles the man's cloak.

"Straw boss, straw boss," the others chant, their dissonant chorus.

"You fuck God?" the skinhead asks.

The antipreacher shivers and shuts his eyes. The punks want him to react, to fall down on his knees and beg for his life. They receive only his strangeness, his trembling.

Gangs. They are the phantom armies of the corporate city. They could be armed. In Chinatown, a mere two blocks from here, adolescent thugs have fired off clips from Uzis at rival teenage bosses; hoods have died in a chatter of automatic fire. These kids, however, rove through the streets without connection to anyone or anything, like sleepwalkers who have gone off dangerously in their minds. They chant slogans that seem to come out of some diabolical trance, using a debased language to spew their hatred. Their street idiom is made of slogans, blurbs, and graffiti — bits, shards, splintered words from psyches caught up in the density and debris of matters and material.

The gang's aimless dreamstate makes me uneasy.

In a mirror image of the corporate people in the towers and of the televangelist and his cathode flock, these kids believe that they need a pack to give them a cohesive identity. They crave a sense of community, a meaning, even if that group and coherence turn out to be brutal and narrow. The gangs wage war on anyone who looks different, affluent, comfortable. These packs don't recognize boundaries. They trash what they don't have. So they swarm and wild, with toxins in their veins, and lose themselves in mindless anger, inarticulate pain. Some are possessed by nothing, floating in ethereal media visions, living shadowy lives, turning their flesh into self-conscious displays of ugliness and self-hatred. I sense how these young people become blank, blurry, and menacing when they stare up at the transnationalist offices. Above in the towers people work, shielded from the clamor, working at terminals while statistics and percentages ream by, in cubicles with filtered water and air. Below the kids descend deeper and deeper into a faceless ruckus.

The kids scatter to harass a middle-aged black man in a raincoat. They heckle an old woman who drags a shopping cart behind her.

They have gone dull and numb in their reception of other people. Only the hallucination remains, the caricature. All things have become a glittering surface, an unresponsive shadow, a confusing shade.

* * *

I walk toward Bay Street, behind the mall, away from the kids and their roaming. We have done little with our luminous acoustic telecommunication marvels to provide them with tenderness, with invitations to learning, kindness, and a core of well-being, with the paths that could lead them to the discovery of meaning, with accurate and multidimensional maps for the zigzagging networks, the magnetic complex. The data rampage can damage the senses, the psyche, through digital saturation. Reject, Tilt, Malled. These kids have chosen names for themselves that accurately describe their feelings of loss and contempt, and incomprehension.

One block to the west I see people huddle on park benches. In a stamp of grass and stubby trees on the south corner, derelicts hug knapsacks and plastic shopping bags full of blankets, clothes, and food. Men sprawl on yellowed grass, clutching bottles of cheap wine.

This is how the cityweb folds around you. Not far from the corner where I saw the kids, I find this defeated group, exiled from the elegance and extravagance of the city's veneer. A crone crouches by a sack, weeping soundlessly. A ragged man hobbles on a crutch and begs for coins. A sour smell; their clothes reek of the chemistry of despair.

The contrast between the panhandlers and the city of mirrors and images jars me. When I observe the smashed-up look of the homeless, the slick geometry of the towers, the poles of poverty and wealth, the desolation and the hightech frames, I know that all this is a sign that we have become a worldclass place: you could step into scenes like these in Buenos Aires, Los Angeles, or Mexico City.

So one city block can focus the extremes of the kids and the derelicts. I cross at the lights with the throngs who scramble back to their offices or go on to the malls, and I consider: could more of the young people grow up to lose attachments and reference, all possible centers in the self? The drive for privilege, security, and gain may stall. The derelicts and the kids register the burnout of affluence — the point where the expanding city begins to consume people. The power rush can make us avid and ruthless. The abundance in the forcefields can manifest itself in our ravenous need to absorb more. But the people on the street have already been left out. They have lived through their own crash. The kids hunt for ways to expend their pent-up rage; the derelicts slip away to Salvation Army hostels, dependent on handouts and charity. Anonymous and rudderless, they all must feel sapped, deprived of life, while they meander in their spiritual isolation and wreckage.

I slow my pace along the south side of the street.

There is a cry from the kids and the derelicts, not uttered directly, barely a whisper. If you listen closely when you pass them, you'll hear their breathing, unamplified and low and private and strained, and their litanies of hunger, sorrow, and loneliness, the quiet howl of those who think they've been shoved aside and forgotten. They rummage by the mall — the maze of cheerful salespeople, material goods, Muzak, and arcade games — as if by a shrine. The moan has no variety. Yet surely it's a muffled howl that pleads for recognition and response, that says they're still alive, but falling, falling. The current moves in them, though it's waning, to be heard only on a lower frequency beside the buildings that overshadow them and the racketing traffic that almost drowns them out.

*   *   *

Chinatown on the west side.

TV screens beside mirrors. Skirling neon. Lit-up pagodas

187

over doorways. Teenagers flaunt mirrorshades and expensive Walkmans. Hi-fi speakers squawk outside gift shops and vegetable stands. Advertising signs struggle for space and attention, proclaiming origins, other centers: Hong Kong...Peking...Saigon... Singapore...Tokyo.... Handicams and 8mm cameras on tripods set up on the sidewalk. The media moved outside...

In the short space of three blocks, I discover that the city's tone, rhythm, and appearance have shifted completely. This is another world; there is vitality in the change of voices, the chattering, the high and low sounds. Faces bob and poke out of doorways and from around corners. I see a richness in the looks, the frowns, the grins. Chinese, Koreans, Japanese, East Indians. Encountering this collage of humanity, I sense the diminished undertones of shock and anger and challenge, and less of the resentment that I'd witnessed in the kids, and none of the dejection that I'd felt in the derelicts. Here I recognize variation, voices colliding, a vibrancy, something simultaneously technological and earthy. As if by bringing their TVs and radios and stereos out to the sidewalks, mingling food stalls and loudspeakers, and by eliminating distinctions between indoors and outdoors, the people here have created moments of belonging by turning the street into a community hall and not a virtual space, a theater, or a passage point to somewhere else.

Lights change, and I hurry over the streetcar tracks. Fewer people cram the sidewalks on the other side. A movie marquee over top of a glassed-in mall, posters showing kung fu acrobatics. Squat storefronts and garages with peeling paint. And the neon spectacular fades behind me.

As I step away from Chinatown, I realize how there are cities within cities in Toronto. The high civilizations of Athens and Alexandria evolved in small places; the visionary Renaissance states, Florence and Venice, were also small. The smaller the size of the community, the greater the chance for human contact and help. In a high-voltage city, people can become both wired in to their surroundings and lost in the concentration of extremes, the wealth and the desperation, the multitude of languages and styles and the cacophony of tones...

* * *

A band of Chinese youths bang out of a lane. Black leather jackets, silver motorcycle chains, polished cowboy boots, styling gel combed thick into their slicked-back hair. They kick ahead, agitation in their faces and eyes.

I get out of their way. I can feel their need to relieve their disquiet, to break loose.

All at once the four of them stop and stare at me. I stare back. For no reason we're squared off, keyed up, impatient, dusted by suspicion.

I'm outnumbered, and I feel my fear spurt up. They scowl, look me over. I wonder how I can escape from the absurd attack I see coming, and I'm fascinated by the looming wild burst. We're sharp to one another, ejected out of the ordinary, nervously attentive to every gesture. I watch us sidle toward a freakish conclusion, apparently powerless to do anything about it.

Mistrust brutalizes the air. I clench my fists. Where did my anger come from? They clench their fists. No one budges. Then I take a step toward them — propelled by a turbulence I've buried, overlooked, left in a space I don't want to explore.

The boy nearest to me grins mockingly.

"You," he fumes.

Suddenly he shrugs, barks to the others — words unintelligible to me — and they nudge by, allowing the pressure to stay unvented in the atmosphere.

The rage without words.

We've been strangers jammed on to a narrow walkway, who have strayed into unmapped psychic terrain, pummeled by the invasive moods of the city, by the masses of people who are often maddened by the need to exercise power, jacked up by the furious impact of indeterminate data, an inexplicable unease ready to riot inside us, all of us uncertain about anyone's motives, now seeing only reflections and distortions of the other, scanning masks and not faces, maybe looking for the authentic beginning, testing the glimpses.

Soul in the Fiber

Then my mind fills with memories. I walk on quickly, steps ringing on cement, and I remember an artist I knew, her unusual work made of fiber and thread, her studio where a stillness had been shaped through patience and thought, solitude and need...

Frauke Voss.

Her house had a soothing air.

I pass gray buildings, crowds packing sidewalks, and I remember how she worked to string patterns together, discovering unities in structure and form, an articulation of the flow, so that she didn't contain the power surge but arranged it into texture and color. And I think of her, setting up her sculpture in her studio near these streets. Her hands on soft fiber, kneading it. She was obsessed by her probing into wave shapes, wombs, spheres, the elusive designs in nature. I imagine myself going to visit her as I did many years ago. She talked in the way that I thought a mystic would.

"It's about finding a form for love. Getting rhythm and color exactly. Pressing your hands into the energy."

I'd nodded and smiled and had wanted to hear more.

Jute hung from the ceiling of her studio. Red twinings gaped like wounds on the floor. Fiber had been wound into Möbius designs, dyed and transfigured into purple vortices. The pieces were so tensed and defined that they looked as though they'd been wired with steel.

I'd thought when I stood in her studio that her work was strong, sensual, and yet it had a revealed quality, a vulnerability that belied their tension and strange texture.

I'd never seen anything like them.

Voss was a thin woman; her skin was pale, almost translucent. She'd once said, vaguely, that she was in her late forties, but it was hard to tell how old she really was. Her blue eyes were so piercing that I'd had to muster courage just to stand in their glare. During my visits I always had a difficult time believing this strand of a woman was responsible for the determined traces I found knotted and tied in the halls, in her living room, kitchen, and workroom.

When I'd first walked into her house — through an invitation from a friend — I felt I'd violated a mood that was introverted, pained, self-conscious. On closer look, I saw how her emotions were being turned inside out. She was wrestling with decaying and dying form, molding what looked like sound waves to me. There was no steel or wire in the work. The fiber had been pressed by hand.

* * *

"You can touch them if you like," she'd said.

"How long does it take to make one?"

"A long time. You have to work with the thread. Dry it. Stretch it. Work your hands in until it comes to a point. All of your body goes into the heave and push. You explore and knot, and sometimes I'm sore for days and days and I can't work because my muscles seize up. You eventually feel your way into a contour."

Her pieces twisted my preconceptions about sculpture. The cube shapes, the hemispheres, the islands of thread, the undulations. They resembled arteries, muscles, and skin in their nakedness. I'd thought that the threads of herself were being repaired, lost energies trussed. Her studio hid a secret. She was leading you in her work to an unbroken time. Quietly, inside the place that was her home, she dyed and stretched cotton and then she slowly coiled it. She pulled from rancor and devastation those harmonious, whole, and bonded pieces.

She was a mediator, cording her perceptions together, capturing the current's track. The forms preserved the patterns she'd discovered. Pores, veins, webs, strings, shells, braids, sacks like wombs, spirals like fetuses. Decay recurred, and so did the disorder. Her sculpture left the impression that it was incomplete, anguished somehow, a meeting of formal order with uncertainty.

"I know I'm learning, but I'm not sure what. I resist the shiny perfect product. I want to show a progress through the senses. Why? I have violence in me. Self-destruction. Dealing with pressure all the time. On myself. On my material. But when I stick my fingers in I always cut my nails short."

I remember that sculpture, like architecture, is called frozen music...

"My work scares people. There's just so much there. It doesn't sell. Buyers stand around speechless. My surfaces are a memory so I can read my own development. See where I've gone wrong. And it's slow. In these days of maniacal omnipotence. Well, there's no finality in the pieces, nothing terminal. It's always arriving."

* * *

She knitted the cotton like connecting tissue. She'd ply and massage the material, her frail-looking body emboldened by her hands' strength. She kept mending, searching for points of union and intensity, link and clutch, seeking inner levels, structural disclosure. To locate cores of meaning she'd sacrificed a conventional sculptural career. From the curves, holes, embraces, the fluid lines and primal pattern, came the issue of rebirth, the nerve ends of the new. Making process visible.

Snow

In the early morning I start out walking toward the citycore, and what I'm looking for this time isn't the morning ritual of crowds and cars. Strong winds churn up. The trees shiver and bend. Some branches snap off, scattering over the sidestreet and the lawns. A storm moves in and I want to feel its rawness.

The wind rushes through the trees, in the cracks between the houses, low-rises, and stores. I know that broadening *ssss* well now. It's deep and bracing, going in and out, insisting that it be heard, prevailing over the traffic.

My sleeplessness shoves me on again and I can't really explain why I'm driven to keep moving. I've been taken inside the city's process and force by the streets: they've led me to the skyscrapers, the impressive trajectory of their form, and they've directed me toward the wrecking, the skinned look of the worksites. But the untamed wind sweeps around the building edges, overpowering their concrete-and-steel presence.

I lean into the wind and cover the short blocks to the business zone, speeding up to match the brisk walk of the crowds. The wind humbles our activity. The buildings seem to shrink, protectively withdrawing against the storm.

The hiss in the wind means snow.

I feel an excitement bolt through me. I'd been unsure, even uneasy, about the meaning of the signs and sound bites, the electric pulse and its networks and configurations. Now I'm certain that it's energy itself that impels me, the unchanneled, elemental, and invisible drawing me forward.

The clouds colored like pewter roll lower and closer. The air turns frigid. I stop at a red light. Cars slide on slick cement. Then the rain comes down. And when the light turns green, I hurry ahead, and because I haven't got an umbrella I button up my overcoat and turn up my collar. People bunch into doorways, their faces red and wet. The streetlamps pop back on, and the air becomes dark.

The rain eases. I look up at the sidewalk at a mist that's like a long curtain. The wind drops away and the mist turns to snow. Thick white flakes begin to fall gently. As the snow becomes feathery, it remains on the ground, blanketing it, transforming the streets into a soft white heaven.

And I respond to the city with an awe that I didn't expect to feel. Through the snowfall, the architectural designs stand out sharply. This city carves a distinct geometrical place, probing the extent of symmetries, arrangements, and order, insisting that you make up a relationship with its sprawl of symbols and structures. I've been absorbed into the wild effects of the current, its fluctuations, its ebb and flow through the frames, outlets, and moments we make and engage: the city vaulting higher, the window-mirrors multiplying individual reflections into masses, the cathode glow and the strobing in the dancebar, people alone, needing others to listen to them.

But the snow slows the city, and brings beauty to it. The crowd crush has been muffled. There's a point to this slowness, another method of perceiving. To see patterns again gives me the courage to deal with what I've so far blanked out. The CN Tower and the top of the Dome emerge through the clouds and eddying air. I walk ahead, smiling, seeing the city temporarily quietened and softened.

* * *

Eight-forty-five a.m. Steam on the coffee-shop windows. The aroma of bacon and eggs. People in suits lounge, drinking coffee and tea from styrofoam cups. Some people look exasperated, others amused. The storm has thrown off their expectations for the day.

I sit down in the last available booth by the window and pull out my notebook from my coat pocket. People saying, "Snow's got to melt soon..." "For jeez sakes, it's too early for a real winter..." This whiteout will give way to the grays, golds, and silvers of the cement, marble, and steel. But the snow scrubs the air, and for the next days the air's sharpness will make the city look as if it's been outlined by lasers.

I note down on paper: rain becomes snow influenced by the wind and cold. Soon the wind will change its course and speed again. Energy and transformation remain the constants...

The city, electronic technology and nature, the personal. Each is touching and affecting the other. Connections are inter-phases of change, often explosive, hard to decode. Arresting the speed makes patterns briefly comprehensible. Yet I sense how the current rises and falls through these points of contact...

Cars stall. A van slips over the curb and stops. Two women trudge through a drift. Fresh squall. Snow swirls into dunes and banks. White everywhere falling.

I turn my head toward the window and listen. The *ssss* in the wind persists, the language of waves, an incessant sound and beat breathing through the machines and around the buildings, haunting us, sometimes inspiring us, always half-heard, half-there.

Drug Rage

Crack in the Street

THE LIGHT AT THE END
OF THE TUNNEL IS OUT

Graffiti scraps. Outraged phrases spray painted on walls down a back street.

THE CRASH OF 87
CAUSED BY THE BLOW PIGS
OF THE WHITE GODDESS
COKE

As I walk along an alley this evening after the snow has melted, I find an outburst of slogans, datelines, and messages painted in red, black, and green. These fragments signal the drugcult, a shadow world. They tell me of the anguish and frustration that many people feel over their inability to talk directly about what seems another invisible influence. In the wired city, everything can be a connection and cast in the language of drugs.

NIHILISM LIVES
IN THE HEARTS
OF THE DISPOSSESSED

Rumor, innuendo, and clues. Someone has covered these walls near the lakeshore, where I'm walking, with indictments. As if accusation and desperate appeals have become a full-time job for a person or a group. While I feel a certain bond with this anger, I know how mistrustful I've become of judgemental moods, the harsh reactionary tone, the single point of view. The electronic milieu releases presences, spirits, agencies, forces; there is a barrage of attractions, possible realities, a generating of revelatory conditions. It's easy to accuse people who launch data swarms, and the machines that escalate and expand the current, of subtle conspiracies and collaborations. End-of-the-world prophecies come easily to those who secretly crave the finality of Armageddon. Yet this graffiti reminds me that there is a darker undercurrent to the thrust in the city.

I remember seeing other graffiti lines about drugs around town.

CRACK OPEN YOUR MIND
IT'LL BE YOU
ONLY BETTER

Wall writing is alternative news. Graffiti appears like cracks in the clean surfaces of new luxury condominiums; it informs you of the disguised lives that people sometime lead, of experiments and compulsion, the surreptitious demand.

Other graffiti remarks come back to me:

SHOOT UP YOUR CORE
    START YOUR RACE
YOU'RE EITHER A DRIVER OR A PASSENGER
OUR HEAVEN
      IS
        ARTIFICIAL

Drugs. The word detonates in my mind. The artificial paradise, transcendence, rebellion. A way of altering your senses, of penetrating the veils of existence, of shutting out the world's noise. I see mental images of coke, coke spoons, crack crystals. Shooting up in the veins, dirty syringes. Then I think of drug wars, witch hunting, and informers.

CAN'T WE STOP ALL POISON
      WITH LOVE?

I've been surprised by the emotion and the range of expression of the protest walls. They're in a vehement dialogue with anyone who passes by and who's willing to listen. They talk of the power we possess to blow ourselves up with chemicals, to inject a radical uncertainty into our experience.

THE MORTAL, THE GUILTY
BUT TO ME
THE ENTIRELY BEAUTIFUL

I remember that one eloquent wall writer echoed a lyric by W.H. Auden, in dripping letters on chipped cement. On a cool night downtown, I find abandoned factories, fractures in sidewalks, and sometimes poetry. I see that everything isn't as slick and lustrous as would appear from the top floor of a bank tower. Strange signs.

THIS VIOLENT FUTURE
ENFORCES SELFISHNESS
AND DESTROYS SELF-SUFFICIENCY
BECAUSE IT DOESN'T WANT US TO KNOW
HOW MUCH
WE NEED EACH OTHER

Anonymous graffiti is a series of comments on the way that the information maelstrom feeds on affluence, on individual availability, the mayhem in minds, the soul isolation of people. You occasionally see street cleaners scrubbing off the letters, restoration experts sandblasting defacements. But the protests keep appearing, the words hitting notes of dissent and bewilderment, the statements making up a visual counterpoint to newspaper headlines and advertising logos.

The graffiti disappears from the walls when I circle outside the Dome stadium site. I begin to reflect: the cult language of drugs has codes that refer to amplification, control, withdrawal, and possession. Users talk about accelerators, sensitizers, the crash. There is obscurity around the motives for drug dealings: people can express a longing for a higher union with spiritual energy, another plane of existence, and a higher income. What happens when you push toward the source, the ultimate deal that may set you loose, that may redeem your life or let you escape it?

Poison and love, and the crack that's in our souls...

Memories return, scenes replay.

I tried all sorts of drugs when I was a teenager. Those were the years when my questioning began, when I sensed the transformations that were taking place in my home. I took LSD and smoked hash and marijuana because I wanted to satisfy a vague yearning and fill what I thought was an emptiness in myself. This was before a simmering discontent flared up on the graffiti walls, a dissent that had once shown itself in a rebellion against established laws, systems, and conventions, and now shows itself in some people's expectations of a vicious apocalypse, a global rage of anarchy and murder; it was before I began to hear rumors about friends, acquaintances, and colleagues who were slipping over the white line of trafficking into the lift of a constant intoxication.

So I'll go back again in my past, remembering how I wandered in the psychedelia of those years.

My friends and I were experimenters who used our bodies and minds like test tubes. Grass helped us to contain the popcult's scramble and blare; grass gave us a relief from pressures at high school, the subliminal messages we got through the media, and our awkward adolescence. We took hallucinogens, smoked hash, looking for teachers and a new kind of learning, a method of transcending ourselves, in pursuit of an originality that would soothe our psychic unrest.

Underground

"The world's turning purple," Terry said.

"You mean it looks purple."

"I mean it's turning purple."

"Like purple haze," Neil said.

"No, that's a song."

"So what do you mean?" I asked.

"I'm entering the purple world. The universe becoming one place. All existing within me and without me."

Nineteen seventy; and this is the way that we talked to each other, while we were sprawled on the carpeted floor of my parents' basement. We passed the hash pipe that was packed with blond Lebanese hash laced with LSD, dope that we'd bought from a counselor at our local community center.

The rec room had become our underground cell. We'd skulked downstairs as if we'd escaped into a hideaway. In the next room there were the hot-water pipes, the furnace, the fuse box, the washer and dryer. I'd papered over the brown wall panels with posters of Bob Dylan and Jimi Hendrix in fluorescent profile, their hair like a tangle of snakes.

Terry had dropped acid earlier in the day. Acid. That's what we called LSD. He explained how the ritual was to be performed: then he toked up the hash, and let it curl up out his nostrils. I'd arranged incense candles around us on the floor. The sweet scent and smoke permeated the basement. Terry had experimented with LSD long before any of us. He thought of himself as a revolutionary Utopian, a countercultural poet. He carried scraps of paper filled with his musings and with quotations from books of poetry. He'd launched our Saturday-afternoon session by reciting a line of Baudelaire's:

"The temptation of drugs is a sign of the love for the infinite."

I thought I'd take his word for it.

"The philosopher's stoned," Terry said, and passed the hash pipe to me.

The stereo rumbled Whole Lotta Love from *Led Zeppelin 2*, through tinny speakers. Robert Plant's vocals sounded like an air-raid siren; Jimmy Page's guitar, like the engines of a jet taking off down a runway.

"When you drop acid you cross borders, man," Terry said. "You won't need words. Once you're out there, your armor cracks."

* * *

Desperados. We saw ourselves with the collars of our denim jackets turned up. The chemicals related to rock and roll, to the news of Vietnam on TV, to the city. The pop rebels we admired were devourers of their stardom. They chased after a sound of their own until they achieve miraculous being — we assumed — on the public stage, in orgasmic showings, while they communed with their mass audience who fed on more outrageous acts. Our favorite stars expanded their presence on stage and through their recordings on black discs, and we wanted to expand ourselves to the point of radical abandon too. No limits.

* * *

We lay on the floor in the dank basement, my parents gone for the weekend. The acid-and-hash fusion inspired our feelings of being secretive, willing to subject ourselves to the indefinite.

A light overpowered me. My mind cleared; my defences dropped. I looked at the wooden floor, thinking that it would become transparent and I'd finally see what was living under the foundation. The basement was no longer a confined space. The acid-hash blend enhanced our revolt against barriers. Our mental worlds were already integrated into the visionary circuits of TV, radio, and movies, but we hoped for greater bonds, incandescent waves of insight.

Terry tamped the hash down in the pipe with his knife. I was mesmerized by the knife's motion, the soft tapping sound.

I settled back. Nothing in the world was disconnected. All things were haloed. The pharmacy had replaced the church then. If we'd had a guide, or the focus of a religious faith, or an asceticism that might have prepared and sharpened our senses and desires, we might have recognized larger motifs, the pattern of breakage and of the need for wholeness. In the safety of my basement, we experienced only the peaking of our responses, the easing of tensions, the light voyaging.

I believe Terry was sincere when he said he'd entered a purple world with LSD. He was always brooding, daydreaming, staring off, scribbling in his notebooks. But I listened to the room itself. The bright tones, the sonic tracing. Neil shuddered quietly, his eyes closed.

* * *

I pulled out more hash from a cube of aluminum foil, cleared the ashes from the pipe, took the shrivelled brown grains, and swallowed them. I understood the grains would dissolve in my stomach, prolonging my high.

Spells, passages.

We wanted the trip in our basement hideaway. The chemicals held out the promise that we'd engage the moods that Rimbaud had described — Terry and I were avid readers of *A Season in Hell* and *Illuminations* — and be ushered into a drug bohemia. But hallucinogens only amplify your state of mind at the time that you take them. So for me it was the riffing guitar and the drumming that crescendoed and a white light that deepened.

"It sounds like Hendrix is alive in Page's guitar," I said to Terry, thinking I'd achieved a rare insight.

"Hey, the guitars are. You've got the point. Jimi is."

On the Inside

Every Saturday afternoon for months we tested new substances in the basement. We learned the names — Purple Microdot, Windowpane, Strawberry Flats — what the highs were like, what to prefer, what to avoid. It was a game, a confirmation of our circle of friendship, a breaking into the technological code. We used the language of radio: wiring up, tuning in, tuning out.

To my surprise I discovered that our group wasn't considered exotic at our high school. We'd thought that dropping acid would enlighten us, put us on the inside of the secret world where music and pure sound and rhythm thrived.

Once I'd talked to my friends and classmates, I found drugs weren't a secret at all. Nearly everyone I talked to had tried LSD, grass, hash, at least once. Older students bragged about how they'd gone on to harder substances — heroin, speed, cocaine. They implied that the three of us weren't really inside anything. Our trips had been smalltime detours; we'd been more seduced by the image of the quest than by the fact.

"Are you stoned enough, man?" Terry asked me in my basement. "Have you got the stone yet, the book of hightech?"

In our acid club, we'd sometimes be stunned by the presences and connections we'd find between objects. We'd feel yanked back to a sort of Stone Age — uncomprehending strangers on a surreal frontier, uncertain of what to do about the rearrangement of our senses. On a bad trip when our moods soured we'd feel heavy, arrested, as if we'd been knocked stone-cold, zoned out of that space, panicking over the same relations that we'd established with the music, the room, and the light. Then for days afterward we'd confess to one another how we felt as if we'd been cracked in two; we were living in pieces, like stones flung in all directions. Terry and I continued to feed our obsessions with music and poetry into this process, accelerating our learning.

High school bored us. The suburbs sometimes felt cramped. I see now: we were speeding up our responses and educations, making our minds fly, conforming our sensibilities to the radiant acoustic flux.

* * *

We soon stopped taking acid together. Without much discussion we ended our drug days. I think we'd become disappointed, and maybe disillusioned. The light in the room had dimmed. What we thought were esoteric, indistinct words no longer erupted from our dreamstates. The reverberations in the stereo had toned down. None of us expressed any interest in using hypos — hitting up smack. All of this seemed like an expensive way to spend weekends for results that were less and less magical.

Unknowingly, we'd participated in the mass introduction to the suburbs of the chemicals that had inspired and deranged and addicted mystics, jazz musicians, and mobsters. What had once been considered initiation drugs for sacraments and rituals were commonly available to us. We never asked about the countries the substances came from, what sleazy greed and viciousness

211

had produced them, who the traffickers were. We'd spend week-ends dropping acid and smoking grass, then we'd return to our week of classes and homework and dating, and the drift in our minds, our search for affinities and adhesion.

I recognize that we shared a premonition, even a prompting, about our future concerns: our distemper was a spiritual one, and we were finding out what it meant to live wholly in the moment and perceive the possibility of infinite states of knowledge and watchfulness, inside vividness and concord and beauty, an extended pitch of mind and emotion that would override the apparent chasm between ourselves and the world.

The White Goddess

Night, but there's no real darkness, only the brilliance of street-lamps and neon. I continue my walk along a wide street. A few blocks on, and I see how the graffiti walls become articulate and dramatic again.

DREAMING OF
THE WHITE GODDESS
BUILDING YOU UP
MAKING YOU A MAN

DREAMING
OF MERCY

Who is writing this? Why is there so much strong language here? It's as if the walls have to speak, the buildings must have their say. I find fragments of speech concentrated on arches and pillars and over signs by the ramps to the expressway. The closer I come to the buildings by the lake, the more words I read.

AUNT CECILIA
THE WITCH TAKES YOU DOWN

The scratchings and splashes of paint warn of a harder chemical substance. They tell of homages paid to the white powder, of enthusiasts who have the inside dope, the scoop in the reality of a seductive goddess whose cult fuses a $40-billion-dollar-a-year trade with the amplification of the ego.

The words and my memories inspire more associations, strands of thought.

The drugs I took when I was young were called soft, light. They were part of our need to discover a direction in the flux. That cult had been a stage for us. We'd been self-conscious actors in what we'd hoped would be a subversive drama, mugging for cameras and tape recorders that didn't exist. When we finished with our experiments, and our spiritual emptiness wasn't made immediately meaningful, we intuitively realized that we'd have to evolve into deeper communications, networks of authentic understanding.

By the time I'd moved into the vortex of the media, of publishing and promotion, the drugs were called hard, heavy. I began to hear about dealings that were high priced, conspiratorial, and influential. Cocaine, heroin, cocaine and heroin together (speedballs): these were the choices of fashion, the designer drugs, for TV people and journalists, editors and magazine publishers, lawyers, politicians, and stockbrokers. The altar of the white goddess, this new lunar muse, was consecrated to money and power.

SNOW
RUNNING
ALL AROUND MY BRAIN

These walls under the expressway are talking primarily about cocaine, the favored high of the supercity. The pure white

214

powder, the more refined the better, its uncanny blankness. Your perceptions clear and you feel physically stronger with coke — or you have the delusion that you've become more vigorous and lucid — and then you descend back into your body's limits. The claque of the goddess grows by seemingly giving its initiates a brief surge of omnipotence.

> CALL MIDNIGHT =
> SHE GIVES THE ULTIMATE
> BLOW JOB

I note the harsh shift in the voices. Nameless shouts, crude signatures, abstract scrawls. Some of the graffiti has the appearance of a transnational ad campaign.

My basement drug use was in part the result of its availability and my parent's affluence. I'd had the money to buy hash, grass, and LSD. There are more varieties of drugs for sale now: legal uppers and downers to cope with aggression and exhaustion; outlawed steroids for athletes to deal with the demand for kickoff acceleration. The hard drug use parallels the look and mood of the city: the lean jabs of steel, one-hundred floor elevations, twenty-four-hour broadcasts, the demand that you can't rest if you want to compete in the rush of commerce.

> MARY LOVED
> JOHN
> RIP

Back alley news. During the time I spent with the crowds that congregate around sources of power and influence — electronic, corporate, financial, and cultural — I learned things about cocaine. I snorted it four times on social occasions at a friend's house, where the coke was usually provided in discreet lines on a table. I wasn't too impressed with its effects so I dropped it. (I also couldn't afford the stuff.) But the alleys, walls, and concrete islands between streets provide an image of decay in the glitter and renovations. Smashed bottles, rusted bicycle wheels, a caved-in TV, punctured cans, the refuse of technology and a refuge for burned-out objects — and all the telling slogans.

In the shadows below the towers, I remember a man whose impulses drove him to the feet of the white goddess. He was someone I cared about, a friend who began fastforwarding his soul...

Informers

Raymond Price was a journalist, a radio talk-show host, and a poet, with a gift for self-promotion and a talent for ruin. "The guy's always on the make," an editor confided to me. This was part of Price's mystery and charm. An Anglo-Irish immigrant to the city, he was perceptive in print, a drinker, generous with money, an eccentric whose wide eyes had a rare vulnerability about them. In those circles where people played parts, looked literary, and let you know that they had the right connections, he seemed both pretentious and true, a living paradox. "A real fake," the same editor said.

I met Price at a reading at a novelist's house. What struck me about him was his brightness. He talked intelligently, his erudition packed into his every sentence. His knowledge of books and writers was formidable. In a tireless monologue, he held forth on the epic orgies of rock stars and MTV directors, the lectures he'd heard Jacques Derrida and Allan Bloom give, the politicians and police chiefs he'd interviewed at conventions and rallies. He tested out ideas with you for articles, then flatteringly promised to mention you in the published copy. In need of friendship myself, feeling shy at the gathering, I'd warmed to his jokes and allusions, seeing some of the con artist in his teasing of "the provincials," as he kept saying.

The air of awareness about him. That he knew more than he said. Always on the verge of letting you know a vital fact. Confessions, revelations.

He had a plastic nature. He took on different appearances in different places. After a reading he could be sharp, condescending in his comments about another poet's delivery, and he would look tall, lean, ascetic, as if he'd been fasting and vigorously exercising for a week. At a bookstore, if you met him there, he could seem modest, kindly, self-effacing, and he would look short, round, almost plump, as if he'd just returned from an orgy of eating. Over dinner his elegant accent could supply a tone of detachment as he entertained his listeners with his observations about cabalism, black magic, and Renaissance Rosicrucianism. On his radio talk show for an FM station he was affable, cozy with visiting literary celebrities, who were usually left bewildered by his breezy familiarity with them. On other occasions he'd sit sullenly at a bar, his face swollen, his gaze hooded. After many drinks, his Trinity College-trained accent melted, strangely, into a Dublin gutter drawl.

Toronto was a laboratory for him. "The media world is made up of chemicals," he'd said. "Additives in the food, ions in the air. The information explosion is full of intangibles, variables, elements in a constant state of becoming, adaptation." He introduced me to a few of these ideas. But while I was probing and questioning, I didn't notice the depth of his obsessions.

The feeling that he was some urban mystic with answers for enigmas and riddles. That he was someone whose wife — it was widely said — really knew nothing about him. That he had debts.

* * *

"You think you know him?" a photographer asked. He was an

acquaintance of mine and we'd been talking after a reading one night.

"I'm not sure."

"Everyone thinks they do. But he's out there. Lots more going on than you know. Pills. Crack. Smack. His capacity is incredible. Believe me."

This informing had come out of nowhere that evening. I'd been seen in Price's company — I enjoyed his banter about books. Obviously, I was someone who had to be enlightened.

"Yeah, I'll put down a line or two. But I've noticed weird things with him. He'll snort up six lines. Go on a bender. Mix booze and speedballs. Disappear for days. Lost in the streets, lost in his mind."

"Then what?" I didn't hide my sarcasm.

"He takes off somewhere to dry out. Locks himself up in a clinic. And he's back. Like Jekyll and Hyde."

I listened and wondered, why's he telling me this?

"But his arms. Hard from the shots. Can't find a vein. Toughened by needles. Started doing it in his *balls*, man."

I stared at this man who was reporting on a mutual friend. The casual manner in which trust was broken.

"How can you be sure of any of this?"

"It's hard to spot. You're Mr. Certainty for ten minutes. Buzzed for an hour. And the man's a liar. A total blanket of lies. A genius, sure. You'll never know you're being used."

He talked like a man with a grudge. He was so angry that he couldn't stop himself from pouring out his bitterness. I didn't believe a word he said. Price had been drunk in public, but so had I, and so had others.

People were projecting images and opinions on Price. In a data matrix, people will think that they have special access to details, points, and facts. Insider trading. Information spurs the system, leading you on to believe that you know who's who and what's what.

What was the truth about him?

This hearsay in shadows.

* * *

I began wondering if others were using pick-me-ups. Was the magazine photographer stoned when he'd freely offered his stories? He'd been wearing sunglasses at the party, for an eye problem, he claimed. His impromptu exposé certainly had an effect: it left me suspicious. Suddenly I was traveling in circles where behavior could be a disguise and people spied on one another.

I was bothered that I didn't know what was going on. Price was a good journalist, and an interesting poet; I respected his talent. It appealed to me that he wanted to start a new life here. I enjoyed his put-on of the dull-witted, and I didn't especially like the puritan moralism that Toronto often fostered. Yet people whispered, "He's a crack head, a blow pig, a dealer." They were saying that he dared others to see him for what he was, that he was waiting to be caught. The photographer had luridly mentioned frosted nostrils, bleeding membranes.

* * *

A Saturday afternoon, and I ran into Price in a bookstore on Queen Street West. I suggested coffee — he suggested a drink. He was talkative, beaming. I felt the urges of friendship again, so I decided to tell him what I'd heard.

"You're kidding," he said, after I'd repeated the rumors over drinks at a café.

"It's what's going around."

"What nonsense. They must be awfully bored. It's all untrue, of course. I drink too much. And I've tried things. As everyone has. But, really."

"This is different. The extremes of the gossip. You should know."

"Conventional morality. What will I do with such old-fashioned thinking? It's all so small time. They don't have much of a sense of humor, do they?"

We joked about it and our conversation turned to a recently published novel that we'd both admired. I did notice that while we talked, he drank four vodka-and-tonics to my one. He seemed sincere in his denials, but he clearly enjoyed being the subject of rumor, even an object of slander.

"This price will never be too high," he said.

Then a look of fear, of utter nakedness, came over his face. I was startled by such a frank glimpse into desperation. Terror — it wasn't a word we used much. But that's what I saw. His raw look passed. He turned away, apparently embarrassed by what he'd shown me, and ordered another drink. Again the contradictions in him. I was concerned, curious, and too polite to say anything. Again the cloud of not knowing.

* * *

COCAINE CAN MAKE YOU BLIND

From euphoria...to paranoia...to psychosis...

I'd clipped this ad from the *New York Times* business section soon after the Twenty-four-hour Drop in the financial markets. Threats, accusations, suspicion. The copy confirmed my intuitions: my circle of friends, colleagues, and peers mirrored the public fear, the atmosphere of allegation and blame.

There was a hypodermic effusion in these end-of-the-decade alarms, the propaganda and blurbs about drugs and their effects. Hypos and hype. The language in the news was being pitched in terms of warfare, conflict, and campaigns, a red alert. It was a hitup of crisis and disaster, an injection of unease. The editorial hyperbole could be addictive with its promotion of highs and panic.

But I admitted to myself that the more I got to know about Price, the more relentless the gossip about him became.

His life looked like an airbrushed image of success. His wife, Tanya, a timid blond from Vilnius in Lithuania, and his daughter, Merike, were attractive, healthy. They'd been used in celebrity photographs for a pop-fashion magazine that wanted to show a happy youthful family. Price in his early forties, Tanya in her late twenties, their young daughter. The picture was shiny, tranquil. Who would have thought that there could be so much doubt haunting Price's eyes? It was rumored that he'd been married four times, that he hadn't been fully divorced when he married Tanya and Merike was born, that he was illegitimate himself. His poetry was mostly plagiarized, a reviewer insisted privately. He was friends with neo-Nazis, coke dealers, hoods who carried weapons under Armani jackets, a lawyer claimed.

More denials when I talked to him. His disarming humor, the gifts of books and passes to movies and concerts. Then the avowals of commitment to his work.

The suspicions about him came to a head over an incident with a best-selling author.

* * *

They had been close friends at Trinity College, Price announced. They had shared women and had belonged to the same literary group, he said. Price seemed to be preparing himself for a reunion with one he called by an intimate nickname.

The novelist arrived in the city, exhausted by his North American promotional tour. A refined, worldly, and taciturn man, he had come to do his last set of interviews and readings before returning to his home in County Killarney, Ireland. After the first meeting between the two at the publisher's reception, it was clear to everyone that they'd never met.

"Now, tell me, what sort of accent does he think he's

speaking with?" the author was heard to ask at the party. "It's most...peculiar. Unlike any I've heard before anywhere. Trinity College, he says? I think not..."

Price's radio interview with the novelist was a fiasco. The author stalked out of the studio, infuriated by the inexplicable delays, the way that Price continually mispronounced his first name, the unfocused questions. It was all over town by evening that Price had been stoned at the time. Coke under his fingernails, brandy in his coffee, blue pills on a tray. Price had sneezed and coughed through their talk, like a man having a seizure.

That night there was a celebration for the author at a downtown hotel. It was an expensive party, extravagant with food, crowded with book sellers and reviewers. I left early; I had things to do elsewhere. The party's host, a magazine editor and an organizer of welcomes for visiting authors, phoned me at home in the morning. He sputtered furiously about how Price had arrived late at the hotel suite, sweating, jabbering.

"No more embarrassments. You tell that prick he's gone too far, if you happen to fall over him. His name is shit. I don't want to be part of his crackpot scenarios."

I told him that I thought Price may have been sick. Maybe none of us understood the man's self-torture.

"Cut the crap. He's off in his brain. He'll betray you too. He can't help himself. He's oozing out of his pores. Look, I don't want to see the guy dead. But he'll drag others down with him. You watch."

I asked myself why Price had allowed himself to be snared in obvious lies. He must have known that this time there'd be no way out.

* * *

He called me that afternoon.

Over the phone his twitchy voice babbled about issues I couldn't grasp.

"Why are they saying terrible things about me? These lies. I've been ill. We've got to help each other. I deny, deny, deny it all."

He pleaded with me to understand. And I heard in his voice the fear that was overwhelming him. I said that I questioned why he created such a self-destructive image for himself. The half-truths, the evasions, the exaggerations, his private fictions, provoked others into complicity and anger. He broke in, his voice shaking, and ranted about a conspiracy against him. "I know who they are." He slurred his words. His sentences began to skitter off into fantasies about the plight of rebels in Toronto. He yammered that he was "a godlike presence above everyone. Women want to fuck me. People are far too interested in me."

I couldn't listen much longer. The messages were garbled. Conversation seemed futile.

* * *

A day after the novelist returned to Ireland, I heard from others that I'd been implicated in Price's stoned behavior. The story went that I'd been the one feeding him lines about the so-called conspiracy, feeding him the lines of coke. The stories, I was told, originated from Price.

I couldn't understand why this was being said. The pack mentality of those closed groups. But it was clear to me that Price was casting us in his personal script, creating psychodramas that involved everyone he knew. The media culture can be a vicarious one that turns spectators into voyeurs with cravings for more hits.

After a few nights of thinking about what had happened, I knew that I'd had enough of the buzz of innuendo, the warp on the words, the deforming images, these slants on what we were or could be.

I decided to see Price.

The Fix

Rosedale after ten p.m. The only loud sound in Price's neighborhood came from the subway nearby. Steel wheels on a steel track, brief, fading.

Alone in his flat, Price wasn't surprised to see me. He looked as though he hadn't changed his clothes in a week. His face was pale, slack. Agelines stood out around his eyes and on his forehead and neck. His eyes softened at first, then his stare hardened into anger, before softening again. I sat down on the living room couch. A bottle of Remy Martin on the coffee table, three-quarters drained. A tablespoon. An empty plastic bag. A candle. A tiny silver razor blade.

"Did I ask you to come? Couldn't have. Doesn't matter. I knew you'd come. I'm honored, in fact. It's really a pleasure."

He'd tunneled down into a zone that I'd never seen before. I almost left, feeling my rage drain out. His voice held me — its mid-Atlantic flatness, the disappearance of his accent.

"You've been asking questions."

"As a friend," I said.

"Of course. But there's more to it, isn't there? You're rummaging around. The great confusion. Trying to figure it out."

His voice wobbled, disintegrating into an accent that was now impossible to identify. But I understood the double edge in his words. I recognized the truth through his eyes: I'd become someone drawn to others who were blowing up, their emotional, spiritual, and intellectual outage. Who was the sleepwalker? Which of us was in a trance? Who was eluding their own needs and desperation?

"You want to know about me? I'd be delighted to tell you. Shall we have an interrogation or a conversation? Or would you rather do an interview?"

His glare blurred, became fixed, then blurred again. He sat up and grinned, and suddenly he looked carved out of chrome.

"Say whatever you want," I murmured.

"You do the shine, and the faces around you become devils. You do the shine, and the next thing, you're on a mission. Total focus. You're streaking. You see vast links. If you do the shine you'll see in the dark. But you don't get it. You're not hip. You think you're reading my book and you're not. When you do the shine you see through. Everyone is transparent. They're out there."

He leaned forward. His shirt was damp, stained.

"Let me explain. Coke movies, coke books, coke ads, coke TV. It's an in club. Is that what you wanted to hear? Movies where squares like you are fucked. Why is this movie funny? If you haven't been ghostbusting, you won't get it. You have to cut more lines, cut deeper, and snort up every grain you see."

His eyes narrowed to slits.

"You want firsthand experience. A dose of reality right up your ass. Well, welcome to it. What do you think you'll find? Something about yourself? Ask Lena. What does she say?"

His tirade silenced me. Its battle of tones, the call for help, the attempt to get me to respond. I knew what he was talking about, though. There was an intense logic to his words, a fierce building up. He appeared to be physically inflating, his body swelling. While he harangued me, I got the sensation I was shrinking.

"Do you want a reason? There is no reason. I know what this is about. Whoever you are. I've got plots for a personal paradise. I'll build a camp in New Zealand. Somewhere the mental telepathy isn't strong. Once you're shining, the mission takes over."

I was about to reply, when as abruptly as he'd begun he stopped. His body sagged; he breathed evenly. I thought that he had, miraculously, regained his composure. He sighed, shook his head, smiled. I thought he'd forgotten what he'd just said.

"Would you like a drink? Some brandy. Tea. Coffee. I have some...brewing." Unbelievably, his accent had reverted to the polite Trinity College graduate again.

The front door latch clicked.

Tanya appeared, smiling. She greeted me warmly and turned to her husband, and stopped dead. Her mouth opened as if she were about to speak. The mess on the table, his state. She sat down slowly on the couch beside me, staring at Price.

He was sweating, nervous, withdrawn, like a man caught in a highbeam. I was seized by a feeling of helplessness. I watched his mood soften again, the shift in his face, his stare that solicited sympathy. What could I say? Tell him to see a doctor? Warn him? That seemed trite, wrong. There was something behind his words, behind his deep mania, that hounded, trailed, pursued him.

The three of us said nothing. Then Price began telling Tanya about what he called "our very interesting discussion."

A short while afterward he ushered me out, and we stood together on the front steps of his flat. His eyes menaced; his eyes showing pain. He seemed to want to reach out and tell me something else. But he wouldn't say what was on his mind. I'd forgotten my anger and now saw the waste, the physical wreckage, the cost of the mental scattering. He was lashed by an inexorable obsessive story that would ride him until he found its finish, and that made him dangerous to himself, and his motives unknowable to others.

After we shared inanities, I left him standing there on the steps, the sense of helplessness remaining with me, the sense of loss. I felt as though I were saying goodbye.

* * *

The firebomb exploded two weeks later.

When the charge detonated at his flat, Price was standing in the living room, drinking orange juice spiked with vodka. Three a.m. Hungover from a night of drinking with the producer of his radio program — as he explained on his talk show — he'd eased out of bed, careful not to disturb Tanya, and Merike in the next room.

Then the flash hit the window.

A fireball spread across the porch, devastating it in seconds. Glass shattered. The front door was yanked off its hinges. As if a ferocious creature had demanded an entrance.

Price was paralyzed for an instant. He watched the orange-red inferno. "Neatly done," he commented to himself, with a detachment that astonished him. Then he became aware of the heat. He ran to get Tanya and Merike out of the house. He found his wife sitting in bed, screaming. Merike was curled on the floor of her room, crying. They fled into the street, wearing only their night-clothes. Terrified, their neighbors had already hit the sidewalks and were huddling on the corner.

From the corner Price watched the blaze. The charred porch, the scorched timbers, the air smelling like gasoline. The flames somehow didn't engulf the rest of the house — though Price never explained why the fire dwindled so quickly.

Police cars and fire trucks arrived within minutes, and the firemen hosed down the ashes. Who had put in the alarm? Price never found out.

"A professional job," the investigating officer said to Price. "If they'd wanted to blow the whole place up, they'd have put the bomb at the back of the house. The old gas stove. Place would've gone up like a rocket. Somebody knew their business. Sending a message?"

Price told this story over the air, narrating it with anguish, and pleasure. He replayed the event in an article that he wrote for a magazine.

"What's going on?" Tanya asked their friends. She knew the picture wasn't complete. The police probed. They talked to Price's colleagues and neighbors. Despite the suggestion about a warning, no one produced any evidence. Price assured Tanya, the police, and his radio audience that it had been a mistake, the wrong house.

Gossip stirred again. Rumors said that the bombing had been a payback. He was in trouble with dealers. A hood had come calling.

* * *

In two months there was a second explosion.

The house beside Price's flat was firebombed, in the same style, with the same effect. "In the early morning hours," a local tabloid reported, "the porch of a Rosedale home was consumed in a matter of minutes by the blaze. This is the second incident in the area. No suspects have been arrested."

This blast sent Price crawling on his bedroom floor. His home was being attacked (so he said later). Tanya had tumbled out of bed, clawing the air. He'd leaped up to reach for her. (They'd sent their daughter to stay for a month with Tanya's aunt who lived in Montreal.) Only then did he realize the fire was next door.

The police interrogated him again. Price hired a well-known lawyer. The questions came. Did he know anything? "What's the link? Illegal drugs? Trafficking?" Price had a reputation. Could he tell them anything that would help? "Give us a fix on this."

Price retreated into his writings and into himself. People said they no longer saw him at many gatherings. He spoke over the radio in a moving editorial about the second bombing, his concern for the safety of his family, what he said was the random danger. Terrorists pick innocent targets. It was impossible for him to know why, he claimed. "Things happen. I can't always lock my door..."

In his concluding remarks, he told his audience that he'd resigned from the talk show and that he wouldn't speak over the air again.

"I'll concentrate only on my poetry from now on."

* * *

So the drugcult takes you into its baffling maze of paranoia and denial. I could only interpret Price from cinders, the fragments of the blast.

I've come to understand that the true fix in the drugcult is power. Explosions, crosswiring, adrenaline, and heat. The addiction is to force. It's about knowing details that make you part of a privileged group, eluding surveillance, learning the use of fictions, pseudonyms, covers. It's about making images of yourself and thinking that you're in control of your destiny. "You, only better." That's what the graffiti had said. It's about recasting yourself into a midnight personality, about opting out of reality's track, risking death in order to burn with outrage at the body's limitations, social decorum, and convention.

Drug use recalls the alchemist's attempt to find herbs that would cure mental affliction and demonic possession. These were, the spiritual doctors thought, the origins of disease, of psychic imbalance. Drugs could restore harmony. But adepts, priests, masters, and herbalists accompanied the pilgrim's transcendental experience; the rites were performed in guarded circumstances. This drugcult is unguarded, the clairvoyance often coming to already darkened, cloudy minds. Higher states of consciousness achieved through drugs imitate the higher states of awareness accomplished through learning. The initiation mystery, the rite of knowledge itself, appears inverted in the drugcult that mingles mass-media hype, surface glamor, the uninterrupted orgasms of rock and roll.

The white goddess offers a path — out of the world and out of your head. But the goddess can turn into a witch, and the result is a firebomb searing off a porch.

* * *

"What's going on?" Tanya Price had asked, her voice tight with worry.

Yet she'd said nothing that night when she'd noticed the spoon and the razor on the coffeetable. I remember the expression on her face. She wasn't surprised — she'd seen Price do this before. Surely she'd watched him deteriorate over that week. Maybe she didn't want to know too much about him. And who can blame her?

What would happen to any of us if we probed too deeply into our lives? What do we truly mask from ourselves? I thought of Lena, my marriage — and my resistance to seeing and knowing what was cracking apart. And what if we were to ask about the way the current can rip and twist through the city? How does it influence us and what is its aim? What is barraging us, clamoring inside us and through us?

I think of Price stoned, talking as if he lived in a dreamstate or a nightmare, his many voices rambling, accents shifting, hiding the truth from those closest to him, merging with misinformation, allowing himself to become a malleable image, a screen on which others could project their contempt and anxiety, often their uncertainty, and sometimes their compassion.

He continues writing magazine articles and poems, giving readings, vanishing for days — according to those who know him — and traveling in Europe, Australia, and South Africa. We've moved apart.

Questions form in people's minds. Who is he? Where does

he come from? Where does he get his money?

Questions fill the space around us. The world seemingly on the edge of exploding. People not knowing. The speculations in darkness. The roarings in the night.

Millennial Jamming

The air is alive with radio voices.

The atmosphere vibrates with intimations of a call, a tone that carries the beat of the pressure in ourselves and the rhythm in the streets, the noise of collective passions and questions, reverberations of need, a hailing that is part shout and part song, now within earshot.

The static gradually bursts out, like a radio warming up. Then the acoustic stimulations surge into a cacophony of young, old, and middle-aged voices, millions of people who plead and demand and speak, asking for listeners, authentic reception.

> "Ah this is Radio One-oh-oh..."
> "Until the morning hours..."
> "Missed getting you in..."
> "Dial a mate..."
> "What's the number you called..."
> "Again, please..."
> "Reaching everywhere..."

"The night exchange..."
"No longer in service..."
"The help hotline..."
"Long distance charges apply..."
"In any emergency..."
"You have reached..."
"No one is in to take your call..."
"Forwarding..."
"You..."

Harmony recognizes harmony; and discord will always recognize — and seek out — discord.

This is due to the forces
of ever-active fire
which exists in all things
and in the course of long cycles
of time resolves itself into itself
and out of it is constructed a reborn world.
— Philo, a philosopher of the Pythagorean school.

(Undated)

Letter to Lena

> Morning in the mountains
> Banff, Alberta

Lena,

I'm writing to explain what I think happened to us. So this'll be rough, loose, confessional. Frankly, I've been uneasy about writing your name down. It had a power I couldn't face. Divorce is hardly unusual these days; it no longer seems like anything special. Yet what I couldn't face with any honesty or courage was you, us, the breakdown of our marriage, and the scattered pieces of myself, of ourselves, that were left afterward.

Lena, I've been remembering your reddish-blond hair, your brown eyes, your long legs. You were, and are, a striking woman. Tough-minded, brusque, active. I never saw you sit still. You were one of the most sensible people I've ever known. And you treated my obsessions with technology like storms that you thought would pass. When we worked as a couple — and we did for a time, when we lived together, before we married — it was because you balanced what you called my airiness with some ground. You worked hard, building your own graphic design company, becoming a part of the local political scene. I see you rushing: out the front door, off to a breakfast appointment; home late, to dash off again to meet with a candidate for election. You liked to organize people. And you certainly tried to organize me. I could do what I wanted — write, teach, wander mentally — so long as I came home. Eventually I stopped coming home. Lena, I didn't believe I had one, so tenuous and vague had our links become.

Yet I remember warmth and affection with you. We began

237

as lovers, became friends, ended up as your average non-communicative couple. I remember seeing you on the dance floor at that wedding — willowy, poised, a little solemn, dismissing the people around you with a glance — and sauntering up to you and saying, "Hold on." What a line you said that was. I liked your sharp talk, your sarcasm. We'd stay up all night in those days, yakking, eating tangy food you cooked, leafing through poetry books for quotes that spoke to us about new love, watching late-night movies, making up dialogue for the shows so that they would fit what we felt. Long nights, with the near-quiet of our muffled cries. After we'd made love, I'd listen to you whispering, while you drifted off to sleep. So much of my life has been spent trying to figure out what others were saying, implying, whispering...

Eventually those times together just stopped. You became business-like. When we married, a few years later, I felt like a ghost at the ceremony. I'd begun to feel that confusion about things; I was letting the data load overwhelm me. I think you sensed this, balked at my turmoil, imposed your own form of rigid structure, and proceeded to discipline your life with meetings, schedules, plans, clear destinations. We became blurs to one another, in our house.

I don't know why our marriage disintegrated with amazing speed. What uprooted us? A lack of maturity? A refusal to deal with reality? Were we living in such garbled forms of communication that we couldn't see what was happening? I've argued with myself, considered angles. Blamed you, blamed situations, blamed myself. Maybe we fell apart because nothing very much had held us in the first place.

You said, "You go so far off in your head sometimes."

But I'm here, I'm here... (I'd replied.)

"Well, things are getting over-complicated..."

Why don't we have children? (I'd asked, a question out of nowhere.)

"For God's sake! We don't have the time! Or the money..."

I tried to warn you in our cross-purpose conversations that I was losing myself in the noise that was both in my head and in the streets. The savagery of that internal process — to be radically unsure of everything. And what were you losing? Why were you giving up? I felt like I was speaking to you across a chasm.

"Don't worry," you said. "Pull yourself together...Don't indulge all this stuff..."

Common sense was the last thing I wanted to hear at that point. I became a poor husband — adulterous, impatient, even more self-obsessed, sometimes self-pitying; I was even drinking too much. I who valued communication above all couldn't communicate with you. I dealt with things by plunging in to turbulence, roaming in danceclubs, in techno-wonders, attaching myself to people whose minds were imploding.

And one day I realized I couldn't live in our house anymore. I felt shut in, closed in. Our place was haunted by solitaries. When we made love, I couldn't always feel you. It was as if we were slipping away from one another physically.

Resumed
in the late afternoon

Let me describe that night, when I sat you down in our kitchen and I said I had to leave. I was clear in my head, but it was an unnatural clarity — an adrenaline high. Do you know how you stared at me? You were calm, though I sensed that you didn't understand. Suddenly I saw you as I once did: bright, steady, consistent. I saw your beauty again: your vigor, your eyes, your hair. I almost didn't leave, thinking we've broken through, we're truly talking. Then you said you'd expected this; you weren't really surprised.

I packed my briefcase in the morning with some clothes, a few books and notebooks. You said at the door, on the edge of tears:

"If you break things like this, they'll be impossible to heal."

But you never said don't go.

Were you secretly glad to have my obsessions out of the house? It was so much easier to blank out pain. You remember how we conducted our separation mostly by telephone? We concocted stories for others so that we could rationalize what we'd done. The vast structures of disinformation can worm into how we act and talk; miscommunication becomes the norm when you deal with masks, blackouts, missing connectors.

I tried to fall in love again. I'd met Pat, someone I thought was a livewire — I only saw her bright blue eyes and blond hair at first — and who turned out to be one of the loneliest people I've ever known. We had a short passionate romance, but we couldn't make it work.

I bolted again, lost track of you. Moved around, with next to no money. Returned to Toronto. Taught, wrote, started to come down. Came to the mountains to work on the book I can't finish — or don't want to finish. There's no quiet for me anywhere. I keep running, and running. Whatever it is that's happening is far from over.

Lena, the pattern we called our marriage has shattered. I know that at points in our time together we almost built links to each other. But we've reached some end, and it's time for me to say I'm sorry for my ignorance, selfishness, and arrogance, and to say goodbye to what we were.

I've been gradually learning that at the center of the information labyrinth — if there's anything that remotely resembles a center — there is this question: what keeps your identity from leaking away? Be yourself, TV ads command. Lena, as if that's the easy thing to do. I'm not sure I ever really knew you, but at least I can try to mend the one thing I have left: my words.

After 8:30 p.m.
and watching the sunset
over the Bow Valley

Let me tell you that over the past months a message has
begun to emerge for me in the communications whirl. On low
frequencies, almost inaudible, no more than an undertone.
Murmuring:

"The breakage is in the perceiver, not in the perceived.
There is coherence in the universe, harmony in the cosmos,
deeper and more comprehensive than we know. We live in fragments but the world has an inner rhythm, music we move to
and yet do not recognize. Our life's work may be to find a way
of throwing off our perceptual blinders and understanding that
the cosmos is a whole. This interconnection of all things is
good, but it is also a danger, because it presses us, asking us to
make choices about what we want to be."

my love,

—

From my field notes, consisting of headlines, blurbs, and newsletters, that help me to describe the nature of the new. Voices from signs and posters, the human jumble, thoughts jumping with premonitions.

HYDRO IS UNABLE TO GUARANTEE
CONTINUOUS SUPPLIES OF POWER.
WE RECOMMEND THAT CUSTOMERS
ON LIFE-SUPPORT SYSTEMS TAKE
ALL PRECAUTIONS NECESSARY TO ENSURE
THEIR SYSTEM CAN CONTINUE TO FUNCTION
DURING A POWER OUTAGE.

Computer Wail

Evansville, Ind. (AP) — ...Two researchers believe they have linked noise made by video display terminals with stress symptoms in women...

"The sound is present in almost all American computers," said Dr. Caroline Dow, assistant professor of communication at the University of Evansville...

"The sound might be compared to the cry of a rabbit caught in a trap," said Dow's husband, Dr. Douglas Covert. "This squeal, to a mother, is a distress call," Dow said.

Crisis Advice in a Hotel

IF YOU ARE IN AN ELEVATOR, USE THE EMERGENCY PHONE.

SIT DOWN AND RELAX, EMERGENCY PERSONNEL WILL GET YOU OUT.

OUR EMERGENCY LIGHTING IS BATTERY-OPERATED AND FUNCTIONS FOR ABOUT 25 MINUTES.

AFTER THAT, THE STAIRWELLS AND HALLWAYS WILL NOT HAVE ANY LIGHT.

IT IS QUITE LIKELY THAT A POWER BLACKOUT WILL OCCUR AT LEAST ONCE DURING YOUR STAY HERE.

Transcendental Data

A data dictionary does not contain the real data that forms an organization's data resources and is handled in the daily operations of its business; rather, it contains data about such data: the location of the data, a description of the meaning of the data, the relation of the data to other data, how and where the data is used, who owns the data, the source of the data... This 'data about data' is sometimes called metadata.

If there is power in an image, if a look can bear a message, then there can be power in a voice, a sound bite, communiqués in the tenor of recorded speech.

Process Words

Nonevent Talk
Downloading Persons
Voice Bonding
Floating Point Routines
Beyond Basic
KEYword
Kernals and Extensions
Sourcing, truthing

Process Phrasing

Reversed audiotapes can reveal information
or thoughts hidden in normal speech.
According to Pentagon Declassified Information,
speech patterns of public figures
can be played backward to reveal
significant terms
that may indicate meaning
for those who know...

So the language of radios and computers converges with the language of recording studios. Our awareness is extended from slips of the tongue to occult concerns, unconscious meaning, paths that lead toward the arcanum.

The Currency Swap

The vice-president for Public Affairs in a transnational investment and loans company spoke to me, when I was back in Toronto, before his retirement:

"What happened after the crashes of nineteen eighty-seven and nineteen eighty-eight? The word was greed. The word is now chaos. What have we got? Mobility and piracy in the marketplace. They call it 'flexibility.' What does that mean? Can you operate without a safety net?

"People like me were raised on the promise of ascent into the executive suite, homes in suburbia, medicare, retirement plans, and old-age pensions. That's over. Government officials laugh when you mention plans. The mood is hustle. You can't promise anything. We live in a mythology of a global economy whose only survivors will be multinationals, brave entrepreneurs, and family mafias. What government experts really mean when they talk about interdependence is everyone's in debt to everyone. What they mean by diversity and deregulation is freedom for the big boys to do what they want. When they say restructuring they mean say goodbye to your job. When they say globalization they mean screw the Third World.

"I'm retiring so I'll say what I want. After nineteen eighty-nine I expected to see the end of résumés from those who'd been fired, downsized, permanently laid off, whatever they call it. But people kept applying. The middle-class unemployed. The ones who weren't told to keep moving.

"Everyday I feel the fear that's just under the surface. Reading stats on VDTs. There's moral hand-wringing, but nothing's done. No one can come up with legislation that will shape the speed of the nonstop stuff. People can't take much these days. The tolerance for criticism is low. But if you feel you've nowhere to go, what can you do but stand there and take it?

"Economic chaos. Good or bad. It's what we have. Take-overs. Leveraged buyouts. Junk bonds. Currency swaps between debtor nations. Offshore money management. Debts so huge that no one can conceive them. One trust buys out another. Staff is fired and shuffled off to branch plants. Families crack apart. And all the big boys want to know is can you run with the ball? Can you uproot yourself?

"I'm retiring early because I belong to another world. The class struggles that typified my youth seem largely over. Everyone involved will want to grab a piece of the action. Find a hole, a need. Meanwhile everyone else runs for cover. Things will be divided between those who have access to information, and those who don't.

"Call it hightech social Darwinism. We burn up products and people. There are corporate heads who are unscrupulous and *vital*.

"This doesn't mean nothing can be done. It's important to look at the enormous power that's in the hands of a very few people. The groups trying to assert some control. The invisible elites. There are issues to be addressed, lines to be drawn. Highly structured plans for the future are straitjackets. You have to think on the run with the pieces flying around you. And see beyond the numbers into the heart of the matter.

"Why did I stay so long? The marketplace is where technology and human nature meet. And I've made money. Much more than I need."

OnLine

"Money is a manifestation of invisible value…"

VDT Passwords

Repeat. Begin. Go ahead.
What's your purpose?
Course. Menu.
Command?

Storage Recall

*No more relation could he discover between the steam
and the electric current than between the Cross and
the cathedral. The forces were interchangeable if not
reversible, but he could see only an absolute fiat in
electricity as in faith.*
— Henry Adams, in *The Education of Henry Adams*

*Firms push to move cellular phones
pagers into all aspects of life*

TALK AND ROLL — LOTS OF TELEPHUN
GET YOUR TRAVELING ACCESS NOW
OUTFAX YOUR COMPETITORS

These blurbs rush over the airwaves, stirring us with their promises, the bits like a form of telepathy in the teleglobe. I've been picking them up as if they were telegrams, keeping my record:

NOW YOU'RE PLAYING WITH POWER
REEL POWER
PORTABLE POWER

The blurbs are headlines. Some actual headlines have the effect of an advertisement. Their persuasive lure comes from the compressed phrases, the hints, the repeating rhythms. The ads and the news are often indistinguishable from one another, the type and the bold copy feeding off each other, commingling, creating an intersection of current affairs with sales.

Lyric

Turn on the noise
Turn it on, turn it up

Sampling

Patterns of reception and transmission
favor the absence of logical sequence
and the stepping up
of surprising parallels,
sudden intuitions,
radical realignments.

It's about momentum and position,
changing your mind,

minding your change...

Bell Telephone Ad (Circa 1940)

Giving Wings
To Words

Radioing

There's been a ringing in my ears for a long time. It starts loudly, coming in from a great distance, then it grows louder, sharper, more irritating. The ringing appears to stop, but then it starts again, a sound unlike anything I've heard before. I find that I'm staying awake and waiting to figure out what it means, this awareness of noise, the responsibility of voices.

Sometimes I shut off my typewriter for the day — wherever I happen to be working — and go for a walk. I hope I'll avoid the ringing. In an instant, even in what should be the quietest places, it's back, just there, impossible to avoid.

When I try to sleep, I wake up abruptly, thinking I've forgotten to shut off some electrical device. I get up and check the TV, the radio. While they could have been part of the source, none of them is the true origin.

The ringing persists. No matter where I am, it won't go away.

Record of a Phone Call

"Maybe it's time to get away. Outside the country," my mother says.

Her voice on the phone, mild and yet probing.

"That's what I've been thinking, too." I move the receiver closer to my ear.

I've just returned to Toronto again after a short stay at a friend's house in Quebec City. But I'm feeling restless, ready to travel again.

"Are you sure there's nothing we can do?" Her voice, though low-key, is kind and concerned.

"I should get out of the country for a while. I'm not getting enough here. The things I need."

"You've mentioned Italy."

"The Adriatic Coast."

"You're thinking about Venice."

I could almost see my mother smile on the other side of the phone.

"You've talked about going there since you were a boy. Well, it's a good time of the year. It'll be cheaper, quieter. But there'll be crazy things. You know Italy."

"Venice is different."

"Maybe. But it may give you the answers you've been looking for. An answer for all your searching. There's a hole in your heart."

"You've known about that."

"It's hard not to see it. All your questions. Since your breakup. Your divorce. You're very hard on yourself."

I think of how I can keep this line open between us.

"Do you ever play the piano? I've been remembering how you used to play for us in the morning."

A long pause. I hear her breathe. We've both been surprised by the question.

"You know I can't. It was a long time ago."

Her voice is faint, but clearly she is moved.

"I still read music," she says after another pause. "My scores. These days the Scarlatti sonatas. And the Brahms intermezzi, of course. I'm reading them." Silence. "It's close enough for me now. Close enough."

We're quiet for a moment. In the restrained manner of our family, we've made the necessary emotional connection for ourselves. Over the telephone.

"Well, then. You'll be leaving soon. Are you all right?"

"Yes, I'm fine."

"Are you okay for money?"

"I have some. Enough. I'll be all right."

"You take care of yourself. Know that we love you. And travel well. Above all, travel well."

Millennial Jamming

Two days before I'm booked to leave for Italy, I decide to return to the hill at Riverdale Park, look out over the city at night, and improvise on the ideas I've been exploring.

What if —

One day in the future all the lights in the city go out. The turbines stop, the telephones become quiet, the traffic lights shut down, TVs dim and computers download, and elevators wedge between the office towers' floors. Hospitals with battery-run backup supplies stay functional, but the banks and the stock exchange with their E-Money, the government offices and transnational boardrooms, the TV studios and radio stations, the cafés and bars and restaurants, are all unplugged. We'd be engulfed by a night unlike anything anyone has known since before the Edison Illumination Company lit up New York City in eighteen eighty-two, extending the hours of the day, turning the streets into a twilight spectacle of artifice, priming the crowds for the first time to watch and wait. The city would wink out and everything would shudder, flicker, and slam back into the time of candles, torches, and bonfires, and the smell of kerosene and wood-smoke.

That moment when the city blacked out would be shocking.

Instant gridlock, mass dismay, stalled lives. People blinking, chattering to one another:

"What's going on?"

"Who's in charge?"

"Lost..."

"You okay..."

"I can't get through."

"Where are you?"

"Anyone...need...help..."

In that break, massive and complete, we would realize how the private and public realms have been fused into a giant network with every part subject to what arises elsewhere.

A newspaper quote:

There is the chance that a failure occurring in London will knock Chicago out...

But the metamorphic existence we lead would appear to freeze. The cycles of boom and crash, of off and on, would temporarily end. We'd see how our lives have been ruled and molded by power drives we have funneled and concentrated, creating superconductors that we call our cities and technologies. Any historical event, any crisis or confrontation, enters the convergence of electronic fields — through computers, fax, telephones, TV, and radio — and is instantly inflated, rerun, and pushed to an extreme. This is now automatic, the process. Only where there are interruptions, fissures, cracks, do we see the pattern, the structure, what goes unrecognized, concealed by the familiar, the clichéd, the routine.

With the city's light and power eclipsed, we'd be incommunicado. There would be no clear distinction between land, sky, and lake, until the sunrise. There would be no hallucinatory corona on the horizon, the fiery sign of your approach to civilization. There would be no beacons on the lake or the hills. We would live without the benefit of a switch.

What would happen then? The citizens of an ancient city-state or a medieval town wouldn't have been terrified. They always knew that darkness was at hand. For us there would be psychic pressure and the buildup of voices calling.

My fantasy fades. It's unlikely that anything so apocalyptic will take place outside of film, novels, poetry, or visual art.

* * *

What if —

We have formed the habit of thinking only in millennial terms, linear structure, terminal points that must be final and absolute. Straight lines create roads that conclude with full stops. Our anxieties about the turn of the century may be magnified by the attention that we give to it. The millennial dateline may be given credence by a book culture that has trained us to think in the pattern of the printed page, of story lines, of crises and crossroads, of a beginning, a middle, and an end. The print tradition suggests that when we come to a climax, we turn to another page to find closure, resolution, a finish, the movement from alpha to omega. Does time travel in straight lines? Do events lead to crises that resolve and explain everything? The tensions we feel may be the result of a clash of conditionings, of our fragmented and specialized literary modes of learning, of our custom of waiting for categorics, definitions — or Armageddon, the final chapter, the last word, the ultimate explanation. This habit may not permit us to recognize that the culture of immersion, sign, computer byte, and sound bite reveals that there is only flow. The attempts to block the flow are the reaction. And the dams and walls wo make hold back the surges of life, forcing pressure to mount.

* * *

What if —

The overloads and brownouts in homes and skyscrapers are part of the way that the primordial consciousness we call electricity communicates with us. Our brain cells constantly interpret experience through electrochemical charging; neurons and nerve ends must fire to keep sense data alive. Electromagnetism in technology and the micro and analogue chip processing in computers have begun to mimic the complexity of the brain itself. This mimicry or doubling could be one reason why we sense the presence of another in the city; why we have the feeling that we're being surveyed, shadowed, canvassed, watched over, even violated and abducted; why we feel there are ghosts in the machines, demons possessing us, ETs visiting. Because we live in a communication space that is emotionally, spiritually intimate, and because technology augments and reflects how and what we think, we now exist in a condition of perpetual mental telepathy with the world. We are sharing minds, dreaming one another's dreams, participating in the creation of images, symbols, and myths. And we have harnessed and imbued ourselves with the energy that shapes the planets and stars, what stirs the cosmic dust. It may be that we're part of this elemental consciousness, the universal process, and that our hopes and terrors belong alongside its surges, and the primordial mind multiplies its impulses through the shapings, outlets, and institutions we make, our humanizing needs. Whatever the electric consciousness may be, a voice struggles to be heard. In the city the howling grows, the speaking and chanting on bands that we can't tune in clearly, asserting patterns that we can't visualize yet. There is the tumult in our ears, a stirring of our language, a shaking of the ground beneath us. The cacophony of bites and segments may be a polyphony, the song of all things joining.

The roar is here, the roar in the street, the roar that's never left me. It's the shout I hear inside every person I've encountered or passed, the shout that is a plea, a prayer, a warning, an acknowledgement of a lack, a crucial question, an ecstatic music, a squall like the cry a baby makes when he's torn from the womb and gulps in air, a grumbling grooved with age and disappointment, a cynical sneer, a snarling threat, an expounding of theories for a life that consistently threatens to unravel, a foolish braying, a frantic probe, both delirious and rationalistic, a call for kindness and healing and solace, that is all this at the same time, these voices that crave sense and structure and cohesion, voices that hug memories of warm bodies while inhabiting frigid steel offices, voices too desperate and chastened to admit that the sophisticated means of storage and story may mean nothing if they are directed nowhere, the voices of people who know the message, who know there is a message, and yet bog down in minutae and the jostle of paperwork and the need for security. It's the sound of the time, and the sound of ourselves, rebounding off the glittering towers, their windows and steel, the sound that rises when we try to crack through or transcend the seemingly endless cycles of misunderstandings and misreadings, the walls and barriers and cul-de-sacs of the cityscape.

Headlines

TRANSFER EXPLOSION
DARKENS CITY

Equipment Pinpointed

Firms Tot Up
Blackout Costs
By Light of Day

BIG MONEY MADE, LOST

Failures Could Happen Again
Officials Warn

No Guarantees

METRO BLACKOUT BURNS
BRIGHT FOR TOURISM

What seems like
a paradigm shift
is paradigm overload

Many meanings collapsing, colliding

dataspace detonation

human spiritual implosion

High-density
white
light

Current in Venice

Bridges

The jet engines hum; the air conditioners softly hiss. I gaze out the window at the blue sky, the cabin darkened to simulate the night. Other passengers doze or flip through magazines, listening to Muzak on earphones. A few hours and we'll be landing in Amsterdam, then a change of plane for me, and the shuttle to Milan.

Flight again. I'd felt the exhilaration of takeoff, the leveling off in the air. Hurtling change, altered points of view. Traveling in the jet mirrors what's happened inside me. Back in Toronto I'd locked up my manuscripts in a box, dropped off my remaining possessions in a security locker. I'd unlatched myself from things, and refreshed by my desire to go, I'd accepted that I had to take another step, and this time leave the country and like a discoverer invent a new life.

Simplify, reduce, detox.

Looking at the clouds shifting shapes and colors — red, now gray — I evaluate where I've been. A time of inquiry, of personal dislocation and pain. I think about the rock-and-roll pulse in the dancebar, the TV screen and the futurist's talk about technognomes and technomads, ideal worlds of light and motion, sexual contact and no physical contact at all, crazed zones of dazzle and thunder, the pressure of momentum, and I remember Price, the drugcult and its ritual of peaking and self-annihilation. People are submitting themselves to ambitious highs and radical amendments of their personalities. In the city, the graffiti walls had dripped words of anger and mourning. Over the air, the frequencies were rammed with opinions, fears, and promises of relief. To decode the true human want behind the noise had been the challenge I'd set for myself, but I'd hit the tilt button, reached my limit, finally wanted out.

After Amsterdam, we fly south across snowcapped mountains, their whiteness like a clean slate. We soar over the Alps, then dip above green valleys and lakes. In this cabin over the land I feel freer than I have for months.

Once we touch down in Milan, I pass through customs and board a van for the train station. I'm slowing myself, acknowledging that I need a less banged up pace, taking the train rather than flying to Tessera and the airport called Marco Polo.

"Why pick another city?" Lena had asked when I'd told her I was off again. Exasperated by my lack of a clear answer, she'd said, "It's just the same in Italy. Why don't you go back out west? You love the mountains." I couldn't explain it to her during our short meeting. I'd imagined the old city veined with canals, the floating place with its closeness to water and wind, the mercurial shimmer of waves under the morning sun, moonlight, and the stars. I saw a balance there, houses built over the tides, people living with the currents. Lena shook her head, and said, "You've lost it, kid." All I seemed to have was chaos. I'd begun to wonder if I'd lost my thread too.

* * *

The train's rumble is constant. I observe flatlands and farmhouses, vineyards and irrigation ditches, along the route from Verona.

My thoughts return to finding a cohesive message in the information flux. Is the electric process impossible to grasp and freeze?

I remember: in the mass-media discharge, extremes meet. Everything can be reversed, repeated, accelerated, amplified, doubled. We lead overdosed lives like people who want to be possessed, and we strive for illuminations and resonances that reveal "The world is vivid. We can become anything." A piece of knowledge I take for my guide: the undercurrent in the noise, the transmissions and receptions, is mutation, metamorphosis, experimentation with the self. The signals may say your identity can be as fluid as an ephemeral image, as mobile as sound. This processing my conjure apparitions, masks, ghoulish hybrids, terrifying specters, and it may make us ponder our nature, what we were, what we are, and what we could be. With all this fired up transformation, it's easy to be deluded about what's true and untrue, to become addicted to power, and to lose your way. That's why I come after balance, the reconciliation of energy and understanding, leaving the whirl behind (if I can), thinking, I'll do without much for a while.

I lean back in the seat, pull up my legs, lay my head on the vibrating window, and I feel how tired I am, fatigued to my core, and I want to sleep, and let the train take me.

* * *

I wake up to sharp voices. The train lurches. Padua, the university city. I don't know how long I've been asleep, but in my compartment four men clutch briefcases and chatter to one another. I sit up and stretch. One man abruptly speaks to me. My Italian is adequate for comprehension, but not strong enough for a full dialogue, so I respond in English. All three men perk up, and our conversation becomes a ferociously fast exchange in a fractured combination of English, French, and Italian.

We talk politics — the internationally recognized subject —

263

and about their businesses, which send them through the European Economic Community, over borderlines. While the train streaks eastward, I begin to smell water in the warm air. We pass villas, swampy land, and apartments that look like prefab cubes transplanted from suburban Toronto. The businessmen explain how life works on the coast. They recommend trattorias, hotels, galleries. When the train pulls into Mestre, the evening sun casts golden lattices of light over the station. I thank the four men for their advice, say goodbye, and push out into town, amazed at how so many people want to point to paths and findings. We're all wandering and probing.

* * *

"Stay in her?" The concierge is wide-eyed.

I've stopped at a two-star hotel so I can cross over the bridge in the morning, entering her slowly, by bus.

"No one stays over there for long!" He suavely gestures with his hands and checks his bow tie. Then he slips his left hand down his white shirtfront and clutches at his chest. He seems to be having a heart attack. "There are palazzi without toilets! She's Euro Disney, but not as well run. And the people! Well. They are...strange."

I'm about to answer that I don't mind any of this, when he, fully recovered, produces a black fountain pen for me to sign the register. An enlistment.

"Do you know most pensioni do not have TVs?" He rocks back on his heels. His bald pate gleams under the ceiling light.

A realm less consuming, the hyperinformation subdued.

"Most stay here." He smiles, showing off a mouth lined with gold fillings. "In luxury."

The hotel's entrance has been painted sky blue with a dark horizon of cupolas and spires that looks suspiciously like a silhouette of that place across the bridge.

"I recommend visitors go to her for only one day."

Weary, I say I'll take my chances, and head to my room, drop my bag, burrow into bed, and fall asleep again.

* * *

The city shrouded in morning mists, a city like a phantom in a cloud. The bus bumps over the causeway, and I feel myself becoming impatient. This bus is crammed with silent people who must work on the other side. Garbage piled on banks, the shallow water basin, and when we pass the sign

VENEZIA

I think, no, that can't be right. The buildings are rotting. In the Piazzale Roma, the bus halts. Everyone piles out, and the driver, a lanky darkskinned man who speaks some English, hauls out my bag from the luggage compartment. "She gets so crowded she closes down. *Basta!* Some say admission will be charged soon!" Taxi drivers quarrel over parking spaces; tourist buses arranged in a semicircle. I smell popcorn, and lift my foot from a pool of sticky pop.

Laughing, the driver sees what must be a stricken look on my face.

"It's off season. She's beautiful before spring. You'll have her to yourself."

I trudge over to the footbridge. Hawkers peddle decals, T-shirts, flags. I suppress my disappointment over the cheapness of the scene and cross the bridge that spans torpid water in a sour-smelling canal, over a smashed gondola run aground on a mudflat, and pick up my pace through the crack between two buildings.

She, they call this city.

The circus clamor falls off behind me. A new sound emerges: my steps echo eerily; a new smell: a salty marsh scent. Shadowed by high walls, under streaks of blue sky wedged above these corridors, I follow a path and pass an open-air market where old men sit at metal tables, mulling over newspapers, indifferent to passersby. In a doorway a huge woman with a broom strokes the back of a longhair cat. It coils and purrs. Tiny sparks of static flare between them. Silver light flashes at the end of an alley.

Sea air, quiet, a slower rhythm.

Where do I turn? My city map is useless. I didn't expect to find dead ends, false fronts, and walls. I walk by shops that display beaked carnival masks, storefronts piled with baskets of fruits and vegetables and fresh baking and meat, turning corners, the slithery corridors leading me somewhere.

Then wave sounds.

Going around a chapel, I step across another small foot-bridge, and I see through a sliver of space that there's an expanse of blue sparkling water filled with gondolas and waterbuses and wooden skiffs, and I step out on a wharf at the water's edge and look over my shoulder at the beautiful surfaces and colors of Venice.

* * *

"*La Serenissima*," the signora at the pensione says.

"Serenity."

"If you like. It's what we call her. I mean that's what we tell people. She goes by many names."

Wordplay. I've been in Venice only half a day and already the signora teases me with glimpses of the city's mystery. She shows me my room in this slim building not far from Saint Mark's, tucked behind what was once Goethe's house. The Venetian rococo style of the place appeals to me. Quiet, clean, private. Near water and moored boats. A destination. A refuge.

"A *scritore*," she says, after I tell her what I'll be doing. She smiles wryly, as if she'd expected me to say something more interesting.

The signora is in her late forties, handsome, of medium

266

height, with what I take to be a northern-Italian look. Her brown eyes, slender face, sleek blond hair pulled back in a ponytail. Uncannily, she appears familiar, resembling photographs of my maternal grandmother when she was young. A coincidence, and yet an inexplicable assertion of the past for me. The signora's manner is brisk but not unfriendly, her English formal. She sounds more ironic than curious.

"Many come but do not like her. They leave after a few days. My husband was a teacher. We are, how you say, separated. People from the mainland. They seldom fit in."

"You have help?"

"My son. And one is never alone here for long."

Voices bank up from below, loudly resounding because the buildings are like canyon walls. Children's laughter blends with footfalls and indecipherable words.

"I'll be staying for a time."

She shrugs.

"We get painters. For the Biennale. Or the light. And professors. For the architecture. Even the occasional visitor who remains. Travelers...of every kind."

When I tell her that I'm fascinated by the strange stillness of the city, her brown eyes glint with humor.

"This won't last if you stay."

* * *

From the balcony off my room, I look out over a canal. A gondolier poles by slowly, standing straight in the stern, singing a melody full of ascending phrases, like questions. An old song about ardent souls. With a powerful calm he guides his empty boat. He seems to imprint the walls and water with his voice. And I turn back to my room, wondering what has truly brought me to this place that poets call the marble forest, the Stone Aphrodite, the city that like Venus rises from the sea.

Wave Reflections

"You have a Toronto accent. I haven't heard it for years," says the man with the coal black hair pulled back, popstar style. He steps away from the crowd in Harry's Bar.

"You've been to Toronto?"

"On a shoot. I used it as a double for New York. No one knew the difference." He smiles at what's obviously a private joke.

So Benjamin Sarnoff introduces himself. I'd come to Harry's Bar late in the evening, after I'd walked through the slender *calli* that wind above the north side of the Grand Canal, near Saint Mark's and the Doge's Palace.

"May I ask you what you're doing here?" He speaks in the overly polite tone that everyone uses in this city.

"Thinking about a book I'm writing."

"In Venice. Where everything has already been said."

"I haven't been here before."

"I remember water in Toronto. Lake Ontario. That wasn't enough?"

"I came for other reasons."

I've walked along canal fronts and watched shadowboats glide in man-made rivers. The slowness of the oaring, the wallowing when the boats pause, the yaw in the dark, a cigarette lit by an oarsman, his face reddens then blackens. The water's sonic peace. I've heard gondoliers skulk out, lonely, finding no customers or traffic that night, oars dipping steadily, quietly.

"I'm scouting locations for a film," Sarnoff says in his guttural rumble, a hint of an accent in his voice.

"About...?"

"Venice sinking. The end."

Now it's my turn to be interested.

"You're a director."

"And a photographer and screenwriter. I make commercials, rock videos, avant-garde documentaries. In Paris. The commercials and videos fund my own work, of course."

Benjamin Sarnoff is tall, in his late forties, wearing a black suit jacket — expensive, tailored — over an open-collar white shirt, torn jeans, and what appears to be handstitched leather cowboy boots. He manages to look dandyish and slummy, almost what you'd expect from a European director. His eyes are lit up, startling. He makes you pay attention to what he says in the bar by rarely raising his voice above a whisper.

"Venice is the perfect backdrop. An art object. Absolutely unnatural. In a state of decay. And she's doomed to sink. A little more each year."

I'm surprised by the automatic way he grandstands. The polished phrases, the quick aphorisms, the theatrical intensity. He's said these things before.

I tell him about my data explorations, how headlines in the media can come to mimic and reflect what happens in your life, my assembling of fragments, memoirs, essays, personal testimony, amalgams of philosophy, criticism, and history. Then I tell him of quiet *calli* at night, nearly deserted canals, the wave reflections on the palazzi under moonlight.

Sarnoff orders a brandy and a cappuccino for himself from a passing waiter, and a soda water for me. I explain that I've stopped drinking alcohol and anything with caffeine since I arrived. To clean myself out, I say. "Such…purity," he murmurs with a smirk. He lights a black cigarette, sits back in his chair at the table we've found by a window, and begins to talk.

"What you've said about searching for patterns. I don't search — I film. I'd rather explode expectations. Film must have exotic space. Artificial worlds displayed as backdrop for human futility. My only principle? Keep the camera moving. The more frantic the scene, the better."

I learn that Sarnoff is an American citizen who lives in Milan, Paris, and Berlin. His father was a journalist for the *International Herald Tribune* in Paris, and his mother was an Italian. She was killed in a car accident in Rome when he was young, and after, his bereaved father took him traveling. "Everywhere," he says. Istanbul. The Dead Sea. Bangkok. The north islands of Japan. "Traveling was my education." He doesn't mention family ties: I have the impression that he travels alone now.

Uneasy, I think he's explaining too much too quickly.

"Why Venice?" he asks.

"Can you think of a better place?"

"Morocco. Japan. Tibet. India. Why so Eurocentric?"

Venice bridges the east and the west, the past and the present. She's a city of transitions, I think to myself.

Instead of saying this, I reply,

"Because I've always wanted to see her. And this time of the year I've found her to be beautiful and still."

"You've found the city's clichés. Pretty sites and pigeons. What is she? Slime and flies beside a cathedral. I love her because she's about to become nothing."

He tenses in his chair, gesturing as if he's shaping a scene in one of his films.

"I want to catch Venice's liquidy end with her whores screaming as the swamp starts to drown them."

Strangely, he seems to be noting every response that I make. It's as if we're both mentally recording the other.

"That isn't what I see."

"What do you think's here?"

"A peaceful place."

"That's the Romantic speaking. There's a Wendy's. Greasy burgers and newsstands selling *Time Magazine* and *GQ*. Italian boys wearing Walkmans that pump hard rock into their brains Don't get carried away. Balance and peace. They don't exist. You've misunderstood her. She has no depth."

"I don't understand."

His eyes are mischievous. "You look for meaning. There's none here or in the media. Image, dazzle, surface. *That's what's good.* Everyone thinks there's more to Venice because of her mystique. Take it from me. She's just a supreme curiosity. With moats."

He's amused by our encounter. But I sense the start of an argument. Before I can interject, he's off, explaining again, striking a pose, clearly taken by his words.

* * *

"In Venice everything is a double for something else. It's why I want to shoot her."

I break into his monologue. "I've been thinking that echoes are links, signs of influence and continuity. The interweaving of all things. It's about call and response, human history talking to us, resurging in our names, in people and their work and desires."

"So you're interested in recurrence. Take the Venetian painters. There are three Bellinis, two Tiepolos, two Tintorettos, two Longhis. You like associations in names? Take Antonio

Canaletto. His name has canal in it."

He pauses to laugh, enjoying his pun.

"And sculptors? There are two Venezianos. There's a librettist called Ponte...bridge. There's echoing in names. Priuli the Doge, Priuli the banker."

He gazes around the bar, appraising the space, it appears, for camera setups, lighting, arresting angles.

"There are misconceptions. Shylock isn't the Merchant of Venice. Gustav Mahler didn't die here. But Wagner did. In the film *Death in Venice*, Visconti made up Dirk Bogarde to look like Mahler and changed Thomas Mann's writer to a composer. Venice's greatest composer is Vivaldi. If you've endured his high-brow Muzak, you know how he repeats himself."

His glance lights on me. Like a framing shot.

"The whole city is supposed to be a Renaissance book filled with correspondences."

I've seen these images of open books in the architecture, their pages etched with hieratic visions, ornamented lettering, unexpected arabesques of initials. The city seems to conceal a wisdom of which I only have inklings.

"And the buildings contain images of tides and energy," Sarnoff says, as if he's heard my thoughts. "Winged lions. Waves. And what does it mean?"

I wait for an answer, realizing that Sarnoff is playing games with me.

"Nothing. You crave connections. My film takes bits from everywhere. Only deconstruct! I'll edit the murder from *Don't Look Now* into an episode from Brideshead Revisited. The city as haven for killers, the city as holy relic. I'll juxtapose David Lean's sentimental *Summertime* with Paul Shrader's *Comfort of Strangers*. The city as lover, the city as killer again. I'll throw Madonna's Like a Virgin video into the James Bond *Moonraker* sequence shot here. And Fellini's masterpiece *Casanova*, with Donald Sutherland dancing with a puppet on a frozen canal. History? I'll have images of

Lord Byron riding his horse in the Piazza San Marco. Promiscuous nuns. Vivaldi fucking the violin section of his all-girl orchestra. Senile doges drooling. Criminals howling as they're hauled across the Bridge of Sighs. Her last days accompanied by rock and roll. Heavy metal bands playing so loud on a barge in the lagoon that her foundations crack."

I expect him to be breathless after his harangue. But he appears to be just getting started. I try to remember if I've seen his films, if I've read his name in newsmagazines. What he describes sounds like the film I saw in the dancebar, the collage of decimated heads. Now he plans to make a pastiche out of Venice, stripping her of her cloak of beauty and mystery and character.

Angered, I tell him, "There are lines of continuity in what you say. Allusions, relationships, themes."

"That's the illusion. Venice is an illusion. The human dream and nightmare made flesh. Pardon me. Made stone. Paolo Sarpi, the greatest Venetian diplomat, said, 'I never tell a lie, but I don't tell the truth to everyone.' Venice is nothing except for people amusing themselves before the shitfilled lagoon swallows them."

* * *

A waiter serves Sarnoff a Remy Martin VSOP, another soda water for me. I'd been so embroiled in his words that I'd forgotten we'd ordered anything. The bar has begun to empty while the night surrounds us.

"If everything is pop culture now," he says gleefully, "then Venice is wonderfully retro. My films come out of parody, irony, cliché. They have no point. Should I apologize for them? Of course. Apology is part of my art. I'm very sorry for what I just said!" he laughs. "You see, I come here because Venice's only invention is herself. Yes, there's the casino...and the ghetto. For Jews —" he pauses, suddenly scowling, "— and the income tax form. Shall we thank her for that?"

Time to let him know that I disagree, to challenge what he's said. But the evening air coming through the open door is mild, cooling, and he's paying for our drinks, and the mood isn't right for debate, so I suggest that we meet again soon to continue our talk.

Benjamin Sarnoff smiles, and turns to look out a window.

Rain

Rain scours away any trace of light and color. She looks stagnant, wizened, gray. The rain exposes an old, raw city.

In my raincoat and hat I walk around the Rialto district. Up the Strada Nuova — the only wide straight walkway I've found — and I see the open markets, flower stalls and cafés shuttered down. Their fronts look grimy. An awful smell wells up from the back canals, the stench of rotting sewage, water that hasn't been flushed out because of sluggish tides. In the rain Venice appears to slouch into pulpy water and mud. Rain hoses down the palazzi, and I'm grateful: it's as if my eyes have been cleared. I see what Benjamin Sarnoff sees; most places need stonework, paint, and support beams.

People retreat into their rooms, hotels, apartments, covered gardens. Bridges vanish behind clouds. Uncrowded vaporetti travel less frequently. Gondoliers jabber sullenly in doorways.

The rain transforms Venice by turning her into a claustrophobic place.

Yet when the rainmists cover the city, she appears to return to another century when there was no electrical wiring, no causeway, no buses or jets. The only way you could get to these islands then was by steamer or hired boat. In this naked state, decrepit and alone, Venice seems stilled, self-contained, detached from what bustles on the mainland. The people here have built bridges to link the districts; but it wasn't long ago that the Venetians constructed the causeway to Mestre. What emerges now in the rain is a mood that seems to accept solitude, and the inevitability of moldy watersteps, blackened arches, and rotted moorings.

Stopping at the Danieli, on the Riva degli Schiavone, I leave a note for Sarnoff, asking him if he'd like to meet tomorrow.

* * *

"Are you going back out tonight?" the signora asks, standing in her pensione lobby.

She's been interested in the walking I do, my "prowling," she calls it. Discreet, reserved, she's still been a good guide for me, knowing where the best views are hidden, what locations are less frequented.

"The streets — I mean the *calli* — are flooded."

"There was a great flood years ago. All of San Marco was under water. Very damaging. Tomorrow they will put planks down for us to walk on. Like little bridges."

"You don't go out in this weather?"

"Do you think anyone would?" She laughs. "You could easily lose your way."

Her humor enlivens her face.

"And do you like the rain?"

"It makes your city look different."

"How so?"

"More rundown. And real."

"She's very real to me. I live here."

"I'm still finding out things about her."

"You will if you want to." She laughs again. Turning to walk to her rooms, she says over her shoulder, "*Buono notte.*"

* * *

The squall peaks furiously after midnight. I get up, swing back the window's shutters, and lean out. The walls are streaming. Water cascades off the ledges. Black sky, and the rain slants down, pounding. It clears off the smell, washing the *calli* and the palazzi, cleaning the canals, opening the city to the rush of the wind.

Finding the Medium

"The question is, what's behind the masks of media power? How can you find a balance for yourself, a way of channeling data? What the messages mean, how truths appear."

"What we are is cracked," Benjamin Sarnoff says, putting on his mirrorshades. "Yesterday I scouted locations in the rain. Churches, palaces. All of them rotting. The only power I have over this is through the caress of my camera lens. I can make an image, a myth. That protects me from facing decay."

We've met in the afternoon, in the café by the water, near the Danieli. The day is warm and clear, and I'm eager to talk.

"Yes, we live in a continual dialogue of masks and faces, images and reality. It's not true that all images, appearances are false. The super-real idols of the media represent authentic yearnings, hungers, needs, and fears."

"This is where you're wrong. The authentic is the illusion. There are only the games we play...whatever you can get away with."

He lights one of his black cigarettes, doing so with a

flourish. As if it's a signal to me or to someone nearby.

"I believe we must accept that we live in a new culture of immersion, sign, sound bite, and computer byte. Transmission, receptivity, and endless variation. One message, many interpretations. All this driven by electricity's presence in our supertechnologies. We have harnessed nature's power itself."

"And what does *that* mean?" He bunches up uncomfortably in his chair, unbuttoning his black silk jacket. Though his jacket is different, he's wearing the same boots and torn jeans he had on two days ago.

"Technology can unbalance us. Information can overwhelm us. We can become lopsided, specialized, out of whack, insensitive through excessive attention to one invention. But each person has to recognize themselves as a medium. I've thought about this for years. It's haunted me. What does it mean to say you're a medium? I'm sure there's a deep meaning here. Our natures are receptive. We feel effects. The causes of those effects seem invisible. The media culture is a sphere of cause, and our bodies are the spheres of effects. Our minds, our souls, are the points of mediation. In other words, I think human beings are the connectors, the go-betweens in the universe. We are the beings between the powers of the cosmos."

He shakes his head, looking skeptical.

"Wait," I say. "There's more. Think of the layers of meaning in the word 'medium.' It refers to a person possessed, speaking in tongues. It also refers to the point of balance, the well-tempered place in our hearts and minds, where we find human measures for raw input. It's the middle way that mystics talk about. The ratio of our senses, moving in a dance of perception. Each person capable of influencing others, leaving traces, the imprint of interpretation."

"You can't achieve a balance in life," Sarnoff declares, almost angrily. "No one can. There's just a glossy surface. I film collages. What makes them work? The seemingly real thing. And obsession. Make people look murderous, sexy, and you've got the beginnings of a mood for a film."

A woman, sitting at a table several spaces away, noisily adjusts a tape recorder. She pops out a microcassette and slams in another, like an efficient terrorist loading a weapon. She holds up a tiny microphone to her mouth, red lips pressed to a silver node.

I continue, "We must deal with what I call projection and emanation. That we can conjure anything. That we underestimate our psychic and sensory ability to take in and change what's around us. We project ideas and intentions on to TV and movie screens, computer terminals and neon ads, and through radio, stereo hi-fi, and the telephone. These technologies emanate their own unique fields. TV, radio, the VDT, fax machines, and the telephone work as passageways, conduits for the electromagnetic current."

"What's real in that?"

"It has something to do with emotion. Love. Loneliness. Pain. Our need to connect. I'm not sure yet..."

"How delightful." He lights another cigarette and frowns into the afternoon light, then twists his chair to the side so that he faces the woman with the tape recorder. He takes off his mirror-shades and stares at her briefly. I turn to her again. Well dressed, elegant, her red hair permed and moussed, she may be an executive taking time to record her thoughts.

Abruptly Sarnoff says,

"Then what?" He squints at me.

I go on from where I stopped. "When we're wrenched out of synch, we become aware of the structures we project and create, the self-reflections and amplifications in the data spill. Now, drugs. I had a friend who wired himself up on coke because I think he wanted to merge with the media's hallucinatory side and the revved-up rhythm of the street. Peaking on waves. But a constant peaking on those waves becomes..."

"An obsession."

"Suicidal. Drugs can be useful for altering awareness. Like

anything you use too much, you can go mad with the highs and lows."

"What happens with this wrenching out of synch?"

"Questions, probes. A perception of what we are, what we do. The struggle to find correspondences."

"How moralistic. And what fictions will you use? God? The Devil?"

"There are tides that push us toward confronting ourselves. The electric media elevate, recall, and tint everything that we are. We should address how media creations mirror, flatter, and stretch us, and the immediacy and speed of that action. This may be why finding a true reflection of ourselves is so difficult. We unleash powerful apparitions and then oppress and perplex ourselves. Behind it all there's the spirit that moves with the energies in our fields. Call it light, sound. It's difficult to articulate. Yet somehow we feel there's a presence in the world other than our own."

"Good God. God! That's not only trite — it's retro! I'll tell you...there's just a city that's a cliché for rock videos. However, I want to film you saying these...unformed ideas."

"How would you use it?"

"In my documentary-fiction about the end of Venice. Lots of talking heads, saying anything."

"It sounds awful."

"Don't worry. It will be."

* * *

After I order a soda water and Sarnoff orders a brandy, we talk on into the evening. People come to the café, linger by the water, then set off, maps and cameras and binoculars in hand. Only the woman with the tape recorder stays seated at her table, busily writing in a notebook, often staring at Sarnoff.

I say, "What we're traumatically experiencing today is the collision of many worldviews. A paradigms clash."

"Explain, please."

"I mean we have many worldviews at once. Competing perspectives. A lot of theories and concepts, not one unified approach. This may be why we suspect there are demons and spirits breathing in the machines. Magicians operating terminals. The supernatural everywhere. Translation — everything's out of control. Where does this impression come from? In part, I think, from the amount of data pouring out from the machines. Our souls feel pushed and pulled. You understand, I'm trying to be lucid. I've been traveling, talking to people, watching far too much TV. I overtaxed myself. I went adrift during my divorce. I felt brittle...uncertain. So I've come to this paradise for exiles, as someone's called her, to think this through, feel it through. I could have gone off to the mountains. Gone canoeing or sailing. But I'm fascinated by cities. These symbols of community, the greatest of all human inventions. In cities you can recognize our longings and worries and aspirations...But back to the changing worldviews. We listen to pundits and experts tell us about what's happening. All this because data runs across borderlines and there don't seem to be any restrictions. All this because the mass-media whirl unleashes our imaginations in repeated images and sound bites. The dreamlife looks real and reality like a dream."

"It *is* a dream. You want meaning when there is none."

"Yet our confusions are real. I think that's why there's a nostalgia for absolutes. It's an imposition of morality on the flux."

"Do you agree with that?"

"It's an intelligible response. But, no. I would say, human receptivity plus energy. We have to recognize the living creature with a soul. We must be aware of what we're tapping into. We draw lines, yet the lines of definition always change."

"Is this possible?"

"Intelligent growth depends on it."

"You're shockingly naive. People prefer absolutes. They love hardlines or decadence. It's easier to say no. Or yes to everything. Which is what I do. You want understanding when people want only what's right or wrong."

"I ran into this with the televangelists. The media force-fields bring pure dynamism. And we seek restraints. Or continuous ecstasy, and release. We have to figure out how to be humane mediators between nature's power, our technologies, and our own restless reactions."

"No car accidents or teenage lust? It'll never sell."

I notice the woman at the other table packing up her notepad and tape recorder, winding up the black cord from the microphone. She glances at Sarnoff and nods slowly. The waiter standing behind me starts writing out a check.

Sarnoff leans over the tabletop. His eyes gleam.

"People aren't explorers by nature. They want safety, secondhand pleasures, a steady income. This is where I come in. I love voyeurism. I'm not concerned with moral effects. The past is nothing but backdrop. What do you recommend? The open life. People will never tolerate it."

His moods flip rapidly. He seems inflamed now, intent on imposing his ego, turning our debate into a test, a battle.

"And you?" Sarnoff swerves in his seat like a man angling for the right position to see a view. "Your attachments. All these ideas flying around. You travel alone. Working, writing, you say. I don't want to intrude, but I wonder about...all these pieces."

The terrifying freedom of the solitary. Why I'd come to Venice: to find a shape for myself.

"What do you put against the open life?" I ask.

"Thrills. Sex. Good and evil as necessary plot devices. A grab for attention."

"And what'll be left for you?"

"An aroma. A touch. A momentary obsession. I find fragments to film. Bits to be edited together as I see fit."

"We've had a century of fragments. All falling back into nothingness. Meaningless drift. Maybe it's time to see things whole. A great radiant network."

He sits back, glowering, his eyes showing conflicted responses.

"The point is, we don't change. We can't." He shakes his head. As if he's repeating no, no, no. "Nothing's connected...it's all...accidents, flight...and the dreamlife...always fading...into a blank."

* * *

Night, and I walk back to my pensione, dissatisfied with what I've said, with what I didn't say. My thoughts are only beginning to achieve articulation. I rerun in my mind the picture I have of Sarnoff shaking his head, retreating into a broken reverie. Old emotions inhabited his words.

The city is ghostly. There's only the sound of waves splashing against docks and poles, watersteps and seawalls. Then I hear the chatter and music of a party somewhere. I walk and think about Sarnoff and his provocative nihilism, wondering if we've actually had an exchange of ideas or another in a series of blind monologues.

* * *

Cloudless sky. A morning doldrum, the water alleys silted. A soft hot mist smothers the city. The walls of the waterside palazzi dry and flake; the cracks in the stones seem to widen. Dazed walkers sway and blink. We are being turned by a furnace into sluggish creatures who are weighted down by closeness and haze and sweat.

Around noon I decide that I've got to find the wind. I climb into the vaporetto for the Giudecca. Once I'm ferried across the basin, I walk around the island, feeling a slight breeze from the sea. I return to my room late, and it isn't until the evening of the following day that I go to the Danieli and call on Sarnoff.

* * *

"He and his wife checked out this morning," the wiry man at the reception desk says. He's aloof in the Venetian manner, courteous but detached, observant, almost suspicious.

"His wife."

"She is his...collaborator. Carries a tape recorder every-where. Interviews people on the spot. I have been...interviewed myself."

"I think I was too."

"So you know who I mean." The Venetian aloofness can become curt.

I sense that he knows more.

"Did he leave a forwarding address?"

"A note. A name. You? Ah. You're to write to him in...Paris. Yes. Most concerned that you get the message. I understand he's negotiating for...a perfume commercial."

I take the note and glance at the contents. There's an address, a phone number, a request not to break our dialogue. I'd been so wrapped up in my thoughts that I hadn't asked him how long he was staying. And I remember the woman at the table with her tape recorder. I'd arrived too late today, missed the contact. It would be some time before I'd have the chance to talk to Sarnoff again. His taunts and games. These glimpses and unanswered questions.

Saying to the man behind the desk, "Thank you." Putting the note in my pocket.

* * *

At the foot of the *riva* black gondolas bob in the surf. A waterbus carries eager tourists over to the Lido. Reflections ripple and dis-solve in the water. I think of Sarnoff, his apocalyptic film, and our uncompleted thoughts, and I think of how I've recorded people because I'm pursuing leads and overtones, because I'm hungry to discover the web between people and events and themes. He'd pointed out the irony that I'd chosen to stay in Venice, where the air is changeable, all meetings are transient, and nothing is what it appears to be.

She's an antique cipher endlessly mirroring herself, drawing visitors with the appeal of refreshment and of linkage with the past.

This city was once a book of messages that we're no longer sure how to read.

Pulse

I enter an empty movie theater. No ushers take my ticket. Yet I have
an invitation, so I sit down, staring at the massive white screen, the
plush red curtains draped beside the stage, the plastercast nude
women who kneel, praying over the exits.

Then she appears, spellbinding me, her face crested with
rich blond hair, her perfume permeating the space. She's dressed
in plain blue jeans and a loose brown sweater. Her skin is flushed
and damp as if she's just emerged from a bath. Her fine features,
blue eyes, full lips. *You know me*, her eyes say, *my body's scent was
left on yours.*

Uneasy, I bolt to another part of the theater. I glance to my
side and she's there, wearing a filmy white dress, slimfitting, showing off her delicate neck, pale bare shoulders, her browntipped nipples. She eases her left hand into my lap, her fingers stroking me into
hardness. Tenderness, such tenderness. The theater and the screen
have none. Only her presence, alluringly alive, is moist and warm.

I escape again. But I find her beside me, wearing transparent clothes that glow, revealing her silky skin, her flat stomach and

firm thighs. I change my seat because I'm anxious about my insistent desire for her. She reaches across for me, and I want to be finally intimate with her, our bodies snugged, arching, coupled deeply in the promise of an engagement that would be rooted in her, and I want to enter between her shapely hips, the lips of her sex slippery and open and welcoming, then come inside her like a flood, breathing in her scent, collapsing exhausted, then starting over with her tracing her tongue down my chest, tasting, sucking, licking.

I invest her with such intensity that she suddenly melds into a stream of women, all similar, until she becomes one, honey-hair trimmed short. I run to another seat, and she's there, caressing my face, staring without blinking, saying, again through her eyes, *Have you moved yet*?

* * *

I'm lost in the early morning. Venice leads me around and around on fluid pathways. Under some spell, I pace over bridges, circling through boatyards and piazzas, everything unrecognizable, everything jarring. I think of the woman in my dream: could I answer her question? did I want to know who she truly was?

I take off in the afternoon on the vaporetto for Murano, where I see artisans blowing glass into delicate shapes, and on to Burano, where I watch fishermen on docks patiently mending their nets. Arrive back on the main island after eleven p.m., and walk again, ending up near the island of San Elena. Staring out into darkness. By the lagoon I smell the marshes, their lush fragrance in the breeze.

I consider Sarnoff's nihilism, and I remember the people I've met in Toronto, offering interpretations, translations, searching, creating, juggling patterns of order and chaos. What have we been doing? Stung by curiosity and perplexity, rage and restlessness, by what we think is the radical randomness of our experience, we prod ourselves toward the alchemy of sense, codebreakers asking for the pulse of meaning from machines, objects, the hardface of the megacity, and each other.

And in the Renaissance Venice was always called she.

Now I know what my dream was telling me. I must open myself, somehow lighten my mind. Breathe in the sweetened air. Walk over the bridges. Surrender to this city's mysticism and sensual abundance, soul and wind and water.

Listening City

Universal Circuitry

"*Americano?*"

Startled, I look up from my lunch.

"No, *Canadese.*"

The waiter grins, runs his hand through his pomaded hair, and then rubs his stubbled cheek.

"I have a sister who lives in Toronto! I'm sure you don't know her!"

He laughs happily, and juggles a plate in his other hand.

At a waterside café, eating carpaccio and green fettucine — spending extra money today — I've been listening to the waves, their lap and hiss.

"And it's close to America. Your country."

"Yes, close."

"All so new."

"Brand-new."

"Must be wonderful. So exotic."

"Exotic?"

"The land, money, space. Close to America and yet not

America. Rich girls looking for things to do. Italy is crowded. And *Venezia* — she's so old."

He scampers around the table, outside the umbrella's shade, smiling, gesturing with his free hand. His apron billows in the wind. He's wearing a T-shirt underneath that shows Madonna dancing.

"Your English is good." I realize too late how condescending this sounds.

His black eyes darken.

"Sure. I learned my English from Prince CDs."

"You'd like Toronto." I note his sarcasm.

He brightens again.

"How long have you been here?"

"Some time now."

"What do you do?"

"I'm learning." I smile.

"Then you're no longer a tourist! You're a guest!"

Sitting here, I feel how the city revives after the doldrums of the days before. Reverberant life. I hear things that come from miles away — liners entering the lagoon, tankers anchoring outside the sluices — and I hear things close up — frittering chat in the cafés, shouts from people summoning others who've disappeared down a pathway. When the wind churns, it carries the sounds of shiphorns and gulls calling and motorboat ignitions, and it seems to be full of intelligences, old souls speaking through the *calli*.

Snapping waves, whitecaps far off from shore. Spray jets like liquid crystal from passing cabs.

Seagulls wheel above fleets of gondolas. Foam lathers in the stone moorings' crevices and cracks.

Today I sense that I've truly become a part of Venice at last, come into her refreshing embrace, the kiss of water and wind.

I think of Toronto, the city of images and mirrors. That place can hustle and overload you; it's an environment of power and noise. What is the answer to the riddle of Venice? If she has an occult destiny and intention, it may be to inspire listening, a quiet receptivity in yourself, to make you aware of the channels and the water, green wakes becoming blue surges.

I sit looking over Renaissance maps reproduced in a history book that I bought at a stall yesterday. Canals lead into the city's heart; channels lead out. A lagoon surrounds the main islands. I leaf through the copies of maps sketched by Giacomo Fianco, Matteo Merian, and Giovanni Andrea Vavasorre. Obviously none of them saw their city from the sky, so they must have drawn their maps in part through intuition. These subtly suggest an ear and a womb. The rounded shape, the sinuous canals. Crestbreaker and seashell. To catch the ebbflow, all the resonances of the sea and the sky.

The hiss in the water...

The shape of the Great Snake in the Grand Canal...

Music forms a way of understanding...

A dialogue between a city and nature...

The wind blowing, love the sound. This is a Pythagorean aphorism and tenet: all things in nature manifest themselves through melody, variation, rhythm, a striving for harmonies, vital accords.

And what about the name Venice itself? It may have evolved from the Hebrew word *phenice* (origin of Phoenician? and possibly of phoenix?), meaning a palm tree, the emblem of creativity, a symbol of the spirit and of renewal.

This is my initiation into Venice. She must be a city devoted to balancing the elemental with the invisible — like one vast duct and flute, a human guide for the air and water currents — to restoring and vivifying touch, smell, taste, sight, and especially hearing. I feel the crosswinds from the sea, taste the faint trace of salt in the wind, and breathe in the tinges of wisteria, gardenia, and salt hay.

Only there isn't any earth here. Venice is entirely man-made, an artificial island secured in sand by wood and stone, built around 410 A.D. by Romans fleeing the butchery of the Goths. The city is a product of ingenious engineering, of imagination and reason working together. And what did its architects secretly, artfully design? A city that is a musical instrument, playing the morning hush, the day's buzz, the night's murmur.

And as I sit, absorbing the talk of passersby — the tonic of their speech — I realize how the buildings and docks conduct sound and conversations, modulate pitch and volume, seemingly let accents rise with the channeled wind. Her mood isn't disdainful or aloof. I'd thought that her serenity came from her age, the solitude and world-weariness, but it seems to have developed from how the stones and the canals amplify a gull's cry, the wind's sweep, a woman calling, and the water's slap.

Plato, in the *Critias*, talked about Atlantis, the lost city of a higher civilization, where networks of bridges and canals joined the various parts of the island kingdom. The myths about Atlantis seldom emphasize how in that place the timbre of human voices must have always traveled in the air.

* * *

Twilight I cross the Ponte dell'Accademia, heading for Calle Querini. The mad Ezra Pound lived out his last days here. Crazed people escape to Venice to be soothed. In this house, number 252, at the end of the closed footpath, Pound brushed aside *The Cantos*, his long poem, calling it fractured, foolish, self-pitying, unredeemable, a work without cohesion or a single point of view, its structure a shambles, his life a failure. He wrote nothing more. Yet he's said to have remarked to a visitor, "Only emotion endures." Other poets have repeated and amended this line which implies that all objects and structures are impermanent.

I've wondered what he meant by emotion. Merely feeling? No, he intended more. I'm beginning to think that he was pointing to the living presence of the past, the value of making connections now, the intangible potential of the future, the inner being of your passion and imagination, the struggle to grasp the invisible source of life, the moving spirit that can only be intuited and heard, what we call the knowledge of the heart.

Near Pound's house, skiffs and barges strain at their moorings. The decks roll, bows dip, wood heaves. Wind over the water, light on the waves.

What endures here is the wind's stirring of the water and air, and the stirring of your senses. People visit and depart, adding their voices, leaving their echoes.

Morning

Vivid spring light through my windows. I wake up early, wash quickly under the shower that spurts hot and then frigid water, and after I dry off, I know it's time to wander again. Slowly memories of my divorce, of all the people I've listened to and talked to, of disconnections and confusions and overdoses, absorb me less. I'm shuttering up these experiences.

I dress, pack up my shoulderbag for the day, take out a notebook and writing pad from my suitcase for the first time since I arrived. Words, thoughts on paper, reestablishing continuity, direction for myself.

I pause to listen to the watersound of the canals. Shafts of warm light stream into my room. I feel alive, everything fine edged, and I walk down the hall stairs and out the pensione door as if the *campo* will stand newly revealed, a voice whispering in my ear — travel on — keep sensing the waves that are inside you and outside you.

But ease your pace. Idle for a while. Explore these islands.

So today I'm out-tripping to the Lido, and I board a half-full vaporetto at the Piazzale San Marco. Cross the basin, out to the Giudecca, where Michaelangelo once lived. Past the island of Saint George, by Andrea Palladio's church, the architectural structures precise and yet almost preternatural in their harmonious shapes. Passing channel markers as if we're motoring through a watery maze. Dock at the Lido. And soon I'm ambling along the beach, watching the morning break over the gulf. A few swimmers shiver in the surf. Shrieks and gull cries carry across the water's luminous surface. And it seems to me that the world is waking up to speak.

"There's no drift, only current."

I turn this phrase over in my mind. It has lodged with me since I first read it in a book on Eastern mysticism. I mull over the statement's enigmatic quality while I stroll. The strangeness, beauty, and ambiguity of those words.

I stop on the beach and realize how it's taken me years to approach their meaning.

What does the phrase mean? Your experience may seem aimless, desperate, desolating, broken by accidents and mistakes, fragmented without hope of wholeness and with your identity dissolving, uncentered, divorced from all correspondence with others, but if you remain receptive, vulnerable to the process, you will learn, and maybe heal. We think we can arrest this fierce education, the flow of life, even though what we can truly do is teach ourselves about the snap and drive of the rough current, sometimes riding it, sometimes overwhelmed by it, building outlets, becoming mediators, learning to reconnect, about kindness, attachments, defects, patience, and need. I went searching so hard for the pattern that would explain everything that my life was consumed in the fastforward. This is what I'd thought, how I'd felt. In some unexpected way I was making my self open, teaching myself about change. I'd needed a spiritual crisis just to find out how to recognize the marvel of man-made islands that live in a perpetual complement with water and wind and light.

Twin girls splash, squealing, into the surf. Fair-skinned,

darkhaired, they leap and giggle when the waves lick their toes and ankles. A tall woman peels off her dressing gown, tucks up her dark-red hair in a white bathing cap, steps hesitantly into the water. She stays close to the girls. Their mother? She's a picture of affection and tender protectiveness, but she lets them wade in deep for themselves.

An old couple shuffles toward a table on the beach. Arm in arm, the man and woman support each other, while apparently complaining and bickering. They smile tensely at me, waving with their free hands, and I wave back.

Climbing up a slope to the footpath, I hike east along the ridge.

And I think of how the current can shock you, seemingly misdirect you. In an amok information field, we receive tips, leads, rumors, feeds, a constant recoding of facts and figures, all of them manic, clamorous. I see the mass media in some perspective now: the radical reshaping of time and place, the systems that can be used for recreation and misinformation, both the heightening and the leveling of experience. We flaunt ourselves through the speakers and screens: we exhibit both the mundane and the extreme. And when you think you've edged toward a core of truths, you may be turned away by a ghost, a lie, a false line. These may be conjured by people who are sincere or passionate, those who are fanatical or corrupt, those who are self-deceived or unformed. Yet if the data rush absorbs you, then the acoustic disclosures and visual revelations, and everything we are, and could be, become at once familiar, tight, fast, strange, and we're singed by promise and dread.

* * *

The hot sun inspires people to flood the beach. I breathe in the salty air with its mingled scents of skin-tanning oil, coffee, and sweet flowers. Teenage girls boldly shuck down to string bikinis, inexplicably leaving socks on their feet, their skin already tantalizingly tanned. Boys shout seductions, sauntering by.

People respond to one another, teased out into the open by the light.

* * *

Drawn back to the beach, I slip off my clothes, down to my bathing suit, and swim out in the silky water. It's warmer near the shore than I'd expected, colder the farther out I go. Kicking forward, I feel the water's press, the mild undertow, then I breaststroke toward land. I flip over onto my back, the water cushioning me, the sun on my face, then I roll and dive, swimming submerged, listening to the slower voices and movements underwater before I surface again.

* * *

My room in the evening. Turning to the windows, I see pale-blue sky. If it's light that's mesmerized me – light in both its technological and natural appearances — then it's sound and rhythm that continue to haunt me. Softly waves crest in the *rio*. This water is making a gentle music. I linger, listening, and look at how the sun at twilight transmutes the colors of the buildings, turning them orange, and gold, and white.

There's no drift, only current.

Magnetic Storm

Thunder rumbles like a missile barrage. A whirlwind of rain. Lightning bolts and streaks illuminate skyscrapers in the darkness. Discharges punch through clouds, rocket off buildings. It's Toronto X-rayed.

The city has declared war on the elements. Air-raid sirens scream. Emergency calls Doppler up and down the concrete blocks. Searchlights trace weird sky designs. A hellish battle zone of tracers and flares erupts. Heat-seeking missiles fire at clouds.

The sky retaliates with thirty million volts, two thousand lightning strikes per second. The heated air expands and thunder rolls, answering the stunning cacophony on the ground. Veins in the sky. Rain pours down in torrents, beating on cement and sheet metal.

I'm driving a car, rushing down a hill. The inside of a car should be a safe place during a storm. Rubber tires usually act as grounding. But I don't feel safe. The car skids ahead. Nothing happens when I press both feet on the brake pedal.

The sky is ripped apart. Lightning shoots overhead. Lasers

and searchlights cut through one another's beams. The air is fiery but cold.

I watch the sky storm and the ground defences become one, battery fire and flash chains entangling. Who's reloading the guns? What's triggered the combat between the city and the sky? There's no time to ask questions. I fight to regain control of the wheel, squirming in my seat. But the car picks up speed.

Rain drenches the sidewalks. Lampposts and streetsigns sway in the windblast. Anti-aircraft fire streaks red in afterburn. Missiles intercept lightning. Sirens wail their song of meltdown.

The motor races. Wheels spin. And I keep thinking, I know how to direct this car; I know how to resist this tumble toward violence, the war for domination and the meshing of nature and technology.

* * *

Calming light. The aroma of baking bread. The pensione humming with warmth and friendliness. Wings flutter, a soft cooing: pigeons flock on my window ledge.

I lie back in my bed, willing the sense of danger and fear from my mind.

I've had dreams about the power in the city before. But this one had a murderousness that I hadn't experienced. Images of the city under fire. The city had struck back, its technologies of defense seemingly autonomous and dynamic, and utterly vicious. Where were the people? It had looked as though the city, the weapons and machines, the rain and the storm, cared nothing for humanity. Only unbridled force mattered — power for its own sake.

I sit up and fold back my white sheets. Though I've spent some months now in this serene city of art, Toronto's powercult asserts itself again.

* * *

A light breakfast in a café near the Rialto.

By the market, up from the Calle dei Fabbri, close to people exploring the shops, I find a seat in the sun. I look over the mooring's edge and see emerald water turn blue, then emerald again, a beautiful transformation. Motor launches and vaporetti shear across one another's bows and sterns. Barges loaded with fruits and vegetables putter toward the bridge. A traffic jam in the Grand Canal. People argue, shout, laugh, swear. A seacab's wake sprays down like a sudden cool shower.

I change tables for a dry spot, take out my notebook and pen and begin to write:

The city went to war with nature in my dream. The sky exploded; rain pelted the towers. It was as if the city had somehow summoned the attack, brought down the thunder. I'd watched from inside the car while buildings became lightning rods and launch pads for missiles. It had been terrible, and impressive. Light had been shooting across the dark.

My perspective was in motion because of the hurtling car. And yet, though the flare guns and defense missiles had fired, I hadn't witnessed a retaliatory annihilation of the city. No smoldering holes pocked the ground where houses had once stood. There had been no surrender.

In my dream I hadn't been able to look away from the detonations. I was riveted by the fury. The city battled the cosmos through the spirit of technology. They jostled each other for mastery, for hierarchy and space. Who was going to win?

It was to be technology or nature. But the missiles and the lightning fused, becoming indistinguishable. Again, there were no people present. Yet what could our role be? Mediation: to balance these extremes of force, finding a humane medium for the allure of mercilessness and destruction, taking the fury in ourselves and our world and turning it toward creation.

I sit back, thinking, remembering:

Lightning burns and creates. It's a symbol of the sacred, of divine wrath, and of new life. The city is a symbol of society's doctrine, of enterprise and shelter.

My dream images showed what the ancient philosophers called the element of fire. The dream may have been about the primordial mind of electricity, the consciousness of energy itself, that drive to scorch, melt down, innervate, and remake.

Toronto.

We've become maddened creators in that city, accelerating nature's flux, accumulating data, doubling information every year through computers — with systems' people collating and storing input without any philosophical center or focus, thus all of it incoherent, aleatory, its gist and intent buried — erecting towers that compete with the sky, shortening seasons by affecting the air and displacing weather fronts, setting up the potential for AI in those computers (forged sensibilities made of microchips and wires that could one day rival our paranoias, longings, and hopes), conjuring cinematic and televisual apparitions that ricochet back to us, so that we ask, "Who are we? What are we doing? Why is all this here? Where are we going?" because we have surrounded ourselves with images and mirrors and sound bites, the spunk of permanent genesis, ignited life constantly hovering on the edge of catastrophe.

I write down in my notebook:

Storms can cause outages. The paradox is an outage can be a blackout, a shock, a shattering of routines and rituals, and it can be a moment when the darkness is brightened, when meaning pours into you. Powerlines cable many angles, theories, stories. It's the world of contraries joining. Electric lines can amplify every tone and voice, and the TV signal can intensify and obscure any expression or gesture or action or statement. The media can enliven and deform experience and their messages can be both right and wrong, a blessing and a burden, a balm and a disaster. The current generates fields that stimulate life, simulate it, and admit all.

* * *

Water splashes against the dock. I glance up from my notebook. The vaporetti are full of people. Each day more tourists jam Venice. Yet this crowding doesn't disturb the concentration that I've redis-covered in myself.

I spend the rest of the morning and then the afternoon walking to the Arsenale, crossing *rios* down to Via Garibaldi, out to the island of San Pietro and the park by the lagoon.

Toronto and Venice. Uncommon magnetic fields. One a place that crystallizes force and expansion, one a place for replen-ishment and recovery.

I plan to stay only a few more days. I've overspent my time, and I'm almost out of money. I'll have to resee Toronto. They were redesigning it when I left, and it'll be new, another place, when I walk down the streets. Toronto may seem small to me, a jumped up city aspiring to be Tokyo, New York, Los Angeles, London, Rome. Like a tourist, I'll want to see everything, because I know how dif-ferent everything will be when I go home.

Through the window of my pensione last night, my city came calling, bringing the roar of turmoil and more elaborations of data, and the next century rising.

Serenity's Echo

Sounding

Sun, warm air, and clear skies.

It's my last afternoon in Venice, and after I eat lunch, I stroll near the Accademia, and think about a story of blindness and listening that may be true.

"I am the last Venetian," Jorge Luis Borges is said to have proclaimed during his only visit to the city. Borges was blind, hobbled by arthritis. He had to be guided through the *calli* and the deceptive pathways, *campi*, and piazzas, by the scholars and translators who'd invited him.

Why did Borges call himself the last Venetian? I believe he'd discovered a Venice within, of the imagination, a place he'd visited many times in his mind to be spiritually refreshed. His Venice was an ideal, transcendent world that he carried with him everywhere. And when he uttered his riddle to his audience of bewildered scholars, he acknowledged a blind man's fact. Tapping your way across narrow bridges, down stone walks, through crowds, you have to let the soundings and echoes lead you. The probing must be done with trust, love, and the ability to respond to reality and to remake it in your mind. When the blind man moved his world moved with him.

Borges presented his hosts with a conundrum. Venice is a republic of the imagination, the property of dreamers, but the imagination also enhances, influences, and molds reality. What we dream criticizes and challenges and even changes what and where we are. This may be the true process of learning and understanding: the joining of the imagined with the real.

But the Venetians will have to imagine daring structures if they want to save their city. Dams, sluice gates, water purifiers, and new foundations. Engineers and technicians desperately work to install machines for the purposes of drainage and to control the overflow of garbage and silt. This attempt to store her up makes me think of the challenge we face in the electroscape. Rigid and conventional frames of reference don't help us to travel well. They don't fully prepare us for the jolts, and cries, and breakdowns. Like Borges, we are blind travelers, carrying with us a dream of beauty and connection, making our way through often treacherous terrain, without maps to guide us during our journey into reforged, unframed realities.

I look at Venice, and I listen to her. She's an exhausted whore and a gorgeous relic. I've found a tourist package, a set for movies, this debauched Disneyland.

Visitors know that the city may sink. They come because she soothes us and yet defies us with her Renaissance ideals. Here art, science, commerce, and politics had once been a whole. World without fragments, all things intertwined. Her presence seems to condemn us for our lack of insight, our inability to completely imagine the possibilities of our time. She reminds us that great dreams can be made into a reality. Venice is lit from within with the remnants of a visionary gleam.

Fugitive city, refuge city. The Venetians chose water rather than walls for their protection. The Piazza San Marco and the Doge's Palace were designed to be accessible, open. Pirates, brigands, ex-slaves, and traders made the floating place a point of departure for profit, exploration, philosophy, meditation, and a republican experiment (relative to the tyrannical theocracies that ruled elsewhere). They sent their ships out to survey coastlines and secure trade routes, battling enemies and finding allies, returning to mysterious inner canals and villas. I can almost feel the drive of those souls who dreamed of an island city and fought to bring her into existence. It wasn't until she fell to Bonaparte in seventeen ninety-seven that the Venetians retreated into secrecy, and she became a place of masks and sexual temptations, a buoyed up antique.

I think of Borges, tapping his way. The old man had accepted the solitude of his vocation, the necessity of grasping paradox, and the importance of dreaming beyond what's in front of you. He must have known that the aging city could shrink him, disappoint him, so he imagined a Venice out of time. He may have been trying to tell his audience that only through inner light and transcendent music can we restore coherence and then bridge back to the difficult world. The last Venetian could be the first visitor to a new realm.

* * *

I have a long way to go before I understand such a vision. As I stand on the path beside the church of Santa Maria delle Salute in the late afternoon, looking across the basin to the island of Saint George, I think of people tapping the ground of their lives like impatient diviners searching for lost subterranean sources. I know how distant I am from Venice. I'm surprised to feel that way. I'd hoped for truths that are less difficult, less paradoxical.

Gulls swoop, picking at half a *panino* in the glimmering waves. The gulls sweep off, squabbling. Plastic *aqua minerale* bottles, greasy water, garbage in the flecks of light.

Lots of questions, few answers.

311

I've come this far only to find that I may have hardly moved at all.

* * *

I'd tried to resist the barewire aggression that I'd found in Toronto. I thought that I'd absorb the peace, the worldly detachment of Venice. Now I recognize that the way forward for me will have to be the way back. "No one lives in Venice anymore," the concierge in Mestre had hinted. He'd been both right and wrong. You can't live here for long. She would leave you feeling bodiless, weightless, like a ghost.

Venice probably won't survive the corrosive poisons in the water and air, another by-product of our supertechnologies. But she reminds us of the energies that were released when imagination and reason, intellect and passion, greed and wisdom, vision and pragmatism combined. Her architecture and art symbolically speak of nature's currents and fields, and of humanist mediation. I think she may even hold a blueprint for the future, like a prophetic model of a space settlement, a world among the stars, kept afloat by lightsails, receptive to solar winds.

The language of bridges, the language of waves, of ebb and flow. These are the hardest to hear over a modern city's din. I'd lost the human rhythm. A deafened person can be the one who's the most out of balance. And I'd often forget to feel for the heartbeat under the data pockets, blocks, and streams, the information rosetta.

* * *

Chattering tourists pass. They're from Saskatchewan or Alberta, judging by their accents. Or Americans from the Midwest? I can't tell. Guidebooks in hand, they're clearly anxious to make use of what must be a short visit.

312

A surprisingly annoyed tour guide describes the sites. She sputters, prattles, her English strongly accented by a northern Italian dialect. She points to buildings, offers her oral Baedecker. The tourists laugh, nod, and produce from their shoulder bags the inevitable expensive camera equipment.

Shutter clicks, a Handicam hum, a zoom lens whir. Another attempt to freezeframe experience, to capture and reproduce later this relic in the flux. These tourists are explorers too. They'll remake the city in their way, with their memories and VHS tapes, slides, and glossies, when they go home.

The harassed-looking guide leads her group past the water-steps by the church, and all disappear around a white wall.

I take out my notebook from my shoulder bag and look through the pages for a quote I'd written down.

> Knowledge has two extremes that meet. The first is the pure ignorance man is born in. The second is attained by those of lofty spirit who, having traversed all that men can know, find that they know nothing and are back where they started. But theirs is a wise ignorance that recognizes itself for what it is. The people in between these two extremes have escaped the first ignorance without reaching the second. Under the color of a useful knowledge they seem knowing — and they confuse the world by mistaking everything...
>
> Pascal in his *Pensées*.

"Wise ignorance." I'd like to think that this is what I've found. Suddenly my doubts gnaw into me again. Fumbling forward, sometimes unable to understand what I've heard and seen, I'm one of those people between the extremes. I'm tempted to make the obvious joke about a Venetian blind or about being caught in a Venetian bind. But finally I admit to myself what I've sometimes sensed: I'm unequal to this task, I don't get the message,

I've projected too much complexity. The communications remain contradictory, and I can't really make out the words, the melody, the underlying harmony, the murmuring in the channels.

I stand on the white stonesteps of Santa Maria della Salute. Gondolas glide on the Grand Canal. Black and sleek, one with a silvertipped bow slips through diamonds of light.

I admire this gondolier's way of navigating. He patiently oars with the knowledge that's been passed on to him and that he's earned through experience. Oscar Wilde found the gondolas resembled hearses. The red and blue shrouds draped over the hulls, the implacable cool of the gondoliers. But the boatman to me is an emblematic figure who's learned from the waves. He skims over the water, his motions confident, silent. He appears content to repeat his gestures, apparently unworried about whether the currents will ever be entirely knowable to him.

While the afternoon sun tints the palaces, hotels, and churches with yellow and orange and gold, he eases his gondola over lightstruck waves.

Twilight

Twilight. Sea blue. Water like glass. The wind keeps brushing the sky clear of clouds. Soon the night will be marked by stars. The European evening, full of repose and elegance and Renaissance magic. I pick up impressions. Red glows bob in the basin. A cloud billowing from the Piazza San Marco turns out to be pigeons orbit ing upward, condensing suddenly into a dark mass, then flying apart, vanishing like smoke over the rooftops, leaving a distant beating in the air, ascending, fluttering out. Venice cradles these changes of light and mood, loving them.

Evening comes. The cafés and churches become shadows. I walk along the Giudecca Canal on the Accademia side.

And in my mind's eye, I see the blind man again. Huddled in a gray coat, a hat pulled low, feeling ahead with his cane. The image could fit many who fled frenzied times to live here. Dante, Byron, Browning, Wagner, Pound. Some of them fleeing the threat of imprisonment; some of them love-haunted; some of them deranged or ill; some of them travelers at the peak of their fame or notoriety. I see the blind man walking hesitantly, his steps sounding over the water, and at my back, when I go home, I'll always hear that tapping, rhythmic, continuous, and exploratory...

Dusk blends into night.

Darkness descends over the city. Her mood gradually softens. This Saturday night becomes darker and darker.

And continuing in my mood while I walk, I see a different image of a blind man. Sinister, black. A figure scrapes along a battlement. His shuffle tortured, imperiled.

An image from Akira Kurosawa's *Ran*, his chaos. In the final tableau of that film, a blind poet-priest who has lost faith in his God, lost the flute for his music, lost his family and inheritance, lost all chance for rescue or redemption, taps his way along the ruined walls of his father's castle. The foreground shows the mass of mourning troops, the funeral for the sons of the king. This is the bitter side of turbulence — endless turmoil, the obliteration of laws, rituals, institutions, and responsibilities — and a blind man teetering on the brink of the abyss, incapable of moving either backward or forward, paralyzed by fear. Madness without compassion, a red hole ripped in the sky, families like a slaughterhouse, brutality and arrogance reigning, and a powerless wanderer, edging into the hollow...

An image from a movie. The story of someone else's desperation. In Kurosawa's view, chaos must always lead to nihilism, savage anarchy. I glance across the blue canal, to the island of Saint George, realizing how hard it is to leave the powerful media reflections of others behind. I've had to find what disorder means for myself.

Wind ripples the water. Wine bottles churn in an oil slick. Nearby on the shores of Mestre lie the oil refineries, the heavy industries, and the docked tankers of the transnationals. These ships are funded by the brokers of the borderless community. They could either allow Venice to perish or they could keep these islands alive. This is what's here and now...

We may be losing our ability to imagine visionary cities. All our cities seem to become Babels, ambitious, mad, and ultimately destructive. But the imagination, the skill, the intensity, and the will that shaped Venice must bring monsters — like the acid that devours the foundations of an elegant villa. It's no answer for me, or for anyone, to withdraw and hide in virtual or cybernetic zones. Here by these canals, the pollution sets in. The rot erodes the hotels, palazzi, and docks, the art and the churches, and we are unwilling to face how abrasive the acids can make us too. The corrosions in the air and water can bring a corrosion in ourselves. But these canals bring both currents, acidic and renewing. That's what the waves carry, the wisdom they convey..

I thought that I'd said goodbye to the fraying I'd felt in me. In the noise of Toronto, I'd heard the competitive clamor, the poignant expressions of estrangement, the craving for space and attention, the frenzy for release. But even here I see bilge stuck like unbridled greed on a door of a sinking palazzo. There are no guarantees that a murderous force in Toronto, in Venice, or anywhere, can be stopped, that the overloaded air and the data rampage won't harden us, make us shut our eyes and ears. The cityroar may override and drown out what breathes truly inside us, ushering in the terrible chaos that Kurosawa depicted...

I wave to a seacab to stop. The driver steers over. The burnished wooden taxi banks and drops down by the watersteps. I ask the driver to take me over to the island of Saint George. He nods, considers, shouts out a fare. We haggle and eventually agree on a fee. I step into the back and settle on the long leather seat outside his cabin. He's a different sort of gondolier, wearing a white sweatshirt, a blue scarf and blue jeans, not the funereal black sweater, pants, and cap.

He launches his cab from the watersteps and into the channel. The bow lifts toward the island's ghostly outline.

White spray, moonlit water.

The cab's hull planes ahead. We pass other seacabs and waterbuses that circle back toward the Grand Canal and the hotels that are lit up brilliantly. About five minutes later, I step out of the cab onto the landing in front of Palladio's church. Two lighthouses close by flash their beams into the basin.

I pay the driver. He hesitates. I wait for him to speak. He asks me if I want him to anchor his cab until I'm finished looking around.

"No," I reply.

He looks amazed — it's Saturday night; all the drinking and the parties take place on the main islands — then he shrugs.

"Be safe," he says in English.

He turns his cab back out and joins the gondolas and taxis that coast and rove through the canals.

The citylights shine to the north. To the south, the Lido and the Adriatic Sea. Under moonlight, the stone pathway in front of me looks empty.

I gaze up at the church walls, darkened and eerie, like a fortress in shadows. Then I think, I may have most of the island and its contemplative mood to myself. So I'll take my time by the moored skiffs and launches. I'm educating myself, learning to take what comes, finding some quiet, patience, and attentiveness to what's here. I walk along the path and look at the building's symmetry, expecting nothing.

Water

Wind moves over the water; water moves under the wind. A soft splashing, then more splashing, slightly louder. After a few moments, I'm aware of the water in a way I haven't been since I first arrived. I'd been heading toward the park on the other side of the island, and I find that I'm at a standstill by the watersteps. I watch waves and wavelets, curling up and back, black and brackish.

A chill from the wind shoots through me. I take a step, then I stop again, shivering. I take another step, then I stop entirely. Moved and awed, I realize I've never seen or heard the water like this before. I've always been aware of the tides and the saltsmell in the city. But tonight I hadn't noticed how the waves were cresting, the water and wind rising, while the night was falling.

Washing up on concrete banks, seasilt and saltweed, the sound of water like whispering.

Around the island the waves ripple in and out. These tides aren't silent — they've never been silent. There's no silence to surround the monastery, the small harbor, the two lighthouses. There's no silence to point to a full stop. The waves beat on, rippling at different speeds, slowing in the middle of the basin, drifting toward the labyrinths of her interior.

Wind blows over the water's surface. Wakes are made, then they break along the docks. In the surface reflection the moon and stars ascend and descend with the rhythm of the water. And I feel the spray on my face, salty to my taste. The tide slides in. The world is breathing.

Light mists. The wind churns up the water and after a time it calms down. In the rises and falls I hear sources, the tide's beat, the waves speaking. The Ursound, the sound of our origins, before books, before technology. And beyond that? The crackle of stellar pulses. And behind that, music that escapes the ear, a message outside the realm of articulate comprehension. Yet felt, there, close to words, close to us.

I'm amazed by the water.

I watch its continuous creation and listen to its incessant hiss. This must have been the primary dream of the Venetians: to walk near the water and be aware of its unruly life; to navigate these tides, subject to their ways; to always have this sound beside you. The water's chaos is temporarily shaped by the structures that people built in this city.

Waves sent; waves received.

Voices flow over the water. They flow like memories of people I've met and known and loved, people remembering, raving, their voices pitched in argument and in simple conversation, expressing their longings, intoning their fears, all talking, searching for one another over the channels. One troubled night there may be a blackout in the place where you live, and you may be faced with loneliness for what seems like the first time. The blackout may humble your opinions and poses, and at that moment you have to find an authentic core of meaning in yourself. Venice is a labyrinth whose secret seems unfathomable, but her core is this water, reminding you of storms, journeys, the fluidity of personality. Voices flow across the basin, not like lost memories but like living presences that can be inhabited and preserved. Lena, Michael T., those in the dancebar, Ava Bernstein, Michael Senica, Frauke Voss, Raymond Price, Benjamin Sarnoff, and my mother and sister and father. All our struggles to be heard, to be human. I know a part of Venice's deep message: we must continue to build bridges between isolated places and people, so that one day we'll be able to receive and understand each other clearly, like voices and their echoes over the water, the guests and hosts of one another.

Spray in the wind.

Tides drumming in around the island.

My face wet, I turn and walk east.

Still

From the island of Saint George, I look back and see the Grand Canal. It appears smooth under starlight. Over to the other side, I see the piazza's spotlit columns. The ratios of the city are clearly visible in the night: the subtle harmonies in the stone, the music of the space. I gaze at the wavering lights of the boats sailing in the darkness back toward Saint Mark's.

I've come to know the Venetian darkness well. The night frames her and makes her look at rest, as if she's floating outside of time, turned back on the mystery of herself, which is the mystery of her identity, her strangeness and audacity. The music bands in the piazza and the chatter at Florian's are a fleeting hum. Sound and light are elusive. Water is elusive. Only darkness remains definite. Even then the night is temporary.

I stand silently, waiting for the moment of complete listening, complete receptivity. High water, low water. Wakes from passing cabs. The slap of an oar. A sputtering motor. An outboard catches somewhere. Laughter and singing. Gulls, herons, wings, calls. All is pitched softer, and higher.

I shut my eyes. I'm as still as I can make myself. Standing here, with my eyes closed, I know that the current has brought me to this island, to the darkness, and water, and to my heartbeat, which I've been trying to hear and to understand.

By the canal and the lagoon, I open my eyes and walk past the lighthouses. I pause, and watch the lights of Saint Mark's once more, and, when I turn around in the other direction, the sea.

The sound of the waves again.

I bend over to dip my fingers in the glassy water. And when I look down into the waves that lap against the dock, I slowly recognize the reflection that ripples there, unstill, forming and dissolving, and forming again. This is where it starts. Each of us an amorphous self, each of us capable of coming undone. It isn't what I expected to find. You, breaking against this dock, not at all something to be entranced with, merely you, a place to begin, what I've tried to face. You.

I scoop up a handful of cold water. Watch it, feel it, leak away, fall away. After, the dampness leaves just its faint trace on my fingers and palm.

Then I walk for a while. And I realize how I've often followed misleading paths. The electronic media can magnify the invisible presence and influence, expose the naked human face, strip us to our nerve ends, give us spectacular moments of connection. But between force and energy, there's an enormous difference. Between fusion and engagement, there must remain an essential difference. Tonight I know that I'm moving away from the information rage, its pressures on the instant and on simulations, the hyped extremes and the cult obsessions with Armageddon, to the music I'm still learning.

On the island of Saint George, my thoughts become peaceful at last.

Venice. Her name is serenity. She could be called solace, or sanity. This secretive place shows me again the mania of Toronto — its elevations of ego, its crashes of identity, its unsteadiness, the ripping down and the rebuilding of structures.

I look toward the Adriatic, the juncture of northern Italy and the sea, and feel the wind sweep in from the east. The lapping tide, the wash of the waves, the touch of the air. An internal calm may be our need, but upheaval is our state. It's taken this meeting of history with the present — Venice and Toronto joining together in my mind — to make me see the great gulf that separates us in thinking and time.

Sunday morning. And by the lagoon after midnight, beside these waters that become quieter as the night becomes deeper, I sense how force and will must be balanced by imagination, compassion, and emotion. Excessive availability of data can make us oblivious to knowledge and wisdom. We career on, inflaming our minds. Yet here I'm starting to grasp links, sources, and fields of possibility. Here I may be truly beginning to listen.

The canals can be sewers, the conduits for the overflow of junk and debris. The water can be sluggish. During a storm the waves can flood in and out. But the canals measure the tides' flow, channeling inward to the city's homes and opening outward to the seas that run on to oceans.

I remember a moment from years ago in my family's kitchen. The power had snapped off. We were blacked out, in the cold, alone.

In our sudden seizure of panic, we stared into the dark, trying to see. And out of the darkness we heard voices speaking to us. Our neighbors called each of us by name, asking if we needed help. If we'd listened closely, we would have heard in those words, this too will change. The flow resumes.

And now in this seacity, I'm settled and reminded by voices, both welcome and strange, that say a breakdown may be repaired through our ingenuity and patience, and that any attempt to see and hear what is real and unreal, nourishing and poisoned, always goes on, toward a still-point of understanding, where the sounding still calls you and the current is still moving...